Copyright © 2024 Megan Parkinson All rights reserved

This book is based on real events. However it is still a work of fiction. Names, characters, places, and organisations, are either products of the author's imagination or are used fictitiously.

No part of this book may be reproduced, or stored in a retrieval system, or transmitted in any form or by any means, electronic, mechanical, photocopying, recording, or otherwise, without express written permission of the copyright owner.

Content Warnings: Waiting for Monday contains content that might be troubling to some readers, including, but not limited to: **strong language, sexual assault,** descriptions of **sex,** references to **attempted suicide,** the **death/illness of a parent** in regards to **cancer.** Readers who are sensitive to these elements, please take note.

Waiting for Monday is Book 1 in the *Melissa Bishop Series*.
Other books in this series include;
Melodramatic

Cover design by: Kayla Coombs
Edited by: Lolli Molyneux

Waiting for Monday

Megan Parkinson

For Rachel, who sat by my mum's bedside every day
during those final weeks — most people will never know
a friendship like that.

And, as always, for my heroic dad.
I love you
X

— **Introduction** —

It is a truth universally acknowledged, that a woman in possession of four brain tumours, must be in want of a funeral director.

Before Mum died we had a multitude of conversations about life, death, the universe and everything. More specifically, there was one discussion we had about *me*. I expressed that, deep down, I felt, and knew wholeheartedly, that I'm not a good person.

"I don't think anyone is," she replied, trying to comfort me. "Not really."

But she didn't know what I'd done. In her eyes then, and probably right up until the moment she took her last breath, I was just her run-of-the-mill daughter. One who plods through life, trying her best, but never really doing anything much wrong.

But I did. *I have.*

I don't really know where to begin. Except for maybe...

Ten years ago. It was a swelteringly hot and miserable summer. I'd just turned sixteen and Mum had dropped me off in the arse-end of nowhere for a 'summer course' with my accordion, Boris, and a chipped brick of a phone with five pounds' worth of pay-as-you-go credit on it.

I'd been subjected to this, by her, all because my first ever proper boyfriend, Alfie, had dumped me, out of the blue, and I was 'driving her up the bloody wall'.

Since summer had begun, I'd done nothing but drag my knuckles round the house, watched pathetic rom-coms on repeat, and eaten the entire contents of the fridge, freezer, and snack cupboard.

"What am I supposed to do for two weeks?" I barked, while Mum pulled Boris's unbelievably heavy case out of the boot of her car.

"Distract yourself!" she snapped back. "Meet new people, play some music, and get your depressed head out of your backside—"

"Some parenting!" I remember actually stomping my foot, like some teenage-sized toddler. "What's Dad said about this?"

Not that it mattered. Dad was back in Yorkshire, at work, probably completely unaware Mum was fobbing me off onto some random theatre company for an entire fortnight.

"He thinks it's for the best," she lied, sucking her teeth. "You get a break, I get a break. And therefore, hopefully, when I pick you up a week on Friday, both of us will be revitalised, refreshed, and be able to get through the rest of the summer without strangling each other."

"You've lost the plot. You've *actually* lost it."

"Can you blame me?" Her eyes widened, genuinely asking. "All I've heard for weeks is, 'Why does it hurt so much?', 'What did I do wrong?', 'I thought I was going to marry him, Mum'. Honestly Mel, you're sixteen! Get a grip."

I felt my eyes sting. "How can you even say that?"

Mum placed a hand on my shoulder to silence me. Stern, looking exactly like her own mum (though I'd never tell her to her face) — *Nana Tia*.

Mum was pulling that hereditary sucking lemons expression, her demeanour loveless, cold, and authoritative.

"I'm doing this for your own good, Melissa."

Looking back, I'd agree with her, but I really wish she hadn't left me that day. Not because those two weeks were particularly bad — They weren't, at all. They were actually filled with some of the more fun, joyous memories I can recall. But being there, on that course, at that time, meant I was introduced to someone who changed my life... And not *necessarily* for the better.

Shortly after Mum drove off in a cloud of dust and grit, a girl approached me holding an overflowing overnight bag and a violin case. She, too, had been abandoned by her parents in a fit to better improve their own summer. She introduced herself, sheepishly, as Wes, and together we wandered around the grounds trying to find someone who could help us.

Traipsing around in circles meant I was able to figure out that I'd been dropped off at a boarding school, empty and rented out for the summer.

Eventually we found a reception desk, where a withered old lady then proceeded to escort Wes and I straight into the lion's den of a dance studio. An array of 'theatre students', head to toe in skin-tight sportswear, turned our way.

"We have our show's band members joining us today," the director, Julian, announced to the eagle-eyed crowd. "I hope you'll all give them a warm welcome."

Julian started off a petty applause and motioned for me and Wes to step forward.

"We've got Wes here, who'll be playing violin."

Wes managed an awkward wave. Her mousy voice squeaked out a "hello" before all eyes then turned to me expectantly.

"And Melissa on the concertina."

"*Accordion*," I corrected him without hesitation. "And it's Mel."

There were a couple of murmurs and I felt my ears burn. I buried my scrunched fists into the pouch of my hoodie and forced an unconvincing smile.

Julian began to ramble on, and the group gradually lost interest in the clearly not-so-entertaining newcomers. However, despite everyone seemingly going about their business around me, I could still feel an unsettling stare fixed upon me. A pair of dark brown eyes right at the back of the room. A boy, slightly tan, with dark hair that was messy and wild; his smile quirky and mischievous.

I shivered, thinking to myself, *stay away from that one*.

"Name's Will," he introduced himself not two minutes later.

Will.

My gorgeous, beautiful Will in his most pure and undamaged form. It brings a smile to my face remembering that version of Will. He was charming, charismatic, and unbelievably ballsy. A mere acorn, with all the foreshadowing traits of the witty, cocky, arsehole of an oak tree I'd grow to know and love.

Within minutes he was asking who I was, where I'd come from and if I wanted to come to his dorm for a couple of drinks with the cast after rehearsal.

"Or you could drink with just me if you want," he'd whispered flirtatiously in my ear, "I won't tell anyone."

For sixteen year old Mel, that was the equivalent to having a rug swept out from under me.

Will came into my life like a bolt of lightning, igniting something in me and starting a wildfire that would burn for the next seven years of my life.

— One —

19th August

Mum's only gone and dropped me off in the arse end of nowhere! Like, seriously — I don't even know where I am in the country! I think it's the south, as everyone keeps telling me they 'love my accent' and try to get me to say words like, 'bath', and 'grass', and that. But put a gun to my head, give me a map and tell me to point to where I am — I'd be dead.

I don't want to be in God-knows-where for two weeks... I want to be at home. No, scratch that, I want to be with Alfie. In his bedroom, watching one of his favourite films, or listening to his music, just chilling. Cuddling him and kissing him... I do not want to be here! Wherever "here" even is!

— Melissa Bishop, aged 16 and completely and utterly lost in all senses of the word.

***

Dad found my legs dangling through the hatch in the ceiling of my childhood bedroom. I'd indelicately scaled my old wardrobe and, with more effort than I care to admit, pulled myself through the hole and into the loft.

"Freckles?" I heard Dad say, with curiosity and amusement lacing his tone. "What are you doing?"

"Mum said I'd left some stuff behind when I moved out." I called back to him, rummaging through the various dust-covered boxes. "While she's busy cooking tea, I thought

I'd save myself a lecture and crack on with sorting through it." I found a box with 'Mel's Crap' scribbled across it in Mum's bad handwriting and smiled.

Glancing briefly down the hatch I saw Dad, with his head craned back, staring up at me. His gigantic oval lenses caught the sharp light of my torch, and he repelled backwards with a wince.

"Bloody blind me, why don't you?" He removed his glasses and pinched the bridge of his freckled nose. "I'm near-enough blind as it is!"

"Fancy lending us a hand?" I ignored him, returning my attention back to my apparent crap. "I just need you to catch this box."

"That depends. What's in it?" I heard him ask knowingly. It wouldn't matter — books, rocks, or an anvil, it was going to get dropped on him regardless.

I pulled the box onto my lap and gave it a gentle shake. *He'll be fine.* I thought, carefully manoeuvring it down my thighs and towards my swinging feet. "You ready?"

"You didn't answer me! What's in—"

He caught it with a pained *'Oooft'* and a couple of swear words that would have made Mum scold him. She always was a bit of a prude — unlike Dad.

"Bloody hell, Mel! Are you trying to get your inheritance early or what?" Dad dropped the box onto the floor, narrowingly missing his brown tartan slippers.

"Right, now catch me!"

I saw his head snap up, "Ye' what?" Despite his apparent horror at the thought of me following suit, he still instinctively raised his arms high, ready to catch me should I jump.

Laughing, I shook my head at him. "I'm joking, you muppet. Now get out of the way before I squish you."

Admirably, he waited a few moments before stepping back, then nervously observed as I proceeded to get my footing on top of the wardrobe. Hunched over like a French bell-ringer, I got the latch shut above me, then clambered my way to the floor.

"Your mum would have a fit if she saw you do that. You could've caused some serious damage."

"Pfft," I huffed back at him, "I would've been fine."

"Not to *you*, to her wardrobe," Dad noted. "If you'd have scuffed that thing, she would've sent you the repair bill." He then affectionately removed some stray insulation that had decided to cling to my hair.

Side by side, it was clear where I got the majority of my looks from. They say it's fifty-fifty, but I don't buy it. Dad and I have matching, unmanageable ginger hair, a copious amount of freckles, and unfortunately, corpse-like complexions. The only clear difference between us is our height. He's tall, whereas I, like my mum, am very vertically challenged.

Ripping open the box, I was disappointed to find Mum's label had been accurate — it was filled with 'crap'. A multitude of sticker-infested diaries, balled up clothes, and trinkets I used to treasure, but at that moment couldn't even remember when or where I got them.

Dad sat cross-legged beside me on the floor, picked up a diary and flicked through the pages, aimlessly. "Do you want me to paper-recycle these?"

My eyes glanced across a few of the covers. I didn't recognise half of them; the other half I regretfully remembered all too well.

"Nah, I think I'll keep hold of them," I shrugged. "Might be able to salvage some material from them."

"Really? This is potential Shakespeare is it?" Dad chuckled, his finger sliding across a random page. "Miriam's big sister has put me off popping candy for life! She told us this afternoon that she was with her boyfriend and—"

I swiped the diary from his hands remembering the incident to which I had been referring with too great a detail. My dad, of all people, did *not* need to read the rest of that sentence.

"Don't go reading my diaries, old man. They're private!"

"Who're you calling *old?*" Dad craned his head back with a burst of laughter. "I'm fifty-two!"

"Over half a century. Yeah, you're a real spring chicken," I drawled sarcastically.

Dad looked at me blankly then began to jut his chin out repeatedly, clucking away.

"You're a nutcase," I chuckled wholeheartedly, before being completely overtaken by laughter when he let out a deafening,

"*Bwak!*"

At that moment we heard Mum yell up the stairs for us. "Dinner's ready!"

Without thinking, we both scrambled for the landing. Reaching the top of the stairs at the same time, Dad wrapped one of his arms around my neck, and we wobbled, like drunken, conjoined geese down the stairs.

In retrospect, I wish we'd not been so hasty. If only we'd stayed, laughing on the floor of my childhood bedroom just a little longer. Didn't know then it would be the last we'd laugh together for a very long time.

Mum was being weird, eating slow and steady rather than simultaneously inhaling and blowing on her food like she usually did.

"Last good meal you're going to have for a while, ey, Freckles?" Dad considered. "Unless Freddie has widened his pallet to more than plain pasta with cheese since I last saw him."

"He eats ham now as well."

"Oh, ham *and* pasta with cheese? Very..." Dad tried to find a word not soaked in sarcasm, *"Adventurous."*

He failed.

"No, just ham. Freddie has it as a separate meal."

"Ham on its own is *not* a meal," Mum interjected, shaking her head and tutting away. "Not right, that boy. How does he not waste away?"

I cast a sideways glance across to Dad, who knew as well as I did that Freddie survived on a special kind of smoke.

Only reason Dad knew about Freddie's habit was because he'd made a surprise visit to the flat Freddie and I shared in Oval.

Dad had been in London for a work conference a couple of months prior and caught the daft idiot red-handed, on the sofa, joint in hand. Dad didn't say a word, just shook his head, visibly disappointed, and told me he would like to take *just* me out for dinner.

I knew from that moment on Dad didn't approve of Freddie, but what could I do? I lived with the bloke. Had been dating him for almost two years, and at that moment in time was about to start drama school. I couldn't leave him. I needed Fred, and knew, though he never said it or rarely showed it, Freddie needed me.

Later that evening, in my bedroom, as Mum and Dad sat in front of the TV downstairs, I re-scavenged through my box of crap. It was a sorry sight. My earliest diaries were a mess of pages, full of intelligible handwriting and spelling so poor it made me wince. They all seemed to fixate on school, my mates, and embarrassingly, more often than not, boys. *Lord help us.*

Where the boy chat was painfully psychotic and worryingly obsessive, I could easily assume I was reading my early teen entries.

I grimaced with every new line that read, 'Oh my God, [insert that week's school crush's name] is so fit!'

And, 'I don't believe it but [so-and-so] chewed the pen I lent them today. I have their saliva!'

I even caught a glimpse of, 'Eeek! I think I might actually be falling in love with [random name here]!'

Eeek, indeed, I thought, internally cringing. I didn't even remember half of the people that one time or another I was adamant I was going to kiss/snog/date or lose my virginity to... *Bloody embarrassing is this.*

I started to form a burn pile. There didn't need to be any evidence of my pathetic high school existence. Except, of course, for the 18th birthday photo Mum displayed proudly on the mantelpiece — I never did build up enough courage to tell her that twenty minutes before that photo was taken I'd made my then-boyfriend cry, round the back of the cricket club, by pulling out some of his pubes with my braces.

A couple more years were flicked through before I finally got to the first diary I recognised. A dark blue, hardback journal, with an optical illusion on the cover. At a glance, it looked as though the image were a flock of doves, but upon further inspection it transformed into a woman's profile, demurely casting her eyes toward the floor.

I checked the year — *God, I would've been sixteen, and a complete and utter, hormonal, mess.*

... Nothing changed there then.

— Two —

19th August

Wes, the only other person in this sad excuse for a 'band', plays the violin — the pissing *violin*! Which is basically the sexiest instrument to ever exist. And here I am with a sodding accordion! It's *so* lame! Because who has ever called an accordion 'sexy'?

Violinists are associated with black, silky, evening gowns, and nights of high class and sophistication. An accordion? Your mind immediately goes to old blokes with three teeth, playing Irish jigs in a pub, surrounded by smoke.

Why did I ever choose to play this bloody thing? Where the hell did I ever think it would get me? Not laid, that's for sure. Maybe the accordion is why Alfie broke up with me... I'm going to be a virgin forever, I swear!

— *Melissa Bishop, the big ol' insecure 16 year old virgin.*

***

Mum had dropped me off at the train station, Dad crammed into the back seat waving like a mad man. He always pretended our goodbyes were as drama-filled as that of a black-and-white vintage film, despite knowing each and every time I would be back up North within the month.

My visits home used to be even more regular, as I'd suffered quite badly from homesickness when I initially moved to London at nineteen. I was up nearly every weekend, drove Mum mad.

"Don't know why you're paying rent on that flat when you're essentially *still* living at home! Food in the fridge, eaten. TV remote, occupied. Washing machine, *always* in use. You wanted to live in London, Melissa, so *live* in London! Go home."

"This *is* her home, love," Dad would tut, wrapping me in a tight teddy bear hug, as if that would somehow shield me from her rant. "You can't tell me you don't miss her when she's gone."

"She's not gone long enough for me to miss her, Ted. She's like a bad rash."

"I didn't know you were so fond of your rashes, love." Dad teased, earning a disapproving look from Mum and a snigger from me.

Mum then tucked her latest literary purchase under her arm and headed upstairs to her study in a huff.

Mum's attitude rapidly changed when I stopped visiting as often. Especially when I moved in with Freddie and didn't come up for nearly three months. Countless hours were spent on video calls, consoling her while she wept about her 'little bird flying the nest too soon'.

Merely mad or purely a devoted mother? I never fully quite figured out which.

Once back in London, I proceeded to hop onto the Northern line and get the tube to Oval. I found myself praying for the duration of the journey, hoping that Freddie wouldn't be in the flat when I walked in. My heart sank when I found him out cold on the sofa, the TV blaring, his ashtray, grinder and joint stubs scattered across the coffee table.

In my head, I pictured myself picking up the nearest sofa cushion and clobbering him around the face with it, but in reality found myself crouched by his side and gingerly tapping his bony chest.

Freddie groggily opened his bloodshot eyes and groaned. I informed him it was nearly seven and he was most definitely going to be late for work... again.

That would make it the third time that month. *They're going to sack him*; I could feel it in my gut.

Ever since I'd told him that starting drama school would mean I'd have to quit my second job, and he'd have to start working full-time, Freddie had been acting more... *What's the word I'm looking for?* Unmotivated? Uninspired? Hell, Freddie had just been acting more *himself*.

I headed into the kitchen and started scavenging for some tea, realising I hadn't eaten all day.

After a good ten minutes, toast buttered, scrambled eggs steaming and covered in salt, Freddie walked in. He was rolling a fresh joint between his finger tips.

"Did you say it was seven?" He grumbled, watching me rooting through the drawers for a clean fork.

Once again, he'd neglected to wash up the mountain of crockery in the sink. None of it had been touched since I'd left Friday evening. The entire time we'd been living together he'd done the washing up maybe five times? — That's me being generous.

I didn't answer him, merely pointed at the grease-stained clock on the wall.

Freddie started to swear, suddenly patting himself down, searching for his phone. "For fu—"

"On the coffee table," I directed him, finally finding a plastic takeaway fork and stabbing my dinner hungrily.

I watched him, too exhausted to be fazed by his usual panic-in-motion tornado. He'd labelled it that past month as 'damage control'.

"I'll have to tell Susan I had an anxiety attack or something—"

"You used that excuse last week, Fred." I chewed, "She won't believe you."

He rolled his eyes at me, his phone pressed to his ear, unlit joint hanging out of the side of his mouth. "She'll have to. There's no way I'm coming in now. By the time I've smoked this, showered, got my stuff together and got there, my shift will basically be over anyway." He put the phone to his ear. "Oh, hi Susan! I'm *so* sorry, I've had one hell of an afternoon, I'm not going to lie. My anxiety has been through the roof—"

I grabbed my plate and headed for the bedroom, already overcome with second-hand embarrassment. In hindsight, I probably should've been angry, but I was used to Freddie's antics by that point. His incompetence had almost become a personality trait.

— Three —

20th August

Right, I'm not even sure I want to write this down but here we go, there's a guy here. *Will.* I told myself when I first saw him to 'stay away' but then he slithered over and introduced himself.

He's really confident, but to be fair has a reason to be because he's annoyingly fit. You wouldn't know he was only a year older than me because he's so tall and built like he goes to the gym six times a week. Tan, with brown eyes and black, messy hair that falls in this really sexy way. Like I said... *Annoyingly fit.*

He invited me to his dorm for drinks with some of the other cast members... I told him it wasn't really my thing. (Sounds cooler than saying, 'I'm underage so I don't drink, mate').

His response knocked me for six. He whispered in my ear that, "The joy of a summer course like this is no one knows who you are. You can be whoever you want, do whatever you want, and no one back home will ever know..."

— *Melissa Bishop, aged 16, feeling like she could reinvent herself, even if just for a fortnight.*

***

When I say the first week at drama school was mind-numbingly boring, I mean it.

I imagined it to be a place filled with like-minded people, eager to perform, thrilled to finally be starting their acting journey and propelling themselves into the industry. In my mind, we'd be learning interesting scripts, studying world-changing playwrights, getting lectures from fascinating professionals, and being taught their tips and tricks.

But, no.

My first week was an absolute joke. I spent six hours on my first day — *SIX HOURS* — playing name games and partaking in team building tasks. It was as bad as it sounds.

A group of us, all in our early to mid-twenties essentially played catch for an hour.

I awkwardly threw a tennis ball to a girl who had legs up to her chin and hair down to her arse, going, "Hi, my name's Mel and I like *magazines*."

For her to then pass the ball to somebody else continuing, "Hi, my name is Kelly and I like *knitting*."

Doubt Kelly has ever picked up a knitting needle in her life, she was just running low on things beginning with K. She'd already used up kick-boxing, karaoke, and knee slides.

Thank God no one in the class had a name that began with U or else we'd have all been forced to believe they liked ultimate disco, under-privileged kids charities, and London's underground bondage scene.

The second day was just as bad. We were forced to sit and listen to our core teachers talk about the importance of breath technique — one of my actual notes from that afternoon was, 'Remember to breathe!'.

God, Nana Tia might be right, I thought as I doodled in my notebook, *My desired profession might be a complete and utter farce.*

If we all got asked to stand around and pretend to be trees the following day, I would've owed Nana one massive (and genuine) apology.

The weeks only went downhill from there. As I was still working night shifts, I had to turn down every invite to a party, pub crawl, or social event that happened once the school day was through. Didn't seem like it would've made much difference until I found myself completely ostracised from all the gossip and banter of the night before — a lost and isolated sheep amongst my flock of fellow peers. It was hell.

Within a couple of weeks I found myself labelled as the 'busy' one, the 'working' one, the 'don't-bother-inviting-her-as-she's-only-going-to-say-no-anyway' one.

Freddie didn't help matters. At the end of that third week he had, as suspected, been fired.

"Termination effective immediately!" He spat, flying into the bedroom as I was changing into my work clothes. "Susan the takes-six-ciggy-breaks-an-hour-manager has the balls to say *my* attitude towards work is unacceptable. Is she serious?"

No comment.

"I *know* people, you know? I could make one call and get them to break her legs. That'd show her."

I shrugged on my coat.

Freddie usually made empty threats regarding people he 'knew'. I took him seriously the first couple of times, but then found out via a mutual friend that the people he 'knew' were his old mates from uni. Known for shoplifting penny sweets, and poorly spelled graffiti on the side of park toilets — hardly the gangsters he always made them out to be.

"Or you could start looking for a new job?" I pitched in calmly, reaching past him for my bag.

Yes, the flat we lived in belonged to his Uncle Steve, which, thankfully, meant we were on family rates, but even then we were cutting it fine with finances. I was a job down thanks to school, my savings already steadily draining away. So, Freddie needed a new job, or I'd be covering his half of the rent again like I'd done back in January, March... and May.

"I deserve better than this," Freddie scoffed, seemingly ignoring me. He puffed out his skeletal chest and rolled his shoulders back. "I was the only one at work who actually did anything!"

"When you actually decided to show up, you mean," I grumbled back.

Freddie, thankfully, didn't hear me, just took the half-smoked joint from behind his ear and rummaged through his pockets for a lighter. He went to spark up, my face fell.

"Thought we'd agreed you wouldn't smoke in the flat anymore," I stated, my eyebrows drawing together. "*Especially* in our bedroom."

Freddie shrugged, playing it off as a simple misunderstanding. "Sorry, with the whole work thing, my head's all over the place. I completely forgot. I'll take it out onto the balcony."

Forget? How could he forget? It was the most frequent subject matter in our weekly domestics.

My biggest peeve was Freddie smoking inside in the flat. It made everything smell; the sheets, the curtains, the carpet, my hair. The regularity with which he smoked also meant that if he was in the same room as me, I was basically getting enough second-hand to be out of it myself. The effects didn't manifest well in my system. There was no relaxation, no wave of calm, or sense of tranquillity that Freddie often boasted about when pleading his case to continue the addiction. No, instead I got paranoia, nausea, and ever-growing resentment for the bloke I seemed doomed to spend the rest of my life with.

A few seconds after Freddie had gone, my phone started to ring.

It was Mum.

"Hello," I answered cheerily, hoping this would save my disaster of a day. I smiled to myself preemptively, awaiting her rant of Dad's most recent (and often amusing) failing.

The previous week had been an absolute corker; Dad had spent eight hours in the garden shed trying to 'reinvent the wheel' only to emerge realising he had, in fact, just made a sledge.

I eagerly awaited for what Dad had done this time. Had he caused an explosion trying to brew his own beer again? Or maybe he'd accidentally put her massive suck-it-all-in pants on a hot wash and turned them all into thongs.

There was no reply.

I wondered if maybe Mum had butt-dialled me but then there was a raspy intake of breath that rattled down the line and curdled the contents of my stomach.

"Mum, is everything okay?"

No answer.

My breath began to quicken. "Mum, you're starting to freak me out."

There was finally some movement, a scuffle of some kind followed by a cough as Dad cleared his throat.

"Evening, Freckles..."

"Dad? Is Mum alright?"

"No, I'm afraid we've got some bad news."

I was still on the phone with Dad when Freddie returned from his smoke. He found me standing in the middle of the bedroom, panic-stricken, holding my phone in front of myself as if it were a bomb. Dad's words on a continuous, devastating loop inside my head.

'She's sick, Freckles... It's cancer, and it's not good. Not good at all.'

"Is she there?" I stammered, ignoring Freddie's goldfish impression as he mouthed, 'What's going on?'

"Yes, she's here," Dad sighed softly. "Would you like to speak to Freckles, love?"

There was a brief murmur and then my mum's quivering voice, reverberating down the line. "Hello, Melissa."

"Right, what exactly has the consultant said?" I asked, rather militantly. I knew I should have been kinder with her, more compassionate, and empathetic, but at that moment I was spiralling internally and in desperate need of something to grab onto.

Within seconds of Dad relaying Mum's situation to me, I had convinced myself that there was clearly some sort of misunderstanding. Dad, or Mum, or the consultant had made a mistake, and it was my job to get clarification and rectify the error.

Mum took a sharp, steadying breath. "I've got four little lesions on my brain, one of which is causing the eye problems, and one of which is causing the other face problems." Another sharp breath. "I've got a lesion on my liver, which is causing the tiredness. The chemo will hopefully sort some of these lesions out, but—"

My heart was beating so desperately, I could feel warm blood swirling around my ears. *Chemo?*

"Chemotherapy means a cure though, right?" I began to feel my bottom lip start to wobble. "So, this isn't terminal, this is only temporary, yeah? Chemo is going to fix you, and make you better, isn't it? That's what it's for."

Out of the corner of my eye I saw Freddie start to chew on the inside of his cheek, his eyes focused on the floor.

Mum made another sort of breathy noise, then her voice mutated into a steady and very practical tone. "Because the cancer is in my brain, the outcome is — *the prognosis* — the amount of months or years I have left to live has now been considerably reduced."

I felt my knees buckle. The whole weight of my body crumpled in on itself and I slumped to the floor. Freddie reached out to catch me, but missed by a good foot and a half.

He didn't join me on the floor, simply stood, arms still outreached, awkward, and completely out of his depth.

"How—" I readied myself for the final blow. "How long have we got?"

Mum started to softly cry, finding the courage to say the words, while I found what little strength I could to brace myself to hear them.

This is it. I thought. *This is one of those moments where everything changes.* An event that scars your heart, sears your soul, and remains with you for the rest of your life.

"We're looking at three to twelve months, love," she gently blubbed. "That's the kicker…"

— Four —

20th August

Tyler is a creep. He's one of the people Will introduced me to last night. Honest to God, with the patchy, spotty riddled beard he's got, Tyler looks like a piece of jam toast that's landed face-down on a carpet. Despite having a minging face, he has a weirdly large ego and has latched onto Wes like a testosterone-induced limpet. I would say I feel bad for her, but weirdly she doesn't seem to mind.

Pippa, Will's other friend, was great fun. Got wilder hair than me (which I didn't even think was possible), muscular dystrophy, and the most wicked sense of humour.

Literally, we were all playing 'Never have I ever' and Pippa drank for everything!

Never have I ever been skinny-dipping. Pippa drank.

Never have I ever taken a joy-ride. Pippa drank.

Never have I ever tried to kill someone. Pippa drank and had to elaborate because none of us believed her.

She said she heard you could kill someone by dropping a penny off the top of the Empire State Building. Closest she could get was the steeple of her local church, where she threw a handful of change over the edge in one go. She gave the vicar a concussion.

— Melissa Bishop, aged 16 thinking she is unbelievably boring compared to some other people.

***

Despite the glorious weather, unheard of for late September, and the raucous rabble around me, I felt cold and completely isolated. I'd spent most of the day finding secret, solitary moments to cry, and the rest desperately trying to feel nothing at all.

End of class meant I had been forced to follow all of my peers out into the sunshine. The second years were throwing a social house party. I had work and couldn't come — no one was surprised.

As they all made plans about where to meet, what time, while wearing what, I felt myself mentally start to withdraw.

'She's sick, Freckles... It's cancer, and it's not good, not good at all.'

It wasn't long before one of them, surprisingly Nazir, noticed that I wasn't myself.

Nazir was a lovely guy in a goofball sort of way. Another loner, though the main difference was that he *chose* not to fit in. I didn't exactly get the opportunity to decide; it was more like I had loneliness thrust upon me.

"God, try not to look so morbid, ginge," he teased, affectionately. "It's the bloody weekend. We've all survived our first month of drama school, you should be thrilled!"

"How much time do you think we can take off?" I asked, distant. "Like, does school have sick leave, or something?"

Nazir took a comedic step away from me and pulled the sleeve of his jumper across his mouth. "Oh, God, what have you got? It better not be chicken pox, because I've already had it twice. Can't afford to get it a third!"

I smiled weakly, grateful at his attempt to lift my mood. "It's not me that's sick, it's—" I paused, unsure if I actually wanted to say the words 'my mum is sick' out loud. As if, somehow, by keeping it to myself, it would make the fact seem less true.

"I just might need to go home for a while, that's all."

Nazir dropped his arm and furrowed his dark eyebrows, genuine concern etched across his face. "How long were you thinking?"

"Three to twelve months," I chirped, unironically.

Nazir's mouth pulled at the corners. "Err... That may be pushing it slightly." He let out an awkward laugh. "I'm sure they'd give you a day or two, but if you're wanting longer, your best bet is to ask Mr Braden."

Mr Braden, being a head of year for the school, had been at all of my many, *many* auditions during the previous five years. He was blunt, ruthless, and not likely to have felt empathy in the last two decades of his life.

I scooped up my bag, my mind already on the next - albeit likely to fail - task ahead of me.

"Where do you think he'll be?"

"You're going *now?*" Nazir looked scrambled. "Jesus, Mel, is everything alright? Has something happened?"

I blinked at him, again not wanting to confess what I was trying so desperately hard to deny.

Nazir seemed to read my mind, and suddenly picked up his own bag. "I'm coming with you."

We walked back to the main building in silence. Well, I was silent — Nazir tried making a conversation out of anything he could pluck from thin air. He started with smalltalk; the weather, the class we'd just had, his new coat, etc. Then moved onto his plans for tea and his latest book recommendations. When it became clear there was something really, *really* wrong with me, as I wasn't entertaining any of his attempts, he clamped his lips shut tightly and adjusted his bag on his shoulder over and over again, purely to give himself something to do.

Mr Braden's office was as stiff and as bland as its owner. The only notable thing in the room were the series of old but shiny metallic awards, sitting proudly on an otherwise very empty bookshelf by the door.

"Three to twelve months?" Mr Braden's mouth practically fell open. "Is that some poor attempt at a joke?"

I shook my head, unsure where this sudden, bold yet empty confidence had come from. The man usually made me feel about five years old with his overbearing presence and cold stare. However, in that moment, he might as well have been an ant I could squish under my ratty trainer or singe with a beam of light through a magnifying glass.

Nazir lingered by the doorway, chewing the cuff of his jumper to a point where the fabric was starting to fray.

"It's a family emergency," I stated, focusing on the many lines now decorating Mr Braden's crusty forehead.

"I'm going to need you to divulge a little bit more information than that, Miss Bishop." His eyes narrowed the longer I stayed silent. "Well," he resigned, when it was clear I had no intention of elaborating. "It doesn't really matter, you can't take an entire year out of your studies."

A spec of foolish hope fluttered around my chest as I asked, "Is there any way I can delay my placement? Postpone it till next year, and start again?"

"No," he answered with little to no thought. "You can have one week off at the most, or I'll need to officially withdraw our offer, and nullify your enrollment at the school."

I took a moment, weighing up my options, a million thoughts firing off in my already jumbled head.

Drama school had been my obsession for years. For a time, it was almost like I didn't know how to care about anything else. I'd given my everything to be at that place; yet with Mr Braden glaring at me from behind his desk, it somehow felt like all my hard work, passion, and achievement had been for nothing.

I steadied myself, my brain at war with itself. One half screaming, *'Tell him what's going on and maybe he'll change his mind'*. The other half, knowing he wouldn't, simply argued, *'Don't bother. There are other schools, Mel. Other courses... But you've only got the one mum, and God only knows how long for.'*

"Okay." I breathed, the air in the room suddenly unbearably thick. "I guess this is my request to be officially dropped from the course then."

Nazir stumbled towards me. "Mel! You might want to go away and think about this first."

I watched as Mr Braden's fists clenched around the armrests of his chair. "There are a lot of people out there who would kill, literally *kill*, for a place at this school. Are you seriously weighing this up in favour of your little family emergency?"

"Doesn't that tell you it's clearly *not* little, Sir?" Nazir snapped, showing a sudden bold disregard. "You need to hear her out!"

Mr Braden was up from his chair within the blink of an eye, looming over Nazir so dominantly that he actually cowered out of his superior's way; all of his momentary confidence tucked well and truly between his legs.

Curiosity and annoyance soaked Mr Braden's tone as he spoke. "I've never met a student show such flippant disregard for their position after showing such desperate aspirations to prove themselves during the audition process. Truly, what has come over you? You are not yourself."

I nodded in agreement. I wasn't. I hadn't felt like 'me' since the moment Dad had told me Mum was sick. It was as though I was suddenly in a body I didn't belong to, living a life that I no longer truly cared about... Because what was the point? Mum was dying, and the world as I knew it was on fire. *Might as well burn with it.*

In a way it was almost liberating to stand in front of a man, who clearly deemed himself *very* powerful and important, and know he couldn't break me. I was already broken.

"I know how much you wanted this place, Miss Bishop. Don't throw it away impulsively. You could regret it for the rest of your life if you do."

Not as much as I'll regret not being by my mum's side for her final months. I thought.

Freddie was lost for words when I burst through the front door. And lost for breath when I started to explain, in very blunt and emotionless terms, that I had dropped out of school, quit my job, was moving back home, and only going to return if or rather *when,* Mum eventually died.

"Are you *insane?*" Freddie protested, as I plucked my overnight bag from the top of the wardrobe and started to stuff it with any clothes in reach. Clean, dirty, mine or Freddie's, it didn't seem to matter, it all got thrown in.

I ignored him, feeling empty; as if I was simply going through the motions as I packed my things. *Hairbrush, deodorant, phone charger...*

Freddie snatched my bag from my hands as I tried to push past him and into the bathroom. "Hold your horses for one minute, Mel! You need to stop and *think*—"

I was tired of thinking. Thinking hurt my brain, made me want to crawl into bed, curl up into the foetal position, and cry until I came up with a better idea of what to do.

"What's there to think about?"

Freddie's eyes widened, and his mouth fell slightly agape. "You can't mess your life up just because your Mum is dying, Mel." Then he clutched his hand to his chest almost comically. "You're basically leaving me over this."

"I'm *not* leaving you," I snapped, making that point very clear before we ended up with another hole in the wall. "I'm going home to be with my mum. She needs me."

"And what about me?"

I blinked, my heart dropping into my stomach as he stared at me with his favourite wounded puppy dog expression.

"I'll come back to the flat every weekend," I promised, the face ashamedly pulling at my heartstrings. "I'll come back every Friday night and head back up north every Monday morning. Will that work?"

Freddie considered it, still looking thoroughly pained and forlorn, though I couldn't put my finger on why. It's not like we spent much time together anyway. We were like passing ships in the night most of the time, only crashing into one another to argue.

Freddie cast his eyes down towards the grubby carpet. "We've got Uncle Steve coming around at some point next week for the rent. What do I tell him?"

I felt the numbing pain in my head start to mutate into anger and frustration. "I have my half of the rent, Freddie. I'll transfer it to you the day Steve comes round."

"And what about next month?"

"What about it, Fred?"

He looked at me like I was playing dumb. "You've quit your job. I got fired and now no one is hiring."

"You haven't even been looking!" I hissed, finally forcing myself past him and grabbing my toothbrush and toothpaste from the bathroom. Freddie looked stung by my bluntness but I didn't have the time or energy to care.

"Do you think I should tell Steve about your mum?" Freddie queried. "He might give us some leeway with the payments if he thinks that's why we're struggling. So, personally, I think it's worth mentioning it to him." Freddie shoved his hands into the pockets of his skin-tight jeans and rocked awkwardly on to the balls of his feet. "But of course, I won't say anything if you don't want me to."

"We're already on family rates, Steve won't drop it any lower." I shoved my belongings into my bag, not forgetting my diary from the nightstand. "I'll see if I can get my old job at *Rogan's* while I'm home, try and get enough shifts to cover what I can of the rent."

"As well as coming to see me at the weekend?" Freddie tensed his shoulders so they came up to his ears. "You won't have the time—"

"Then what do you want me to do, Fred?" I snapped, almost launching my bag at him. "You can't have it both ways. Either I go home to Mum and spend my weekends working to cover the rent, or I go home to Mum and spend my weekends with you and *you* cover the rent. Which do you want?"

Freddie rolled his eyes sarcastically. "I'd like to not be homeless if I'm perfectly honest with you, Mel."

I felt myself actually growl. A rumble in my throat that caused spit to cling to my teeth. "Right..." I breathed deeply, desperately wanting to keep my growing rage under control. I didn't fancy leaving things poorly with Freddie. That would've meant feeling guilty about it for the next month and Freddie using it as ammunition the next time he was losing an argument. 'Remember that time you abandoned me? Penniless and borderline homeless?' He would no doubt twist it.

"I'll come see you every third weekend and work the rest," I decided for us both. "If Rogan will even give me my old job back." I scrubbed my face, frustrated, "How does that compromise suit you?" I saw Freddie nod glumly out of the corner of my eye as I checked my phone. "I'm going to Kings

Cross. There's a train to Leeds pretty much every half-hour, so I'll be able to—"

Freddie's eyebrows furrowed. "You're going right this second? Can't you wait till the weekend?"

"No." I zipped up my bag and grabbed my coat. "I'll text you when I get there."

I gave him a brief, obligatory peck on the lips and headed straight for the front door. He didn't stop me, I don't think he dared. Just grumbled a "Bye, then," before the door slammed shut behind me.

— Five —

20th August

I was actually starting to enjoy myself last night until Pippa asked me if I had a boyfriend or not. My mind jumped straight to Alfie and I swear to God, I thought I was going to vom. What a pisstake! Instead of chatting to the new, cool, interesting and funny people around me (Tyler not included) I was forced to think about Alfie!

All the usual rubbish; Why did he break up with me? What did I do wrong? Blah. Blah. Blah. I made some pathetic excuse to them all about wanting an early night and needing to go to bed — they must all think I'm a right loser.

As I went to leave, Will was suddenly next to me. "I'll walk you to the girl's dorms," he said, "I'm guessing you don't know where they are."

He guessed right, I didn't have a clue.

Why am I not surprised Will knows his way to the girl's dorms in the dark?

— *Melissa Bishop, aged 16, being escorted to her room by a tall, dark, stranger. How very Austen!*

***

My chest tightened as Mum's words scuttled across my head like a bad case of nits. *We're looking at three to twelve months, love.*

Stations whizzed past as I calculated timeframes. The minimum time we had left would've taken us to Christmas, *ho ho how depressing.*

The maximum time frame would've given us a year. One whole year to cram in a lifetime's worth of things I wanted to do with Mum.

I clenched my fists as the frustration and rage stewed inside of me.

Then something new and unfamiliar sent shivers up the back of my neck. I heard the carriage doors hiss open and close several times behind me, the hairs on my arms starting to bristle. Like a deer, I was acutely aware that someone was staring at me. Even though my back was to them I could still feel their hunter-like gaze burning into the back of my skull like a red-hot poker. I hoped it was the train conductor, suspicious of my ticket situation, rather than a psychopath — knowing my luck, it was more likely going to be the latter.

Choosing my moment, I eventually glanced over my shoulder and found myself entrapped in a whirlwind of mangled panic and joyous nostalgia.

Will Green, holy sh—

"Mel?"

In the space of a heartbeat, Will had managed to dart over from the luggage rack to my quivering side. He loomed over the empty chair beside me, forcing me to notice he'd gotten more muscular since I'd last seen him; *puberty has clearly given him second helpings.*

"Will!" Instinctively I stood, raised myself up onto my tiptoes and wrapped my arms around his neck. I was expecting my nose to be filled with the familiar scent of fruity deodorant but instead was pleasantly surprised by the overwhelming tang of musky cologne.

I inhaled deeply, my eyes closing momentarily. I swiftly withdrew, hoping Will hadn't heard or noticed my manic sniff.

"You look—" he motioned his hand up and down my body and I felt an overwhelming shame sweep over me.

The words he was looking for were, '*A mess*'.

My ginger mass of hair was scraped back into a bedraggled top knot. My hoodie wasn't even mine — it was Mum's and therefore three sizes too large. And to top it all off, my slipper socks were overflowing from my holey, muddy trainers. Plus my laces were undone. *I couldn't look more horrendous if I tried.*

"You look amazing," Will lied, his eyes finally locking with mine. They were still as chocolatey as ever, though newly flanked by a soft set of laughter lines.

"So do you," I noted, very much *not* lying. Will, annoyingly, looked incredible. With his crisp, white shirt and neatly pressed pants, shiny shoes and perfectly coiffed dark hair. I hoped he'd smile widely and I'd see spinach between his teeth so I could feel better about myself, but no. He smiled and his teeth were bloody perfect, crystal white and spinach free.

"God, how long has it been?" I laughed nervously, offering the vacant seat beside me and subtly trying to fix my hair so that it wasn't quite as wild.

I knew how long it'd been. Our last encounter wasn't exactly one I was going to easily forget, but it felt like the appropriate thing to say.

"Got to be a couple of years, hasn't it?" Will half smirked, no doubt his mind was throwing up the same memory mine was. "Thought you lived in London now," he said, thankfully moving the conversation in a different direction. "Aren't you heading the wrong way?"

"I'm visiting my folks," I smiled, ricocheting back his merry tone. "Don't *you* live in London? Aren't *you* heading the wrong way?"

"Moved back up this way about a year ago, when the pipe dream finally ended," he sighed. "I'm working in statistics now, boring I know. But at least it means I'm with my mum in Skipton."

I almost choked. *He's that close?*

"I still have to go down to London for work every now and then, but I don't mind." Will rubbed the back of his neck, his arm flexing. "Reassures me that I made the right decision moving. Don't know how I lived there for so long. The air, the noise, the water."

"Suppose, you don't really notice how bad it is while you're still in it." *Like a lobster being boiled slowly alive in a pan*, I thought, morbidly.

My eyelashes fluttered rapidly once I realised I hadn't blinked since Will had sat down. I was too busy soaking in the sight of him. I couldn't believe he was next to me after so long of being God-knows-where.

Will rested his head back against the chair, his eyes never glancing away from me. His talent for maintaining eye contact without being creepy was still as intense and impressive as ever. "How're the folks?"

One daft as a brush, the other riddled with cancer, I mused to myself before answering aloud. "They're fine..."

Saved by the announcement overhead, I looked out of my window and saw Wakefield Westgate station starting to slide out of sight.

"How long are you up for?"

I froze, unsure how to answer such an innocent yet trauma-filled question.

"A bit." Seemed like as good an answer as any.

Before I knew it, a phone was thrust into my hand. "Pop your number in, then."

"Would have assumed you already had it saved," I teased slyly, causing Will to nervously make up the easy excuse of,

"I've gotten a new phone in the last couple of years. A couple actually, so sadly your number isn't in that one. But do me a favour and rectify that, would you?"

I didn't need telling a third time.

After passing his phone back to him, Will comically held it to his ear and I felt a soft vibration in my back pocket.

"It's ringing," he whispered, a mischievous grin playing on his lips. I went to reach for my phone but his hand caught my wrist, and an all-too-familiar warmth spread over me. I felt like butter, sizzling away in a Will-shaped pan.

My phone went still.

"Hey, Mel, it's your sexy friend Will. Hit me up while you're up North for *a bit* so I can take you out for a drink. Or six. Again, it's your sexy friend Will. Bye!"

He hung up and shoved his phone back into his pocket just as the overhead announcement called out across the carriage: "We will shortly be arriving at *Leeds*. This train terminates here. Please take all your belongings with you."

"Right," Will ruffled his hair and stood, "I better get back to my seat. Make sure that my stuff isn't being nicked." Will pointed to my heavy rucksack on the overhead shelf and pulled a face. "Want me to get this down for you before I go? If it is actually yours. I'm not putting my back out for any old sod."

"It's mine," I laughed, getting to my feet. "But I'll get it, it's fine."

Will had already swung it down and onto the now empty seat between us. I was thoroughly impressed, considering it took me five minutes to get it up there.

He reached over the bag and enveloped me into another delicious cologne-scented hug. "I mean it about that drink, you know?" He then kissed my cheek, his lips lingering just a fraction too long. *He hasn't lost his touch.*

Thankfully, my feet were still under me when Will finally released me and I was able to disembark from the train without falling flat on my face.

Platform 6 became the concourse. The concourse became the car park, and before I knew it, I was standing in front of Dad, back in the pits of reality.

No offence to him, but he looked like he should be partaking in a veteran documentary talking about the horrors of war.

The car ride was long and uncomfortable. Dad had instigated the awkwardness before we'd even set off. He reached over the temperamental handbrake of his vintage yellow Mini, and gave me a hug that seemed to last for an eternity.

The taxi stuck behind him, waiting to pull into the pick-up point, honked twice, but Dad didn't give a toss. Merely buried his face into the bulk of my frizzy bun and squeezed the air out of me, refusing to let go.

"It's good to have you home, Freckles," he said, his voice muffled by my hair.

I wriggled and squirmed in response, gravely aware that we were holding up so many people.

Finally, Dad released me and it took him three goes to get the engine started; the understandably irked taxi-driver honking a third and final time.

The whole way home, Dad was like a broken record, either mumbling incoherently some type of pleasantry, or muttering, "your Mum will be so happy to see you" barely loud enough for me to hear. My stomach churned every time he said it. Seeing Dad was one thing, but Mum was an entirely different ballgame. Almost like puddle-jumping and deep sea diving; both involve water but one is exceedingly more treacherous than the other.

We hadn't spoken other than the apex phone call so I really had no idea how Mum was doing, or even if she *would* be happy to see me. I had a strong suspicion she wouldn't be, especially when she found out I'd dropped everything to come swanning to her side.

"She'll be fast asleep by now, but just a word of warning for when you see her in the morning," Dad unconfidently said, pulling onto the drive. "Your Mum is..."

My mind raced through all the worst-case scenarios of how he could finish that sentence. Laughably, they came in the order of; 'dying', 'insane', and finally, 'now a nudist'.

God, I hope not. Mum being permanently naked *and* terminally ill was a combination that would have well and truly tipped me over the edge.

"Your mum is taking her prognosis a little differently at the moment," Dad finally stipulated, killing the engine with a nervous smile. His headlights died along with the mechanical hum of the car, and we were dropped into darkness. The only light around was that coming from the lone street lamp half way down the hill.

"What does that mean?" I asked, my eyes growing wide with ever growing concern, trying to make Dad's figure out in the dim light.

"It means she's not as convinced by the consultant's prognosis as she was when she first got the news."

That answered nothing. If anything, it made me more confused.

"Your mum seems to think she's not *that* sick."

— Six —

21st August

This place is demented. I've only been here three days and I already want to leave. Other than Will and Pippa, the place is filled with weirdos. The musical director, Eileen, is the worst of the lot. Literally, she shows up hours late to rehearsals, stays for about twenty minutes, then leaves again, telling me and Wes to 'practice'. *How?* We've not been given any music! She smacks the living daylights out of the piano and conducts like she's trying to swat a fly with a tea-towel.

Apparently she's a piss-head, and during the first week of the course before Wes and I arrived, she was found in a bush one morning. *And,* according to the rumour mill, the bottle of pop she carries around with her is actually full of booze.

Then again, there's also a rumour going around that on the first night some of the cast played truth or dare and one lass ate a drop scone pancake with a lad's... *'juice'* all over it. So rumours don't mean much around here!

— *Melissa Bishop, aged 16, deciding never to eat a drop scone pancake ever again.*

***

"What the *hell* do you think you're doing?!" I screamed, charging down the back garden path and towards Mum's tiny allotment.

I'd been woken up at God-knows-what-o'clock in the morning by a crash, bang and a wallop outside of my bedroom window. Looked out to find Mum throwing down a giant mental ladder and a rake at the base of her beloved crabapple tree.

She was then up the tree, wielding said rake, while I blustered towards her, barefoot and still in my pyjamas.

"Are you mad?"

"Melissa?" Mum called back, bending down and revealing her podgy, round, red face amongst the leaves. I couldn't help but notice that her right eyelid was slightly droopy, covering up the top half of her brown iris. She'd informed me that one of the lesions was causing 'the eye problems' but she hadn't exactly elaborated on what that meant. It was as though the wind had changed while she'd been attempting a wink.

"When did you get here?" she asked, innocently.

"Late last night. Now get down now before you kill yourself!" I barked back.

"Always the one for the dramatics," I heard her mutter as she stuck her head back amongst the foliage and tutted. "If you don't like the idea of being a reenactment of Newton's most famous scientific discovery, I recommend you take a few steps back!"

I went to scream some more but found myself ducking and running for cover. Apples seemed to have started falling from the sky. "Jesus!"

"We'll have no blasphemy in my presence!" Mum chirped from somewhere high up in the tree; the apples momentarily cease-firing. "I did warn you!"

"Dad!" I yelled, once the fruity attack had ended. "*Dad*!"

He came bounding down the garden path, his dark blue dressing gown billowing out around him. "What is it? What's going on?"

"She's up a bloody tree," I hissed, stepping forward and pointing out a pair of squat legs half-way up the ladder.

"Ah." Dad joined me, looking up and starting to scratch his not-yet shaven chin. "I see."

"She's going to hurt herself!" I squawked, frustrated that neither of them seemed to understand the seriousness of the situation. She could slip, fall and hit her tumour-riddled head. Then we wouldn't even get twelve minutes together, let alone twelve months. "Get down *now*!"

There was a puff of laughter before Mum's face appeared again; her cheeks rosier than before. "Don't think you can show up out of the blue and start ordering me about in my own home, madam."

"We're not *in* your home, we're outside," I bluntly pointed out.

"Technicalities," Mum huffed before bellowing, "*Take cover!*"

I jumped backwards but Dad, being clueless, was hit with an onslaught of shiny, two-tone crabapples.

"Agh!" he howled. His hands flew to protect his head as he ungraciously came bustling over to my side.

Part of me wanted to burst out laughing; this was something that a few months prior would have had Dad and I in stitches, but I couldn't so much as manage a smile.

Finally, Mum emerged from the branches. She was wearing her full gardening gear; muddy gloves, her old, paint-splattered, dark-blue boiler suit, and her waterproof, grass-stained, yellow anorak.

When she placed one of her purple wellington boots on the top step of the ladder, she beamed, proud of the copious amounts of produce scattered across the ground.

"There we are," she said, before looking at Dad and I and scowling. "Don't just stand there imitating codfish! Grab the bucket and help me collect these up, would you?"

Dad jumped straight to it but I was too busy steaming at the ears to move a muscle. I watched as she made her way down the ladder, rake in hand, clearly a lot more out of breath than she was letting on. She had to stop twice.

"I can say hello to you properly now." She tapped the blunt end of her rake into the ground and leant against it, her breathing irregular and cheeks bright red. "Nice surprise to have you here, love. To what do we owe this pleasure?"

"You shouldn't be climbing trees in your condition," I snapped, taking the rake from her and throwing it on the ground before she accidentally took out her good eye and rendered herself near blind.

"You make it sound as though I were pregnant, dear," Mum muttered, her thin lips twitching at the corners. "Which I can assure you, I'm not."

"No, but you're *sick*!" I barked, unable to take her forced humour or blindly ignorant stance any longer.

Mum's head whipped round to poor Dad, who was innocently going about collecting the apples, muddying his tartan slippers and fingertips in the process. "What on earth have you been telling people, Ted?!" she snapped at him. "First Christine next door, and now Melissa!"

"Mum, *you* told me," I countered, stepping in front of Dad protectively like some yammering shield. "The other day, you rang me when you got the terminal prognosis from the consultant."

Mum wafted her hand at me dismissively. "*Terminal?* Funny word, isn't it? Makes it sound so factful, so immediate. So... final." She bent down and started collecting apples, inspecting each one before placing it into the bucket. "Prognoses are funny things. People think they're sacrosanct, when in reality, all they really are are someone's opinion on matters."

I turned slowly to look at Dad, hopeful to find him as bemused as I was — Mum was raged and unintelligible at the best of times, but this was something else.

"What is she on about?" I asked him, bluntly.

"Your guess is as good as mine," he shrugged, picking up a few more apples.

"The consultant *thinks* that I have a reduced amount of time left to live," Mum continued, ignoring us both. "That doesn't necessarily mean it's true. The consultant *says* that my prognosis is terminal, but for all he knows I could be well on my way to being a medical marvel."

"You're joking, right?" My head whipped back. "You are having me on?"

"I am confident I will surpass my life expectancy and live a long and happy life, Melissa. No doubt, I'll be studied by academics the world over for being one of those few cases who defy all laws of logic and reason."

"And how do you plan on doing that?" I asked, gritting my teeth. "How do you plan on *not* dying?"

"By sheer determination."

I almost swore.

I'd only properly sworn in front of Mum once and earned myself one hell of a clip around the ear for it. Frankly, I deserved it. In hindsight, it *was* an overreaction to call a headbutting goat at the petting zoo a 'jammy twat' — we live and we learn.

I rubbed my temples, my head starting to hurt. "I can't believe this. I can't actually believe what I'm hearing."

"You'll see." Mum continued with her attempt to pick up the heavy, overflowing bucket of apples and failed. "You'll all be looking on in admiration when I stand in this exact spot in twelve months' time." She gave up with the bucket and played it off as though she hadn't even tried.

"Now, Mel, make yourself useful and carry these crabapples into the house. You're going to freeze if you stay out here in nothing but your jim-jams."

"She's lost it!" I yelled, throwing both arms in the air as she strutted away from me. "She's officially lost her marbles!"

"If I'm perfectly honest with you, Freckles..." Dad began, tying his dressing gown tightly around his waist. "I don't think she ever had any to begin with."

He then took up the heavy bucket before dutifully following his nutter of a wife back towards the house.

Mum thought that I was merely staying for the weekend, until she saw my bedroom — it was like I'd never moved out. My giant rucksack had somewhat exploded. Clothes were shoved into drawers, piles of books stacked high on the nightstand, battered trainers piled precariously behind the door.

"It's utterly ludicrous, Melissa," she scolded me, shortly after breakfast. "You can't stay here!" she ranted, most of her attention on an absurd amount of crabapple jelly boiling on the stove top. "For a start you have school on Monday—"

"I dropped out."

"I beg your pardon?"

Dad choked, causing him to dribble tea down his already coffee-stained knit jumper. "Ye' what?"

"I dropped out," I repeated a little louder, crossing my arms over my chest and leaning against the only kitchen counter not covered in sterilised glass jars. "Wish I hadn't jumped the gun now, since you're *apparently* not even that sick."

Mum pursed her lips, looking as though she was sucking on a lemon. "I hope, for your sake, this is a joke."

"Why would I joke about quitting school?"

"Why *would* you quit school, Melissa?" Mum waved a wooden spoon at me as though it were a teacher's ruler. "You'll have to ring them and tell your professors this has all been some terrible misunderstanding. They need to reinstate your placement, effective immediately."

"Too late for that, Mum," I huffed. "Don't know why you're getting so uppity about it, you didn't even want me going to drama school in the first place."

"That doesn't mean I condone you dropping out at a moment's notice, simply because I essentially have a cold."

"You don't have a cold though, do you? You have *cancer*," I said bluntly, immediately hating how my words caused Mum to physically recoil.

"It doesn't matter what I have," she breathed, taking a moment to compose herself. "Our approach to it should be the same regardless, and it should not go further than this room."

"Meaning what?"

"Information about my health should remain between the three of us." Mum waved her spoon between Dad and I. "No one else needs to know."

"Well, poor luck on that one because I already told Freddie," I interjected. "And you're forgetting the consultant also knows."

"And Christine next door," Dad added unironically.

Mum glared between the two of us. "I'll be better in no time with the treatment being offered to me so those who know, know. And those who don't should remain ignorant. Do I make myself clear?"

"Yes, mein Führer," I drolled sarcastically, causing Dad to snigger into the rim of his mug and Mum to hiss at me.

"You expect me to let you live here, when you have an attitude like that?"

"Weirdly enough, yeah I do," I bit back at her, genuinely hoping she would kick me out so I could have a good reason to go fleeing back to London without feeling guilty about it.

"What do you plan on doing about the flat?" Dad interrupted before Mum and I descended into a full-blown row.

"Freddie's still there, but as he's out of work again—" I bit my lip, regretting the words before they even flew off the tip of my tongue.

"Oh, *what a surprise*," Mum whirled, returning her full attention to the giant pan of bubbling crabapples.

I continued, the image of myself throttling her with a tea-towel playing merrily in the back of my head. "As I was saying, Freddie is still at the flat, so I'll still be paying my half of the rent to try and make things fairer for him since I'm the one that's suddenly changed everything."

"Do you need any help with that?" Dad asked before draining the rest of his tea.

"No," I swiftly replied, never liking the fact Dad seemed to offer money he didn't have at any possible opportunity. "But thank you. I'm actually going to head to *Rogan's* this afternoon and see if I can get my old job back."

"You're seeking *employment* up here?" Mum groaned, placing a hand on her curved hip. "For goodness sake Melissa, how long do you plan on staying here?"

Till you die, was the only reply my brain could come up with.

— Seven —

23rd August

It was moronic. I know that now, but what choice did I have? We've been here nearly a week and learned basically nothing. We haven't even played the second half of the score and we're supposed to start tech run on Monday! I blame Eileen, who is officially the worst musical director of all time.

This morning she played the piano for a millisecond then said something about having a migraine and effed off. I lost it... And before I knew it I'd grabbed her stupid bottle of pop and sniffed it. Don't have much experience with alcohol but I've spent enough time around my Auntie Angela to know the stench of white wine. Wes said I should put it back where I found it and forget about the whole thing. But what good would that have done? I had to tell someone.

Long story short, Julian just announced to the whole company, grown-ups and all, that "Eileen is stepping away from the production due to personal commitments that were unavoidable." *Fancy way of saying she's an alcoholic.*

Everyone started losing their minds. No one knows what's going to happen now. The show could be cancelled, the course could end early and everyone sent home — because of me.

Wes glared at me through the entire announcement. Probably plotting how she's going to tell everyone it's my fault. They're all going to hate me, Will included. I need to tell him before Wes does...

— *Melissa Bishop, aged 16, with more toes than brain cells.*

***

Rogan's had clearly had a make-over in the five years I'd been away. Instead of it being a cry for help by a man yearning for his old bachelor life, it was a plant-and-flower-infested cocktail bar. Not to mention uncharacteristically heaving with customers.

Where had Rogan's dart board gone? His plasma TV, forever on the sports channel, never to be changed over? *In fact,* I wondered as I weaved between tables towards the bar, *where the hell is Rogan? Fat lot of good coming here to get my old job back if he isn't even around anymore to hand it to me.*

If *Rogan's* was under new management, Operation Get-My-Old-Job-Back would've been well and truly out of the condensation-drenched window.

"What can I get for you?" a blonde, chipper girl asked while she slapped a piece of mint between her palms.

I looked past her and into the kitchen, "Don't suppose Rogan is working today?"

Without even hesitating the girl twisted her head, calling into the back. "Rogan, your girlfriend's here!"

"Oh no, I'm not—"

Before I could finish my protest, Rogan appeared like a troll from its cave, wiping his hands down his front and smearing whatever he had been cooking onto his apron.

He shook his bald head furiously. "That joke ain't funny, Katie. What if my missus was in?"

"Then I wouldn't be making it," Katie snorted, before turning back to me. "His wife scares the hell out of me."

I'd only met Rogan's wife, Pat, a couple of times. She scared the hell out of me, too. There was something about the way she would burst through the door, flicking her ciggy butt and accusing Rogan of having another affair at the top of her lungs, that put the fear of God into anyone in her wake.

Rogan finally looked at me and his grin grew wide. "Cheese-*Melt*!" he cheered, coming around the bar and wrapping me in an embrace that stunk of frying oil, cigarette smoke and coffee. "Long time no see!"

"Hiya, Rogan," I mumbled, not wanting to jump away too quickly so as to offend him. I needed a job after all.

"Blummin ummer', have you been on a hot wash since I last saw you? You've shrunk!" He pulled away and took a good hard look at me. "You need fattening up, lass! Let me make you something, on the house."

I shook my head, flattered but nauseous at the prospect of eating his grease-riddled food. To eat at *Rogan's* I had to be one of two things; exceedingly pissed, or blindly hungover. At that moment in time I was, regrettably, neither.

"No, I'm fine, honestly."

"Give over, I don't mind." He handed me a menu. "We've got eggs your way on sourdough, with or without smashed avocado. Pesto fried eggs, with chorizo and sundried tommys on rye. Or you can have sauteed spinach with— What are you laughing for?"

I was! I was laughing and I didn't even realise it. I knew all the words Rogan was saying but had never heard or expected them to come out of his tobacco-stained mouth before.

Where's his chef special of a double decker cheese burger with a side order of grease gone? I wondered with a sly smile before asking aloud, "Have you gone hipster?"

"Oh, God, don't even get me started," Rogan groaned, rolling his eyes. "Missus wanted more of a say in goingson around here, and when stuff she chose for the menu actually started to sell, I gave her full rein. She clearly knew what she were on about, so couldn't exactly say no, could I?"

I wondered how on earth his missus knew anything about sourdough. Pat took me as the kind of woman who knew every brand of cigarette, not every type of fermented bread.

"So, I'm guessing Pat was also responsible for the decor change as well then?"

"The what?"

"The dec—" I shook some sense into my head, remembering who I was talking to. "Did she also choose to get rid of the dart board and the TV?"

"Oh, yeah," Rogan nodded, gesturing out to the Eden around us. "This is more welcoming, apparently. Don't know how, though. Not like you can have a chin-wag with a bush, is it?" He tapped the menu, ever the feeder. "So, what you having?"

"I'm honestly fine, Rogan. I'm not even hungry."

"Drink then, or a coffee? No, wait, you don't drink coffee. Tea's your poison, isn't it? Let me make you a brew."

"Rogan," I half sighed, half laughed. "You don't have to make me a brew."

"Then why did you bother walking in?" he resigned with a hearty chortle. "Crappy customer if you won't even order anything. Never mind that it's free!"

"I need a job."

"Oh?" he froze. "Things crashed and burned for you in The Big Smoke?"

"Not exactly," I grumbled, thinking that, ironically, it was things up north that were ablaze. "I'm just going to be home for a while and could use the extra cash."

Rogan stuck his head into the back room; clearly the rota hadn't been moved during Pat's redecorating spree.

"What're you after?" he raised his left eyebrow, his forehead lines deepening. "Because I haven't got much, not gonna lie. Danny works Mondays and Wednesdays, so does

Rich, and then the rest of the time Katie is here, since she's got no life."

There was a jolly, "Oi!" from somewhere behind me amongst the crowded tables.

"I mean, I could— Do you mind closing? I could give you the last couple of hours of the day, and like lock-up duties and that? Cash in hand?"

I tried to repress my grimace, thinking that even if *Rogan's* decor and menu had changed, the clientele most definitely wouldn't have. That would mean the closing-up shift would still consist of scrubbing down abused toilets, and convincing unruly customers that 2 a.m. *was* a perfectly good time to head on home.

"Sure," I agreed, thinking of Freddie. *God, I must really love him...* I contemplated, suppressing the knowledge that he would never take such an awful job for me. Hell, he didn't even take *a* job for me, let alone a dire one.

I thought getting my old job would make me feel some kind of positive tingle in my bones, but then I heard "*Lil' nips!*" as I was walking out of *Rogan's,* and my spirit was practically torn in two.

I looked across the road and saw my *Cousin Willow*. Of all the people in my family, she was the one I would've most liked to have seen squished under a bus — if she'd timed her step off the pavement a little better I would've witnessed my wish first hand.

She crossed the road and engulfed me in a sickly fake lovey-dovey hug.

"I didn't know our little actress was home!" she squealed in my ear before pulling back and taking a good look at me. "How are you?"

"I'm fine. Are yo—"

"Yeah, I'm good, just gone and got my hair done."

That much was obvious, Willow's hair was something I'd always been envious of. Where mine was ginger, her's was ice blonde. Where mine sprung out like a lion's mane, her's remained silky smooth and effortlessly straight. *Cow bag.*

"It looks lovely."

"I know, our Jackie works wonders." Willow took some of my hair between her long fingers and hummed. "I bet she could have a crack at getting this frizz out for you."

She pointed a glittery acrylic nail to the white shopfront where she'd emerged from. "She could like, chemically straighten it or something? Or shave it off and fit you with a wig." Suddenly Willow burst out into an ear splitting giggle. "I'm only joking, Lil Nips. Jesus, you should see your face!"

I forced a weary laugh and tried to free my hair from her tight pinch.

"You been for food?" Willow asked, her laugh cutting off. She looked up at the silver *Rogan's* sign above us and pulled a disapproving face. "Heard it's a right dive in there."

I clenched my back teeth together and forced a smile. "It used to be, but it's recently had a refurb."

"Oh," Willow fluttered her fake eyelashes at me, making a poor attempt at feigning interest. "I'll have to take a look then when I'm next about."

"No—" I interjected, slightly panicked, hating the thought that Willow might show up randomly one day while I was working. She was the kind of person who would revel in making me wait on her every whim and leaving no tip to make any of it worth it. "Doesn't really take me as your kind of place. It has egg on the menu, for a start."

Willow's nose wrinkled. "Ew."

"Exactly," I continued, notably letting out a sigh of relief. "You're better off trying *Alcool* on the other side of town."

"Might do," Willow shrugged, flicking her freshly blow-dried hair off her shoulder. "You still got a boyfriend then? Or lost this one too?"

"Don't worry, Freddie's still about."

Willow blinked and comically looked up and down the street. "I don't see him."

"He's still in London."

"You left him on his own?" Willow remarked, admiring her own nails. "You must *really* trust him."

"*Freddie?*" I practically snorted. "I think I'm good," I laughed, tickled by the thought that Freddie would even have the energy to go out and find another woman let alone muster enough drive to do something with her.

Willow suddenly kissed my cheeks like she was a French aristocrat and tittered, "Right, well, Lil' Nips, it was lovely seeing you and all that. I'll let Mummy and Daddy know you're about, I'm sure at least one of them will want to see you. Ta ta."

Before I could even muster up a goodbye, Willow was skipping back over the road and towards her shiny convertible.

It must be nice going through life being that thick.

— Eight —

23rd August

God, I don't half feel like a wally. I packed my bags and headed over to Will's dorm. The big, mischievous grin he gave me nearly knocked me for six.

"Has someone sent me a kiss-a-gram?" he teased, leaning against the doorframe. "Please God, say yes." His smile soon dropped when I blurted out what I'd done.

"I'm going to go to Julian and ask to go home. Even if the show isn't cancelled, I still think I should leave."

"You can't," Will reached out and pulled me into a hug. "You haven't done anything wrong here, Mel. Not your fault Eileen was pissed all the time. You did the right thing telling someone." He then pulled away and the loser inside of me actually thought he might kiss me. He didn't, just asked, "You want to stay for a bit? I've got chocolate."

I would've stayed all night if he'd asked me to. And not gonna lie, I was disappointed when he didn't.

— *Melissa Bishop, aged 16, falling for a guy she barely knows because he's nice, fit, and feeds her chocolate.*

***

For the next few days that followed, Mum gave me the full silent treatment. She locked herself away either in her study or her bedroom, refusing to speak or listen to anything I had to say. Dad was the only one allowed anywhere near her, therefore he essentially became Mum's messenger, under strict instructions to pass on anything she had to say to me with the exact tone and intention she'd originally said it.

This led to Dad attempting a comically poor impression of Mum while I made dinner. "Until I can compose myself well enough to talk about the fact you've thrown all your future prospects away, I will be—"

Dad drew a blank, returning to his usual stance and regular tone. "Bugger this... Basically your mum is still upset and until you say sorry or wait for her to come around, she's going to continue as if you aren't here."

I raised both eyebrows at him. "Me? Apologise? *Me?* What have I got to say sorry for?"

"I haven't the foggiest." He shook his head and pulled one of the chairs out from under the kitchen table before plonking into it heavily. "I think it's quite sweet, you coming home to spend some time with her. *Stupid,* but sweet."

"Thanks... I guess?"

"Your mum, on the other hand, thinks you should have consulted with her first. She also said something about you being unreasonable, and something about... Oh, I don't know, and to be honest, I don't think your mother really does either."

I had a rant brewing on the tip of my tongue. I didn't need to consult with Mum; I was twenty-three years old and had lived independently for nearly five whole years. I did in no way need her opinion on things, and with how unreasonable and irrational *she* was being, frankly, I didn't want it.

However, there was something in the look on Dad's face that stopped me. I filled the kettle instead.

"Let me make you a brew," I sighed.

"Thank you, love." Dad reached out for my hand and squeezed it. "It's been a very stressful and emotional week for all of us... She'll come around eventually. "

"Has she got time to come around?" I asked, unironically, acutely aware we'd already lost four days together due to her stubbornness. We both knew Mum was notorious for holding a grudge. She didn't speak to me for two months when I spent my first Christmas with Freddie in London instead of at home. And didn't speak to me for a week when she found out I'd gifted her a moustache trimmer.

"She seems to think she has all the time in the world."

"We both know she doesn't," I stressed, the kettle boiling along with me. "Or at least I *hope* we both know. Please tell me you know that? I can't be fighting two delusional parents at once."

"Don't worry, I'm with you. I know how bad this is. I saw her cancer scans, she lit up like the Blackpool illuminations." He bowed his head mournfully. "However, *she's* the one who's sick, Freckles. We need to follow her lead on this to make it as pleasant a time for her as we can."

"So we go along with it?" I shook my head, baffled. "We just let her do as she pleases? Be that climbing up trees, shutting herself in her room for days, or even going about life as if *nothing* is wrong?"

"What do you expect her to do?" Dad calmly ricocheted. "Lie in bed and feel sorry for herself?"

"I don't know..." I poured Dad a tea, then made one for myself. "I came up to spend time with her," my phone buzzed away in my back pocket. It was only Freddie so I ignored it. "But now I'm here I'm wondering why the hell I bothered. Part of me genuinely thought she would want me here."

"I think that a part of her does," Dad considered, taking the steaming brew from me gratefully. "Not that she's going to ever admit it."

My phone started buzzing again.

Dad glanced at my back pocket, his wispy ginger and grey eyebrows drawing together. "Think somebody wants you. Either that or you've got a hive of bees living in your arse."

I glanced again at my phone, one new voicemail from Freddie.

"Two seconds, Dad." I placed my phone to my ear and waited with great anticipation. Freddie and I had barely spoken since I left. A few text messages here and there but nothing significant. He was making it clear he was still upset with me for leaving and I was pretending that I didn't care.

"Hiya, Mel. Just ringing to see how you are. Not an emergency or anything like that, just wanted to check in. Also ask how your Mum's doing and if there's anything I can do—" I found myself actually taken aback by the softness in his voice. Dad could clearly hear the message too. By the look on his face, I got the impression Dad was also impressed by Freddie's momentary lapse in character. Freddie's voicemail continued. "So, yeah, just ring me back when you can... Love you... Bye."

There was a click.

"*To return the message, press one—*"

I swiftly texted back.

Just about to have my dinner, ring you in a sec. Love you too x

"Is he drunk?" Dad joked with a light chuckle before adding with all seriousness. "Or stoned?"

"Probably," I huffed. "But at least he's showing an interest."

Mum poked her head around the kitchen door the same way a naughty child might try and re-enter a room after being told to sit on the bottom step. "Who's showing an interest in what?" she asked, her head remaining the only part of her in the room. She directed her eyeline and question to Dad, but when he didn't respond, her head tilted my way.

Clearly her need to know all was stronger than her passion to hold a grudge.

"Freddie was asking after you," I answered after letting her stew for a few seconds.

"Oh," she hummed, finally allowing one of her fluffy slippers to step over the threshold. "And what have you told him?"

"Not had a chance to speak to him yet. Was going to wait till after dinner."

"What are we having?"

"I've made a cheese toastie. Do you want one?"

Mum pulled a face that was undoubtedly her way of replying *no*. "What are my other options? I can't eat anything too heavy as I have my first treatment in the morning."

"*Say again?*"

"Ted, will you be at work, or free to drive me to the hospital for nine?"

"Woah, woah, hold on a sec, Mum," I snapped, not even realising I'd started wafting my fork at her. Stringy, melted cheese flew about like a cheddar-based bungee jumper. "You've got your first chemo treatment tomorrow and you're only just telling us?" My head whipped round to face Dad accusingly. "I say *us*, did you know about this?"

"No..." Dad grumbled under his breath.

Mum sucked her lips together, wrinkles forming like a picket fence under her nose. "Was that no to taking me to the hospital or no to not knowing, dear?"

"No to not knowing," Dad shook his head, befuddled.

"So, you are free to take me to the hospital then?"

Dad sighed, then raised his head and smiled as supportively as he could manage. "Yes, I'm free to take you to the hospital. I can let Emmot know—"

I went to protest but Dad shot me an uncharacteristically stern glare. *She's the one who's sick. We need to follow her lead on this to make it as pleasant a time for her as we can.*

I swallowed my brewing fury and bit into my toastie.

"I'm going to go ring Freddie," I grumbled, leaving the kitchen before I said something I would no doubt regret the moment it came flying out of my cheese-filled mouth.

"You done eating already?" Freddie mused as soon as he picked up the phone.

"Not really," I mumbled, pulling on my coat and heading out the back door, my cheese toastie in one hand, phone in the other. "Mum just sprung on me and Dad that she's going to have chemo for the first time tomorrow morning."

"Oh..."

"Needed a reason to get out of the house, calling you seemed as good a reason as any." I shoved the last of my toastie into my mouth and zipped my coat up to my chin.

"Glad I could help?" Freddie said, with either a sarcastic scoff, or genuine laugh, I couldn't tell. "So where are you if you're not in the house?"

"Heading to the shed on Mum's allotment. Only place where I'm out of earshot, yet still have signal and won't freeze to death." I pulled my coat tighter around myself, feeling the sharp October wind whip against my face.

"Right," Freddie interjected, making my feet stop in their tracks half way down the garden path. There was something in the way he cut me off, then inhaled deeply, it was as if he was gearing up to tell me something.

Tell me it's a new job.

"Probably a bad time to tell you that Steve's coming round tomorrow for the rent then, isn't it?"

I almost threw my phone into Christine's back garden. *Why didn't I see this coming?* I raged internally, slapping myself round the face for falling for his sickly sweet and phoney voicemail. *I should have smelled a rat from the moment he asked how I was!* I inhaled deeply, letting the icy air keep my blood from boiling over. "And that's why you're ringing, is it?"

"Well, technically, Mel, you rang me."

I bit my tongue, trying to stop myself from shouting profanities down the line.

"How much do you need?" *Say half,* I thought with a snarl and glimmer of foolish hope.

"As much as you can send over, really." Freddie sounded like he was actually trying to try and muster up a whimper. "Full amount preferably, but I don't want to put that kind of pressure on you if you don't have it."

Bit late for that now isn't it, Freddie? I thought coldly, a twist like barbed wire tightening around my heart.

— **Nine** —

24th August

They've found a replacement, so we have a new musical director and the show isn't being cancelled. *Wa-hey?* I guess.

Wes isn't speaking to me but no one has noticed since the MD has split us up. Apparently it's to help reduce our workload but it feels more like damage control in case me and Wes decide to make an official complaint. You know, since we were essentially locked in a room with a raving piss-head for a week.

I've now only got one solo; *The Cassiopeia Serenade*. It's as wanky as it sounds. A soft, romantic piece sung by a naive, simple star-gazer. Tell me why I wasn't surprised when Will revealed himself to be the one cast as the star-gazer?

I was just opening up Boris's case when he walked into the music room this morning. I might as well have had a big neon sign above my head saying, 'I THINK YOU'RE FIT' from the way I must've gawked at him. He was wearing loose grey sweatpants and a white t-shirt, for God's sake! I didn't have a hope in hell of being any other colour but tomato red.

Will depressingly showed more interest in Boris than in me. "Where's the piano bit?"

"It's a free-base button accordion, so it doesn't have a piano bit. Instead it has buttons on both sides."

Will frowned at me, pushing his bottom lip out in a really adorable way. "Balls. I was thinking I could have a go."

"You still can."

"Yeah, but I'll be crap. I would've been half good if it'd had the piano bit—"

It's nothing like the piano, I thought mischievously. Buttons or not, you still have to move the bellows to make a sound; and make a sound just to move the bellows.

Will found out how hard that actually was within the next five minutes. "Jesus Christ!" He laughed, sitting cross-legged on the floor, confused as hell and red in the face. "This is mental, and heavy as. How much does this thing weigh?"

"You get used to it," I giggled at him while he continued to dumbly prod and press the keys. Boris sounded like he was protesting from the way he was burbling out notes.

"I'd be able to see the keys a bit better if I was stood up," Will announced, getting to his feet but losing his balance completely. The weight of Boris threw him backwards, resulting in Will looking like an upturned turtle, sprawled out and pinned to the floor.

We both burst out laughing... God, I haven't laughed so hard in weeks.

— *Melissa Bishop, aged 16 and hating that she might be developing an awful, genuine crush.*

***

I was still raging about Freddie when Dad found me foraging through the kitchen cupboards the following morning.

He appeared at the door, big empty mug in hand, no doubt already on his third refill of the day.

"You know you have absolutely no food in?" I scolded, looking past forgotten tins of kidney beans and useless packets of instant sauce.

"What are you talking about? There's some cup o'soup right there," Dad pointed over my shoulder at a half-torn box, filled with one sorry sachet.

"Okay, I'll rephrase that. You have no *real* food in." I gestured to the uncharacteristically bare kitchen counters. "There's no more bread, no eggs. I mean, other than a thousand jars of crabapple jam and what is essentially war food, you've got nothing. Seriously, when did you last do a big shop?"

Dad thought back, looking a little stumped. "Err... What day is it?"

I shook my head, baffled, and nudged past him, "We're going to the shop."

"We can't, Freckles, your Mum is needed at the hospital in half an hour for her treatment."

I mentally slapped myself, surprised I'd been able to think of anything other than that. "Right, well, we'll all go, and while you two are in the hospital, I'll take the car to the big shop."

Dad's face fell. "I won't be going in with her."

"Why not?"

"She says she'd like to do this bit on her own... Keep some things private."

I had two options, lose my nut *again* or stay calm and support my dad, who was clearly having a harder time of it than he was letting on.

"Do you want to come to the big shop with me, then? While we wait for Mum?" I asked, choosing the second option and surprising even myself with my rapid maturity. *Who knew Melissa Bishop dabbled in personal growth?*

Dad pondered on the idea for a moment before breaking out into a timid smile. "That sounds like a plan."

Dad seemed to delight in his time out of the house. It made me wonder when he'd actually last stepped outside of the front door, other than to collect me from the train station.

He pushed the trolly giddily up and down the aisles while I tossed in bits and bobs. Every now and then I noticed him pick up speed and lift his feet off the floor, really relishing in a millisecond of immature fun.

On the dairy aisle the trolly got the better of him and he almost went crashing into the shelves of milk.

"That would've been embarrassing," he joked, righting himself, and getting the trolley's wheels centred. "I could've *moo*-ved you to tears if I'd done myself an injury."

I rolled my eyes, taking a tub of double cream off the shelf behind him.

"If you buy two single creams, you can make our own double cream. All you have to do is mix them together," Dad joked to himself, before turning magenta when a woman beside him politely explained:

"That's not how cream works, love."

I tried to suppress my laughter as Dad awkwardly walked away to join me by the cream cheese.

"She must think I'm a right idiot." He tutted, his cheeks still a bright shade of pink.

"She's not the only one," I teased, throwing him a wedge of manchego. "Do you think Mum will want some brie putting in as well?"

"Hmm?" Dad's childlike cheer immediately vanished from his face and I felt deep regret for bringing up Mum at all. I should've kept my mouth shut and let him enjoy his few moments of freedom.

"Do you think she'll be alright on her own?" Dad asked me as we were paying at the till.

"Oh, she'll be fine," I said, unsure whether my over-the-top reassurance was for Dad's benefit or my own. "She'll probably be glad to get an hour to herself."

I very much had to eat my words the moment we got into the car and Dad's phone started to ring.

"It's in the front pocket of my coat," Dad said, jutting his chin towards the pouch closest to me.

I checked the ID and was panicked to see a photo of Mum from years ago smiling back at me. "Mum?" I answered, trying to keep my voice level so as to not throw Dad.

There was nothing but sobs coming down the line, and the occasional pained groan.

"Can you come and get me?" I heard Mum weep, every choke of breath making my heart beat faster.

I looked across at Dad whose eyes seemed to be giant horrified orbs from behind his oval lenses.

"*Please...*"

I noticed my surroundings start to whizz past me as Dad picked up speed. The old Mini's engine spluttered back at him in protest the more he pushed his foot onto the accelerator.

"We're on our way, Mum," I told her, wondering if she could even hear me through her sobs. "Is there someone with you? A nurse, or a doctor or someone you can get to help you?"

"Please hurry..."

"We're coming. We'll be there in two minutes," I lied. We were more likely to be fifteen minutes away, even with Dad breaking the speed limit for probably the first time in his life.

— Ten —

25th August

Rehearsals were going amazing till Pippa went and ruined everything.

Will and I had been spending all our time together, laughing and chatting about any old crap, and sometimes even doing what we were supposed to be doing and running through the solo.

Will stares at me everytime I start to play Boris, forgetting he is meant to be singing.

I actually thought it might be because he likes me — he doesn't. *He can't like me*, I know that for a fact now, thanks to Pippa.

She came knocking on my dorm as I was getting ready for bed. I opened the door and she let herself in, muttering and chuntering something under her breath.

"I've got something to tell you," she finally said, before sitting on the edge of my bed and rolling her eyes. "Don't hate me but I would want you to do the same for me." She didn't wait for a reply, just came right out with it. "He has a girlfriend."

Pippa didn't need to specify, we both knew who she was on about.

— Melissa Bishop, aged 16, wondering why she feels so devastated that someone she barely knows has a sodding girlfriend.

***

We found Mum looking like a dishevelled bag lady outside of outpatients. Her face was blotchy and sore from crying, her body shaking from what I initially presumed to be the cold. Dad parked up beside her, not caring that half of his Mini was sticking out and blocking the exit.

"We're here, Mum. We're here," I spluttered, clambering out of the car and wrapping her trembling body in my arms. "What do you need?"

Mum's face was scrunched up in pain, her words inaudible as she tried to catch her breath.

Dad pulled his thick coat over her shoulders and led her to the car. "Come on, Terra, love."

I climbed into the cramped back seat with her and let her rest her head on my shoulder. As Dad weaved his way back out of the hospital car park, I could feel Mum's tears seeping through the fabric of my jumper.

With our God-given roles subverted, I stroked my hand down her chestnut hair and cooed words of comfort. "It's alright, Mum. It's okay. You're alright, we're here now."

It was as if she couldn't hear me. She just wept. Wept and sobbed into my shoulder, her body a quivering mess racked with unspeakable pain.

"Everything hurts," Mum finally choked, wiping her running nose with the cuff of her sleeve, her face scrunched up in agony. "Everything..."

I saw a flash of Dad's panicked face in the rear view mirror and felt myself slowly go into meltdown. I genuinely hadn't a clue what to do. Never in my life had I seen Mum - or anyone, in fact - in such agony. How do you comfort someone who is in so much pain they can't register anything else?

I took her hand and squeezed it tightly. "Give it to me," I whispered, rocking her like an inconsolable babe. "Give all the pain to me, Mum. Let it pass on to me."

Let me take it from you, I thought as she gripped my hand as fiercely as she was able. Her face looked almost unrecognisable as she clenched her teeth together and cried.

"Pass it through to me..." I breathed, praying that she'd be able to somehow hear me through her suffering.

Call it divine intervention, call it fantasy or delusion on my part, but in that moment, Mum went still and my whole body tensed up. As if she'd been sedated and I was being tasered at the neck. Mum somehow had heard my plea and managed to pass all of her pain onto me.

I took it willingly, feeling her relax in my arms that were now searing as though my blood had mutated into molten lava.

To this day, I still don't have an explanation for what happened in the back of that Mini. Only that Mum was given a moment's peace, and I was given an insight into what it must be like to be burned alive.

"She's asleep," Dad said, joining me in the living room and passing me a steaming cup of tea.

"Did you manage to get through to the hospital?"

He nodded. "Apparently pain is a common side effect of the treatment."

"That kind of pain is *normal*?"

Dad shrugged, collapsing into his favourite armchair in the corner of the room and letting out a deep sigh. "The pain usually comes later, not immediately after. So they said it could be more likely that she was in shock. Or the stress of it all was causing her to... Oh, I don't know."

"What happens now?"

"Well, the nurse said Mum'll be fatigued for a few days, and her appetite might be a bit off. We've just got to keep an eye on her and make sure she's staying hydrated and getting lots of rest."

I rubbed my eyes, my body telling me it was late at night despite the silver and white carriage clock on the mantelpiece indicating it was only one in the afternoon.

"Haven't you got your first shift back at *Rogan's* tonight?" Dad asked, noticing me check the time.

"Yeah, eight till late. The boss has me locking up so I probably won't finish until two."

"You sure you're up for that?"

I sipped my piping hot tea and rolled my eyes. "Doesn't really matter whether I am or not. Got to do it, haven't I?"

Dad looked at me pitifully, a deep sorrow in his eyes. "If it's money you need—"

"Dad," I raised a hand, silencing him. "To be honest, I could do with the distraction."

"Work is a distraction, is it?"

"Best one on offer at the moment, sadly."

My brain suddenly spat up the image of Will and I felt myself blush despite my better judgement. *Now that would be a distraction and a half,* I thought indulgently, hiding my rosy cheeks with my mug so Dad wouldn't see. *If only...*

"Are you back at work tomorrow?" I asked, trying to move the conversation, and my train of thought, onto something more appropriate.

Dad shook his head. "Don't tell your mum, but I've explained things to Emmot and taken some temporary time off."

"You think Mum would disapprove?"

Dad laughed half-heartedly. "I think she'd hit the roof. I get under her feet enough as it is."

– Eleven –

26th August

Everything got moved to the theatre this morning as we've started the tech run. My sheet music wasn't in Boris's case so I had to run back to the rehearsal room to try and find it.

Found Will instead. The last person I wanted to see after what Pippa had told me. Was going to turn and bolt but then I noticed he looked kind of lost.

He was lying on the floor, staring at the ceiling. I decided to join him. We were like that for ages until he suddenly reached out, took my hand and placed it on his chest. Honest to God, I could have died.

His touch gave me goosebumps all the way up my arm. It would have been a perfect moment if Pippa's voice wasn't nagging away in the back of my head, screaming, '*He has a girlfriend.*'

Will shifted onto his side and leaned into me, I couldn't believe what was happening. Then, "I know you have a girlfriend." Yep. The words practically fell out of my mouth and stopped him dead in his tracks. "Pippa told me all about her last night... Lucy, isn't it?"

"Yeah," was all he said, before lying back onto the floor. He still had hold of my hand. "Sorry, I just really wanted to—"

"It's okay," I cut him off, knowing I wasn't going to stay morally strong if Will suddenly started telling me how much he wanted to kiss me. Knowing me, I'd probably grab his face with both hands and snog his face off. *Sod Lucy.*

"I don't think it's right," I mumbled, not that confident in what I was saying.

"…Fair enough."

I spent the rest of the day kicking myself. Why didn't I just keep my trap shut and let him kiss me?! I don't know this 'Lucy'. I don't owe her anything. Why couldn't I simply let him kiss me and, for once in my life, enjoy myself?

Because I'm an idiot. That's why.

— *Melissa Bishop, aged 16, truly believing that kissing another girl's boyfriend might not actually be as bad as everyone says it is.*

***

Katie is mad, I concluded at the end of my shift when I was finishing off mopping the back room. Every now and then, I caught glimpses of her through the doorway, dancing to a tune that was only being played inside her head. She was wiping down tables to a hummed cha cha, and clearing the bar while she mimed a mysterious musical.

"I'm cashing up the till now, Mel. Do you want me to go through it with you?" she asked abruptly, causing me to half jump out of my skin. "It's pretty standard, but still part of the training." She flicked her blonde hair off her shoulder and threw a thumb back towards the bar. "It'll only take a sec."

I leaned against my mop. "I have worked here before, you know?" I stated cooly, hoping that Katie would interpret it as the intended, *'So you don't have to go through all the training with me'*, rather than, *'So you can shut up now'*.

Thankfully, she understood me perfectly and smiled softly. "Oh, that makes sense. Was wondering why you came in and took to serving like a chicken to water—" Her eyes crossed. "No, I mean goose, don't I?"

"Close..." I aided, a bemused smirk pulling at the corners of my mouth. "At least a goose can swim, but I think the phrase is 'taking to it like a duck to water'."

"Knew I liked you," Katie pointed at me. "Like I said, you've cracked it tonight. Most newbies hover around me like a bad smell. It took Danny well over a week to approach a table on his own. And don't even get me started on this lass who worked here last year. She was bloody useless. She came to work ready for a disco, and we're all doing a line dance. Do you know what I mean?"

Not in the slightest.

"You've worked here for a while, then?" I asked, going back to mopping down the floor while Katie took the last of the glasses out of the dishwasher.

"A couple of years," Katie polished the glasses with a rag, lifting one up every now and again to the light. "Rogan said you usually live in London, wanting to be an actress."

I rang out my mop. "*Wanting* being the keyword there," I mumbled under my breath. "Moved there when I was nineteen, not done much except a couple of independent projects with some mates from acting class. Thought interest from the industry might come when I finished drama school—"

"That's exciting!" Katie smiled so wide her dimples deepened into her peachy cheeks. "I've heard it's hard to get into the big ones, especially for the proper degrees."

I nodded, watching the dirty water swirl around the mop-bucket and feeling my chest tighten. *Drama school to mopping up Rogan's again in the space of a week...* "Took me five years to get accepted but I had to drop out, so I guess it's kind of irrelevant now."

Katie's face fell, and so too did the whole merry atmosphere of the space between us. "Were you not enjoying it?"

No I wasn't, was instantly at the forefront of my mind and on the tip of my tongue. It hit me like an anvil.

For the first time since walking out of Mr Braden's office, I actually thought about class. I hadn't been enjoying it all, if anything I'd been hating it. The pretentiousness of it all. The forced creativity and unbelievable amount of pressure from every which way. Maybe I'd wanted to quit school regardless? Mum's prognosis had just been a perfect excuse to do it without feeling any guilt. Maybe that's why I'd committed to dropping out so quickly.

"It wasn't what I expected it to be," I finally answered, not wanting to leave Katie hanging. "I still want to be an actor," I thought of my mum, and her trembling body in the back of the car. "Though life happens, doesn't it? And we don't always get what we want."

"Sometimes we do," Katie countered, leaning against the dishwasher, her eyes sparkling as a clearly delectable thought came bounding into her head. "Wanting it is only the first step. You've got to work your arse off to actually get it. Lots of people *want* to win the lottery and yet—" she laughed, "they never buy a ticket!"

I found myself smiling. Katie's humour and bubbly personality were undeniably infectious. *Maybe working here isn't going to be so bad...*

"What do you want to do?"

Katie wrinkled her nose playfully at me and raised her last squeaky clean pint glass. "What makes you think I don't want to be a bartender for the rest of my life?" She pursed her lips. "We can't all be famous actors."

"Fair point," I laughed.

"No, but seriously," Katie continued, not looking at all like she was being serious as her smile was almost as wide as her face. "I wanted to be a florist when I was five. Then a vet when I was ten, but I learnt they have a really high suicide rate."

"What?"

"Yeah," she nodded rapidly. "Most people who become vets love animals, right? And what do most vets have to do a lot of?" Katie drew her thumb across her neck as if slicing it open. "You're literally being paid to kill the thing you love the most." She shrugged, "Anyway, long story short, vet became astronaut, astronaut became botanist, botanist became baker... And now I'm back to wanting, eventually, someday, to be a florist."

My eyes flickered around the main room, retaking in the abundance of green, the plethora of flowers, only a small fraction of which were visible from the kitchen. "So *you're* responsible for all that?"

"Most of it," Katie pointed through the doorway to a hanging spider plant by the entrance. "Pat started with one and it looked really lonely so I suggested bringing in the rest."

"It's nice..." I thought back on the former appearance of *Rogan's* and found myself shaking my head, baffled by the transformation all over again. "Massive improvement from what it used to be."

Katie was suddenly next to me, smiling in the same sweet and welcoming way she'd been when I first met her. "Everything has the capability of change, you know?" she stated rather militantly, her eyes kind. "All anything needs is time."

Yep. She's definitely mad.

– Twelve –

27th August

The word 'awkward' doesn't even begin to cover it. Pippa noticed, but then again, it's so obvious a blind cat would probably be able to see that Will and I are off with each other.

"It's not my fault, is it?" she asked me during Julian's third meltdown of the morning.

I wanted to tell her, *Yes. Yes, Pippa, it is your fault. You shouldn't have told me Will had a girlfriend, then I could have snogged him in ignorant bliss.*

But I didn't. Instead I shook my head and watched Will from the band pit while he stretched on stage, surprised there wasn't literal drool running down my chin.

Will has no right to be as fit as he is! There's nothing else for it — I've just to hope and pray that he's stupid enough, or fancies me enough, to try and kiss me again before Mum comes to pick me up in four days!

— *Melissa Bishop, aged 16 and back to having the crappiest time ever in her whole bloody life.*

***

Mum's recovery from her first treatment was slow, steady, and agonising to watch. Not only did she point-blank refuse to admit she was struggling, she blatantly ignored every sign that her body was very much unable to keep up with her determined mind. It took her twenty minutes to get down the stairs, and even longer to get back up again when she realised she'd forgotten to put on pants.

Dad and I had no option but to conduct a plan to encourage her to rest. We decided it would be beneficial over the following days to drip feed the subject of sleep into the conversation, thus hopefully training her subconscious to make her stay the hell in bed.

"No one siestas in the UK, do they?" I asked Dad across the kitchen table, while I painfully watched Mum try and make herself some lunch. She could barely hold a knife to cut up some grapes, let alone smear brie onto a buttered cracker.

"I *see Esther* all the time at work. She's in accounts, cracking lass," Dad joked, Mum managing a weak smile while she poured herself a glass of orange juice.

"Think it's something we should adopt. A midday snooze after lunch. Toddlers and babies always do better after a nap, why should adults be any different?"

"Think siestas are more common in countries with a hotter climate, love," Mum added, pulling out a kitchen chair and sitting between Dad and I.

"I'm happy to whack up the central heating if it means getting a couple of hours of extra kip," Dad laughed, giving me a subtle wink when Mum nodded along, humming in agreement.

There was then a hefty knock on the door, too aggressive to be the postman. Dad and I looked at each other, Mum completely focused on her lunch.

"Who's that?" I hissed across to Dad.

"Sorry, Freckles, I've lost my ability to see through walls since you were last here," Dad whispered back before getting to his feet and heading for the front door.

I followed him out into the hall, and my stomach dropped when Dad revealed Uncle Kenneth standing on the front door step. He was wearing his muddy green wellies, brown camouflage coat and flat cap. He couldn't have looked more like a potato-wholesaler if he tried. He's an orthodontist.

"Ted, sorry for the drop-in. Been walking Bernard and—" Kenneth's eyes landed on me and he suddenly started grinning from ear to cauliflower ear. "Mel! Our Willow said you were up but I didn't want to believe it till I saw you myself."

"Why? Not like I'm Bigfoot—"

"More like Santa since we only see you at Christmas," Kenneth completely side-stepped Dad, letting himself, and all the mud off his wellies, into the house. He then wrapped me in a hug that forced me to inhale his wet-dog-scented coat.

"What can we help you with, Ken?" Dad nudged, thankfully causing Kenneth to release me so I could breathe clean air again.

"The bloody in-laws are driving me round the bend," he waffled on. "Wanting a big surprise do for Angela's 50th birthday."

She's not going to like that, I laughed to myself. *She only just accepted she was older than 45 last year.*

Dad clearly thought the same as me but was much more talented at maintaining his poker face. "And is this your way of inviting us, Ken?"

"No. Not to say that you're not invited, that is, but God, I haven't even got to that bit yet. Was actually wondering if my sis was in," Kenneth rambled. "See if she'd do us a favour of making the cake for free. Save us a bob or two, wouldn't it?"

Mum appeared by the kitchen door as though she'd been summoned. "I thought I heard you, Kenny. How're you doing, love?" she said cheerily, taking a timid step forward, her plate of lunch still in her hands.

"Alright, Terra—"

The three of us froze. We were all looking at the same thing, *Mum's eye*. I'd gotten so used to it since arriving that I hadn't even noticed how the droop of her eyelid had worsened over the past week and a half. It was nearly fully closed.

"Did I hear something about you needing a cake?" Mum went on, either genuinely oblivious or determined to not give any of the three of us a chance to mention the droopy-eyed elephant in the room.

"Yes, I—" Kennth stammered, momentarily lost for words. Then, "Sorry, Terra, but are you having a stroke?"

Ever the charmer, our Kenneth.

Mum's hand instinctively flew to her poor eye self-consciously. "The cake, Kenneth. Are you wanting tiers? Icing? Any particular flavour?"

Kenneth seemed affronted that his question had gone unanswered, so he looked at Dad and I for help.

I tried to follow Dad's lead and keep my mouth shut but that familiar frustration and annoyance at Mum's antics started bubbling anew in the pit of my stomach.

Put out that Kenneth was also ignoring *her* questions, Mum turned her back on him and headed for the stairs. "I've got some books in my study if you want to pick out something for me to replicate."

Kenneth pulled a sour face then cleared his throat with a half-arsed cough. "Seems as good a plan as any." He took a step further into the house.

"Wellington boots off, please, Ken," Mum chimed, notably out of breath four steps into her ascent. "Can't have you traipsing mud *all* over the house."

Kenneth rolled his eyes and began to pull off his boots ungracefully. "Ere', what's wrong with her face, Ted?" he half-whispered, half-hissed once Mum was out of earshot.

Dad shuffled awkwardly. "I think she said it was a cold."

"A *cold*?" Kenneth's top lip curled. "What kind of a cold does that to your eye?"

"A bad one," I added bluntly.

Uncle Kenneth managed not to talk about Mum's eye for about ten minutes before he finally broke. I had my ear pressed against the study door when it inevitably happened.

"Come on, Terra, just tell me. What have you done to your face? You look like you've been in a fight!"

"I told you, it's nothing."

"It doesn't look like nothing to me. Did you get stung by a bee? Hit yourself with a kitchen cupboard, or… You can tell me if it was Ted, you know?"

I felt my fists clench, ready to burst through the door if Mum so much as entertained the idea that Dad was at all to blame for her eye.

"Don't be ridiculous!" Mum thankfully snapped back. "Ted wouldn't so much as squish a spider let alone put a hand on me! For goodness sake, Kenneth, you're letting your imagination run wild."

A growing sense of dread started to sweep over me as I realised that if Uncle Kenneth was going to jump to horrific conclusions, then so might everyone else, especially if we all stayed lip-tied and sworn to secrecy. Clearly, Mum had had the same epiphany.

"If it stops you from rattling off and spreading rumours, fine, I'll tell you. But I want an absolute promise from you first that what I tell you does not leave this room."

"Bloody hell, Terra, you're starting to freak me out here."

"To put it simply, I have a tiny little lesion in my brain that's causing the muscle in my right eyelid to relax slightly."

"A lesion?" Kenneth cut in, "What's a lesion?"

"A tumour, Ken. I have a brain tumour. Four in fact, not that the quantity makes a difference, in my opinion, but there we are."

There was an agonisingly long pause.

"Oh, sis, I thought I'd die first..."

I'm surprised there wasn't a Mel-shaped-hole in the door of Mum's study from the way I burst into the room.

"Have you decided what cake you're having Uncle Kenneth?" I blurted out, my whole body shaking with fury and blind panic the moment I saw the devastated look on Mum's face. "Mum's got loads of good options so I bet you're spoilt for choice."

Uncle Kennth blinked at me before coming to. "Err, we didn't really get round to making decisions on the cake, to be honest–"

I looked past him and at Mum's cluttered roll top desk. Amongst all of the stacked papers, magazines, books and ring binders, there was an open photo album filled with all of Mum's past celebratory bakes. From Christening cakes to wedding cakes, birthdays to her annual Christmas pud. I flicked to a random page and pointed at the three-tier masterpiece. "That one looks good. Perfect for a 50th."

Mum peered at the centrefold. "That was the cake I made for Mum and Dad's ruby wedding anniversary, Ken. A lemon and poppyseed sponge with buttercream icing. Would that be something Angela would like?"

"She loves lemon in her G&T. Can you make gin and tonic flavoured buttercream, Mum? Might go perfect with it."

"I can give it a go."

"Brill. That's that sorted then isn't it, Ken?" I forced a wide smile. "All picked out for you so if it goes tits-up and Auntie Angela doesn't like it, you can blame me and Mum."

Anyone would have thought Mum and I had rehearsed it the way we bounced off each other and eventually escorted Uncle Kenneth out of the house.

The front door shut behind him with a slam aggressive enough to let him know, if he was still in any doubt, that he had said *completely* the wrong thing.

"What a dick," I cursed before turning to Mum and finding her exhausted at the bottom of the stairs.

"Agreed," Mum muttered, her top lip curling. "He is a dick."

– Thirteen –

28th August

Opening night tomorrow. Loads of the cast's family and friends are coming to watch the show. Not Mum and Dad though, *obviously*. I'm not surprised, because why the hell would they ever want to see me play a couple of hundred bars of weird music, while teenagers in tin foil dance around pretending to be stars?

Will's solo is stand-out. He can sing, dance, and act. Seems like Will's got it all — girlfriend included. *Ugh.*

I actually managed to get a full sentence out when he approached me at lunch today. "Have you got any family coming tomorrow, Will?"

He nodded.

Pippa gained a mischievous twinkle in her eye. "Does that include your brother?"

Will's face dropped and he death-stared her.

"Have I missed something?" I asked, dumbly.

Pippa burst into a fit of giggles. "Will's brother is famous, didn't you know, Mel? *Jordan Green.* He's on the West End, and he's as fit as!"

Will groaned as pretty much all of the girls in the cast, at the mere mention of his brother's name, came scurrying over. All of them repeating the same as Pippa — Will's brother is apparently every musical theatre girl's wet dream.

— *Melissa Bishop, aged 16 and very grateful she knows absolutely nothing about the Musical Theatre Universe.*

***

Uncle Kenneth hadn't actually made a promise to keep Mum's condition a secret, so none of us were really surprised when our phones started to blow up.

It began that evening as I was heading upstairs with Mum's dinner. I'd expected, and hoped, to find her in bed, but instead found her in her study.

I pushed open the door with a cheery, "Helloooo," only for my chime to be cut short. Mum was in her chair looking a little lost and confused, a box of medical supplies on her lap.

"You okay there, Mum?" I asked, timidly stepping towards her and offering a bowl of pasta out as if I were making an offering to a temple statue.

"Mmm?" she hummed back at me, still more focused on the white and blue packets in front of her than the food I'd brought. "I found these in my bag. The lady gave them to me when I went for my treatment the other day, but I can't for the life of me remember what they're for."

I kneeled down beside her and inspected one of the sachets, hearing the distant ring of the house phone downstairs.

After squinting to read the tiny text printed on the back, I recited, "Antibacterial mouth gel," causing Mum's face to light up with memory.

"Ah, that's it! They're for my mouth ulcers," she poked a finger into her chubby cheek as if pointing at the stinging culprits. "These must be to stop any infection."

"Probably," I forced a smile and gave her a weak thumbs-up. "Well, that's good... You know what they're for now."

She looked up at me, her good eye glistening with pride. "Clever girl," she leaned back in her chair and assessed me. "You need me for something?"

I raised the bowl of pasta again, and provided her with a fork from my back pocket. "Dinner is served."

At that moment, Dad came bustling into the room, the house phone pressed against his chest, a noise emitting from it that sounded a lot like a dying cat.

"It's your mother," Dad relayed with as much fake joy in his tone as he could muster. "She knows."

It took nearly an hour to get Nana to calm down, the phone passed from Mum to Dad, to me, to Mum, to Dad, like the worst game of pass the parcel ever played.

Dad took the brunt of it, keen to see Mum eat her tea rather than waste her energy and breath on a woman who clearly didn't want to hear, 'There's nothing to tell you, Mum. I'm fine,' on a loop. Nana wanted *details*.

Dad's only piece of advice before handing over the phone was, "Keep it simple, and if in doubt, Freckles, answer a question with a question."

"Does your mother's condition mean you're at home for the foreseeable future, Melissa?"

"What really *is* home, Nana?" I said, in a tone taken as philosophical but very much intended as sarcasm.

"Because, you see, with your Gramps golfing in Portugal and ignoring all of my calls, I could do with some company. Not to mention I've done a spring clean—"

"It's October."

"—and I've pulled some lovely items from my wardrobe. They're far too nice to go to charity, and pieces I'm more than happy to pass along to you, dear. Especially this teal evening gown I have set aside. Much too large for me now, thanks to this brilliant diet I'm on. But I really do think the white lace collar will bring out the green in your eyes."

"My eyes are brown, Nana."

"How about you pop over next week and try it on, along with the other items I have out?"

I'd rather crap in my hands and clap, I thought, looking at Dad with a desperate plea for aid. When initially answering a call about Mum's health condition, I did not expect to somehow be roped into trying on Nana's ratty old clothes by the end of it.

"Yep, sounds good. Now, my pasta is going cold so I'm going to have to go. Text me the time and what day you want me around. Love you, bye."

I hung up knowing Nana didn't have a clue how to text, and probably didn't even own a phone that *could* text.

After the Nana Tia tsunami of contact, Auntie Anglea was at it, ringing Mum to tell her how sorry she was and asking a million intrusive questions, her justification being she needed as much information as possible in order to get her head around it all.

Mum almost threw the phone out of her study window when Angela said, and I quote, "You read all sorts of stories about people losing loved ones to cancer, just never thought it would happen to *me*."

Before that call had come to a close, Auntie Beatrice was ringing Dad's mobile, then Cousin Iris was on the house phone, shortly followed by Great Uncle Matthew, distant Cousin Toby, and then some random woman named Amanda.

"I'm part of your Grandmother Tia's house group, love. We've just been told the news, absolutely heartbreaking. But you've got to remind yourself, dear, everything happens for a reason—"

I hung the phone up with an ungracious snarl before collapsing onto the living room sofa and rubbing my temples. *I need a drink*, I groaned to myself. *Or six...?*

The image of Will's face, smiling away, appeared in my mind again, bringing with it a much-needed second of calm. Then the itch of doubt started to scratch the vision of him away.

You really want to go there again? I asked myself, already scrambling for my phone. *It would be one hell of a distraction, but...* I scrolled through my call history and found the only number without an ID.

You know what? Sod it, you deserve a night off. The dial tone reverberated against my ear.

"Hello?" Will answered, his voice ashamedly making my chest tighten and eyelashes flutter.

"Hi, Will. It's... Err... Mel. You okay?"

"Oh, finally decided to call me back then, ey?" he asked and I actually found myself genuinely smiling for the first time all day. "Took you long enough."

"Yeah, sorry, life has been a bit mad."

Understatement of the year.

"Sounds like you could do with those six drinks then, eh?"

"You read my mind," I half-joked. "Don't suppose you're busy? Like, are you free tonight?"

"Yeah, actually, I am free. Do you want me to pick you up from somewhere and whisk you away for a couple of hours?"

Try not to sound too desperate, I told myself, milliseconds before coming out with the embarrassing reply of, "Oh, God, yes, please!"

Too late.

— Fourteen —

29th August

What an absolute disaster! And, surprisingly, I'm *not* talking about the Will situation. I'm talking about opening night.

A fake dagger that turned out to be not *that* fake meant Tyler got a tiny puncture in his arm. Despite only causing a spec of blood, Tyler reacted as if he'd had his whole arm sliced off. He wailed, he shouted, and he got all the attention he'd been so desperately craving. Someone had to step in and take his place for Act Two. Only, his stand-in didn't know the lines, so spent the rest of the show with their nose between the pages of the script. Threw everyone off. Like I said, absolute disaster!

Only positive thing to come out of it was during the interval, while Tyler was getting bandaged up, Will stuck his head into the band pit and kissed me on the cheek before whispering, "Drinks in my dorm tonight. You in?"

Hell yes. My prayers have been answered. I know I've only got Will in my life for another couple of days and even though he's got a girlfriend, I'm going to soak up as much time with him as I can.

— *Melissa Bishop, aged 16, head over heels for a bloke she's only known for two weeks. Saddo.*

***

Rather than have Will show up outside my parents house and give Mum an actual stroke, I instead suggested he pick me up from the bottom of the hill. That meant I could tell Mum and Dad that I was going to work, raising no impertinent questions. Not to mention I'd also be well out of curtain-twitcher Christine's sight. So, no chance of her ratting me out when she next claimed she'd run out of milk and gave Mum the latest unofficial neighbourhood watch update.

It was borderline laughable, considering how long I'd been living independently in London, that I would need to consider such things, but I hadn't completely forgotten the pitfalls of living in a small country village. Everyone knew everyone, and everyone was far too interested in whatever business they identified as their own — which was essentially everything.

Will honked as he pulled up on the pavement beside me, then wound down his window.

"What's your hourly rate, sexy?" he joked, looking me up and down and actually making me blush. I'd tried to gauge my outfit correctly but had limited options considering I hadn't packed much to begin with. Ripped jeans and one of Mum's old (and therefore oversized) hoodies seemed as good a choice as any. I looked considerably better than I had at our last encounter, which was all I'd really wanted to achieve. My outfit was most definitely not date attire as it couldn't, *and shouldn't,* have been conceived as a date by either of us. I didn't need a date, I needed a drink.

Will is merely my alcohol mule, I reminded myself before answering his tease with an easy, "Accuse me of looking like a prostitute within the first two seconds of seeing me. God, you haven't changed have you?"

"That's why you love me," he replied, reaching over and skillfully opening up the passenger door for me from the inside.

I hopped in and immediately felt the hairs on the back of my neck stand up on end. Not the best of signs considering I had tried to convince myself since the moment I hung up on him that this was a good idea. It would be casual, fun, and a much needed break from the pains of reality.

"So, what's the plan?" I asked, just as Will revved up his engine and started to drive through town.

"You tell me. You're the one who wanted the getaway car."

"True..." I fiddled with the hem of my jumper nervously, aware that even though Will's eyes were firmly on the road, he was still giving me his full attention.

"You've got two options," he started, clearly picking up the vibe that I wasn't in the best mindset to be making decisions. "We pick a bar and drink ourselves senseless before dragging ourselves, most likely, to a kebab shop. Or we cut out the faff, save ourselves some cash, and head straight to mine. We can indulge ourselves in some wine, a home-cooked meal and... No one else will be around to bother us."

The latter, I internally squealed. *Definitely the latter!*

"Sure, whatever," I managed to unconvincingly croak out instead.

"Mine it is then," Will stole a look at me and winked, "Glad I hoovered."

Will's place was *nice*. Hell, who am I kidding? It was breathtakingly stunning. To a point that when he pulled onto the stone paved driveway, I half believed he'd taken a wrong turn.

"Jesus," I gasped under my breath as I stepped out of the car. I was met with an illuminated path leading to what could only be described as a bloody country estate. "Thought you said you worked in statistics?" I nervously laughed, feeling overwhelmingly ashamed that I'd chosen to wear my tattiest trainers. "Sure you're not a drug lord or something?"

"Only on the weekends," Will teased back, locking his car before dynamically gesturing for me to take the lead up to the house. He placed his hand on the small of my back the moment I reached his side. Without warning or want, the contact made me almost buckle.

What are you doing? I internally yelped, letting him guide me up the path.

"So..." I stammered while he unlocked the giant wooden front door. "You said you lived with your Mum?"

"I don't think I did. Mum lives near here, but God, I don't live *with* my mum."

"Oh, right..." I didn't know whether to feel more anxious or relieved.

My jaw nearly dropped the moment I stepped over the threshold and into the opulent hallway. The high ceiling would most definitely have engulfed my parent's house, and the front room was bigger than the entire flat I shared with Freddie.

Freddie.

Bile crept up my sandpaper-like throat. *Sod Freddie,* I cursed to myself again, before beginning to take off my shoes. *He's not even bothered to check in on you since you sent him the full rent! Sod. Him.*

"You really don't have to do that," Will smirked, making my cheeks burn.

"Are you joking?" I replied, pulling my trainers off with a determined *oof*. "I feel like I should be wearing an evening gown or something, not jeans and one of my mum's old jumpers."

"You don't have to be wearing *anything*, if you don't want to," Will flirted, looking me up and down and making me turn an embarrassing shade of beetroot. Thankfully, he then turned and walked further into the house, so I could take a solitary moment to catch my breath.

Once my skin had returned to its normal colour, I followed him into the most beautiful living room. A grand piano took centre stage, surrounded by large leather sofas, a not-yet roaring fireplace, and a glass-top coffee table that I could have sworn was bigger than my bed back at home.

"This is..."

I didn't need to say a thing, I could tell by the smirk on Will's face that my reaction was the same as that of everyone else who graced his halls. Probably one of the main reasons he'd chosen to live in a place like this — it made people swoon without him having to do a thing.

Will disappeared through a door and a few minutes later came back with two glasses of red wine, and the bottle tightly tucked under one arm.

"Here you are, as promised," he said, passing me a glass. "Now, when I said home-cooked meal, what I actually had in mind was something more along the lines of some chips and dip."

"That your pièce de résistance?"

"No, but talk more French to me and it will be," he beamed, before sipping his wine and placing the bottle down on the coffee table. "Make yourself at home and I'll be back with the best hummus you've ever tasted."

I did as I was told and nestled into one of the large sofas. It was the kind of sofa that, if you weren't careful, could nurse you into an easy sleep and bury you in a mountain of throw pillows and flannel blankets.

"How's visiting your folks going?" Will called from what I assumed was the kitchen.

I didn't answer, pretending I hadn't heard him. This was supposed to be a getaway, not an opportunity to talk about all the toxic goings-on at home.

"Guessing not great since you're spending your evening with me and not them," Will presumed correctly, popping back in to take a good assessing look at me and drink some more of his wine.

I still didn't answer, revelling in the fact this all felt weirdly familiar — except our roles had been reversed.

"Fine," Will shrugged, finally taking the hint that I was most definitely not there to talk about my parents. "Keep your secrets."

"Not a secret," I replied flatly, tallying up how many people I'd spoken to about Mum's condition over the last couple of hours. If anything, this was the opposite of a secret, and something Will didn't need to be a part of in any capacity. It would only burst the bubble he was currently creating around me. *It's not about keeping secrets, it's about staying sane.*

"How's your family?" I finally piped up, letting a mischievous, knowing smile pull at the corners of my mouth. "How's your brother doing?"

Will's default smirk fell instantly away, and I noticed him clench his jaw, irked. "Jordan is fine."

"Really?" I continued to push tauntingly, "He's still thriving on the West End, isn't he?"

"Yes..."

"I saw him in a show last year. The one he won that award for. He was..." I pretended to be lost in blissful nostalgia and Will started to scowl, "...as talented as ever. You must be so proud of him."

Will stiffened before hitting my torment back with a "You still auditioning for drama schools? Or did they finally decide to give you a pity pass and let you in?"

I faked a laugh. "Oh ha ha. I did get in, *actually*—" I nestled myself deeper into the sofa, suddenly uncomfortable. "Though had to drop out due to... a *little* family emergency. I've not given up on the *pipe dream*, as you called it, but my options are a little bit limited at the minute."

"You've gotten further with it than I did, Mel. You should be proud of yourself regardless," Will replied, momentarily earnest. He then began to sniff the air comically. "I think I smell something burning."

"I didn't know chips and dip required the oven?"

"They do the way I make them," Will joked before disappearing again, giving me a long while to get up and have a nosey around the room. There were paintings but no family photographs, generic ornaments but nothing too personal.

Anyone could live here, I thought, assuming that Will liked it that way. *He never was the one for opening up.*

I was running my hand across the top of the piano when Will returned with a platter of dips and a giant ceramic bowl of tortilla chips. As he placed them down on the coffee table, a nostalgic thought tickled me into playing a couple of notes on the beautiful instrument. "You play piano, don't you?"

"Be pretty weird me having one if I didn't," Will joked, watching me from the sofa. "But it's been a while, I've gotta admit."

"I remember you saying something about being able to play Boris if he had piano keys."

"Who?"

I laughed, the name actually sounding weird coming out of my own mouth. I hadn't played Boris in years, let alone spoken about him. "My old accordion, he was a *Borsini,* so I called him Boris."

"Oh," Will nodded along, though evidently none the wiser. He took a bite of a guacamole-smeared chip. "Do you still play?"

I shook my head, feeling a little foolish about bringing the whole thing up. It made me think of the silly little girl who was too embarrassed to play her accordion despite the fact she really did love it. "It wasn't exactly the coolest instrument."

"I thought it was cool."

I sat opposite Will on the adjacent sofa and took a handful of crisps. With every careful bite, I became more aware that if I dropped a single crumb or speck of hummus it would most definitely stain my immaculate surroundings. "I used to joke that the accordion was the unsexiest instrument ever. Anything else, like a violin or a piano, you could play naked and look sexy as hell. An accordion? You'd be worried about getting a nipple caught in the bellows."

Will laughed, pulling me out of the past and into the heated moment in front of me. "See, I think you're wrong there. A violin, *or even a piano,* leaves nothing to the imagination. You're fully on show if you're playing either of them naked. But an accordion, you've no idea what's behind it... waiting for you." Will subtly licked his lips and I felt as though the fireplace beside us had suddenly been ignited and fed with gasoline. "I think that's sexy as hell."

I tried to put all my concentration on chewing rather than the image of Will naked, but it was proving exceedingly difficult. Especially considering Will was staring at me with a sly smile spread across his face, and a mischievous twinkle in his eye — almost as if he was daring me to ask him to strip and play.

I thought I'd been in danger earlier in the evening; now I was practically drowning. I could have indulged in it, swam in it till I wrinkled in delight. But no, my barely functioning brain decided to snuff out whatever fire was crackling away inside of me by spewing out four simple words.

"I have a boyfriend."

Will didn't even flinch, he simply continued to stare at me, a mix of amusement and admiration combined. I might as well have told him 'I don't eat fish' from the reaction I got.

"So?" Will finally replied, before taking a long sip of wine. "I have a girlfriend."

"You do?" I blinked.

Will pulled a face, like he was trying to work me out, and coming off short. "Don't sound so surprised, Mel."

"No, it's just..."

I was stuck between a rock and a hard place, and from the glint of winning smugness in Will's eye, I could tell he knew it. I could hardly have had a go at him for being there with me when he had a girlfriend, when I was also there despite Freddie.

We were both as innocent - or as guilty - as each other.

"What's his name?" Will asked, still looking at me funny.

"Freddie."

"And how long have you been together?"

"About two years." I answered sheepishly. Forgetting a boyfriend who'd only been official for a couple of days, or at a push, a couple of weeks, would've been understandable. But two years? That was essentially as bad as forgetting you had a second head, or a third boob.

I was feeling horrendously ashamed of myself and decided to put the spotlight onto Will instead. "What about your girlfriend? How long have you guys been together?"

The answer to his question would decide who out of the two of us was more in the wrong.

"About four months."

Bollocks.

Will seemingly read my mind and started shaking his head, chuckling softly. "We met through a mutual friend. She's his sister, actually, so you can imagine how happy he is with the whole thing."

"Not very?"

"Exactly." Will smiled reassuringly before asking, "How'd you meet Freddie?"

Will saying Freddie's name disturbed me. I hadn't realised how much my happiness had depended on being able to keep these two worlds separate. Or how important it had been, for my own sanity, to push Freddie to the back of my mind.

"He was working in a bar that I went to with a couple of friends from acting class. They're all a lot more outgoing than me, so instead of dancing on the tables and eventually getting kicked out, I hung out with Fred at the bar. Got his number and…"

"Happily ever after?"

"Something like that," I grumbled, shoving a few more tortilla chips into my mouth and seriously considering downing the rest of the bottle of red wine in front of me. I didn't want to talk about Freddie. I didn't want to even think about him. All it did was make me feel the same upset and fury I'd felt the other day when he'd gone from 'love you' to 'pay the full rent, would you, babe?' in the space of one phone call. *Pillock*.

"How do you think your girlfriend would feel about me being here?" I asked, deciding it was better to keep the spotlight on Will and not me.

"She'd probably be fine with it," he shrugged, before a familiar look deepened the laugh lines around his eyes and caused my chest to tighten. "We're just two old friends catching up, after all. Having a drink and an innocent chin-wag. Not like I'm throwing you down onto that rug and doing things to you that I *know* you like... Is it?"

I must have passed out because I don't remember what came after Will spoke, only that I came to with my mouth dry, my arse frozen to the sofa, and my jaw practically on the floor.

"You're still *so* easy to wind up, aren't you?" Will mused, getting to his feet and topping up my glass of wine. "We're not doing anything wrong, so just chill and enjoy yourself, okay?"

"Okay," I gulped, not entirely convinced.

— **Fifteen** —

29th August

When Will said, 'Drinks in my dorm tonight, you in?' I naively thought that meant drinks like on my first day. Him, me, Tyler, Pippa and the others. But no. It was *just* me and him.

We sat on his bed, him at one end, me at the other, our toes meeting in the middle; playing a game of footsie.

"So, now that you know about Lucy, suppose I better ask you if you have a boyfriend or not," Will suddenly said, causing me to almost choke on my own spit.

"No. I don't," I replied, desperate to add, *because unlike some people, if I did have a boyfriend, I wouldn't try and kiss someone else.*

Will must have read my mind as he started to smirk at me. And I kid you not he came out with, "Do you want me to try and kiss you again?"

Is he being serious? I screamed internally, unable to take my eyes off him. I couldn't believe it, and was genuinely wondering if maybe my prayers had been answered a little *too* well.

"I'm up for it if you are," Will continued, clearly loving the fact he'd made me lost for words. "And if you haven't got a boyfriend, then I'm the only one out of the two of us doing anything wrong… Aren't I?" Will sat up and shuffled down the bed towards me, my heart pounding. "Do you want me to kiss you?" he repeated, while I practically gawped at him, lost for words.

He's enjoying this, I realised with a slight twinge of anger bubbling up inside of me. He knew I fancied him but he wanted to make me say it. He wanted me to beg for a kiss!

I may be inexperienced. I may be naive and bloody stupid at times, but I'm not going to make someone else's boyfriend cheat. I'm not that kind of person.

"No, I don't," I snapped, causing Will to stop dead in his tracks. "So, get back to your side of the bed before I slap you."

He did go back, not stung one little bit. "Let me know if you change your mind," he teased, with a wicked smile.

I hate him.

– Melissa Bishop, aged 16, feeling anything but hate for the charming, flirty, bugger in front of her.

***

"I can do what I like, Ted!" I heard Mum yell from her bedroom as I was pulling on my coat, readying myself for work the following evening. "I don't care what those bloody pamphlets suggest or what those doctors have said!"

"Everything alright up there, Mum?" I called, holding onto the bottom of the bannister for support while I pulled my trainers on.

"Ignore us!" Mum yelled back, before Dad appeared like a wound-up tin monkey on the landing.

"Can you *please* come up here and tell your mum she is not fit to drive!"

"I'm out of jam sugar, Ted," Mum barked, still out of sight. "And those crabapples are going to rot if I don't do something with them today!"

Dad shot me a desperate look and I clambered the stairs to his aid.

Mum was glaring at me with her good eye from the moment I stepped into her bedroom. "Before you even start, I am a grown woman, Melissa. I can drive if I so wish."

"Not when you're half-way to becoming a pirate, Mum. All you're missing is the parrot."

She shook her head, outraged, "I don't think you understand the severity of this situation!"

"*Me*? You're the one suggesting getting behind a wheel with only one eye working."

Dad stuck his head in, his cheeks the same colour as his hair. "You wouldn't be covered on the insurance if something were to happen—"

"What makes you think something is going to happen? I'm an excellent driver." Mum put her hands on her hips, "Never had a point on my licence in all my life."

"Only because you've never been caught."

"Irrespective," Mum ground out. "I *still* need jam sugar."

Dad groaned and rested his forehead on my shoulder, "What do I do, Freckles?"

"Hide the keys," I mumbled back to him. "With only one working eye, it will take her twice as long to find them."

"What are you two whispering about?" Mum asked bluntly, taking great effort to pull her woolly jumper over her head.

"I've convinced Dad to drive you to the big shop and let you get your jam sugar."

"*Let me*?" Mum retorted. "Oh, I have to ask permission now, do I? Will his lordship give me permission to go downstairs? To eat dinner tonight? To make myself a cup of tea later?"

Dad's head shot upright, and I could feel him whistling like a kettle as his wispy red eyebrows furrowed. "Can I do your shift at *Rogan's* for you?" he grumbled into my ear, "and you stay here with her?"

I raised my work keys to him, "Go ahead. I could do with an early night."

There was the smallest of smiles and a flicker of genuine temptation as Dad's fingers twitched by his sides. Then, "I'll get my coat on and meet you downstairs, Terra."

Mum sucked her teeth in response.

Dad gave me a quick peck on the side of my head before trudging off down the stairs, grumbling some concoction of profanities under his breath.

"Are you off to work, then?" Mum queried, giving my all-black outfit the once-over.

"Yeah, and I'm locking up so won't be back till late."

"Does Freddie know you're working such unsociable hours?" Mum queried with a curl of her top lip. "Has he got his own job yet?"

I ignored the bile that was creeping up my throat, and simply shrugged. I'd tried my hardest to not think about Freddie all day. The previous night, with Will in front of me, it had been easy to cast him from my mind. Will was distracting me with easy conversation, flirty banter, and a rogue touch of my hand when he took my wine glass from me to fill it up. With all of those delectable fixations no longer in play, Freddie was sitting in the front of my mind, making me feel enormous amounts of guilt. All of my former fury at him eradicated.

"We've been a bit too busy to talk the last couple of days, so I don't know how Fred's doing, Mum," I confessed with a shameful bow of my head. "I was going to ring him on the walk down to work."

"I see..." Mum then pulled a face, never one for hiding her disapproval, and I took my que to leave.

"Alright, Mel?" Freddie answered groggily, after waiting till the last ring to pick up.

"You sound half-asleep."

"I *am* half-asleep," he grumbled back, before sniffing deeply, clearing his airways and waking himself up further.

"Have you only just woken up?"

"I've been busy at work all day, haven't I? Thought I'd get an early night. I'm dicked."

I froze.

"*Work?*" I was practically speechless. "You never said you got a job."

"You never asked," Freddie cut me off bluntly. "Not heard from you in a week."

"It's been four days," I hit back, refraining from explaining that he had also failed to pick up the phone and ring me.

Freddie's sharp intake of breath indicated to me that a rant was on its way. "I already felt bad enough having to ask you for the rent, but to have you then ignore me on top of that was a right kick in the bollocks, you know?"

"I haven't been ignoring you, Fred, I've had a lot on," I interjected, thinking back over the events of the past couple of days; Mum's treatment, the aftermath of Mum's treatment, the family all finding out, dinner at Will's... *Oh*

God. "Sorry, Freddie..." I backpedalled, the guilt engulfing me.

"You should be sorry, I was really looking forward to telling you I got a job, now that's ruined and all."

I started to drag my feet against the pavement, kicking the odd spec of gravel. "You can still tell me about your new job Freddie," I sighed. "I want to hear all about it."

Freddie grunted, then told me with little to no enthusiasm, "Well, Elliot called in a favour and managed to get this new warehouse shop in Peckham to hire me. Literally all I've got to do is hop onto the 36 bus and I'm there. Not like all the faff I had to do for Susan to get across town."

"That's great, Freddie," I said, a genuine smile taking over my face. "Honestly, that's the best news I've heard all day."

"You don't have to patronise me, Mel."

My smile vanished. "I'm not patronising you, Fred. I'm just saying that it's great you finally got a job."

He scoffed, the noise making my stomach churn. "What do you mean by *finally*?"

I wrapped my coat tighter around myself, adamant it was the cold wind that was suddenly making my eyes sting.

"I was actually thinking you were ringing up to speak to me, tell me how much you miss me, but now I feel like I'm on the phone with my mum. Do you also want to know if I've washed my pants? Eaten anything green? Watered the bloody plants?"

"Maybe I shouldn't have rung," I resigned with a pitiful sigh. "Sorry, Fred."

"No, I'm glad you did," Freddie chuntered back, his voice softening. "I miss you, you know? It's weird not having you about."

My heart fluttered slightly, I couldn't help it. "That's nice to hear..." I trailed off, swallowing the acorn of bile that had been lodged in my throat. "It's been absolute chaos here."

"I bet."

The line went silent, me giving him an ever stretched opportunity to ask me to expand. He didn't.

"Right, well, I'll talk to you later then, yeah?" he finally said, before yawning loudly. "Like I said, I'm wanting an early night. Work has knocked me for six and I've got an early start again tomorrow."

"I understand," I replied softly, reverting back to being exactly how he needed me to be, positive and supportive. He was working hard, changing his ways and missing me after all. Or at least that was what I was telling myself, to stop my pain, shame, and frustration from boiling anew.

"Night, babe."

"Night."

– Sixteen –

30th August

Wrap parties are jokes. Especially ones that are full of seventeen year olds who are drinking alcohol-free beer and somehow still getting rat-arsed.

I stuck to the lemonade. Was ordering myself one at the bar when I felt a hand slither around my waist. I fully wanted to believe it was Will but couldn't quite manage to convince myself that he would be so ballsy in front of the entire cast, crew, and all their families.

"What're we having?"

My body shivered. It *was* Will.

I turned and was pleased to see his sexy face so close to mine... But something wasn't quite right. His eyes were too dark, his jawline too sharp. Then it hit me — it *wasn't* Will. It was his clone, his double, his twin. Except this version of Will was older, broader, and... *sexier?*

"Name's Jordan," he introduced himself with his free hand, the other still firmly around my waist. "Can I buy you a drink, princess?"

"No, you can't," an irritated growl replied from over my shoulder. I turned and saw Will, a dark shade of red, standing behind us. I could have sworn I could see steam billowing out of his ears!

"Didn't ask you, lil' brother, I asked *her*." Jordan's eyes landed back on me and my arms erupted in goosebumps. *Clearly the skill of making a girl turn to jelly from one look runs in the family.*

"She's underage, Jordan," Will gritted his teeth.

"*She* also has a name," I bit off before I could stop myself.

"Oh, I like you," Jordan flirted, giving me a squeeze. "Name or no name."

I can't lie, it was amazing knowing I'd basically turned on a guy who was way, *waaay* out of my league — pissing Will off in the process was an absolute bonus.

— *Melissa Bishop, aged 16, playing with fire and loving the way it burns.*

***

I've never been a keen observationalist but even I could tell that Katie was in more of an odd mood than usual. She was messing up orders, forgetting to check the toilets, and had tried to clear a table while the customers were still eating. Twice.

"Third time's a charm," I said as she came towards the bar with a tray full of dirty dishes and table eight's bill.

"What a moppet," she groaned, placing the tray down and nearly tipping all the plates onto the floor. "You won't be surprised they didn't leave me a tip." She ruffled her blonde hair with her fingertips. "Do you ever just feel like a zebra that's lost its spots?"

"Can't say that I have."

"Alright, what about boyfriend trouble? Have you ever had that?"

"Once or twice," I nodded listlessly, watching as Katie lolled against the bar with a groan, holding her pretty head in her hands. "Your fella giving you a headache?"

"Oh, he's accusing me of making a melodrama out of a molehill again. What else is new?" Katie wafted her hand at me, "Don't really want to get into it."

"Ooo, but why not?" I encouraged, trying to lift her mood, since seeing Katie blue was equivalent to dunking a sausage roll into a mug of tea — just plain wrong. "I could do with a good bitch and a moan about someone I've never met."

"I don't want to bitch about him because he hasn't *technically* done anything wrong."

"I'll have a moan about my fella first if that makes you feel better about it," I joked, not realising that would somehow completely turn Katie's solemn mood upside down.

"Yeah, alright," she cheered. "What's yours done?"

"I was jo—" I rolled my eyes, suppressing the smile that Katie's eagerness was bringing to my face. "He got a new job."

"What a bastard," Katie beat her fist against the bar. "I'll kill him if you like, I always carry a shovel in the boot of my car. Well, it's actually a trowel. Does the same job, just takes a little longer."

I started laughing. Katie, for all her lunacy, was addictive. "Why do you travel with a trowel?"

Katie shrugged. "I help my granny with the gardening every Tuesday. Can't use her tools as they're always covered in sunscreen. So, is your boyfriend relocating? Is that the problem? Does his new job require him to ship off to Australia or something?"

"I wish," I snorted, hearing the bell for service jingle in the back room. "He's been needing to get a new job for weeks. He's gone and got one, and not told me. I don't get it."

Katie's eyes crossed. "You've lost me, chuck."

"He's broke and has been for a while," I sighed, Katie following me into the back room with her tray. "Been living off the money his parents send him once a month, and that barely covers his weed habit. So, I've been picking up the slack and been begging him to get a job for ages. I move back home, and he gets a job. You'd think I'd be happy but I've only just found out. He was such a dick about it, following it up with saying he misses me, so I can't even get mad at him."

"Mad at who?" Rogan asked, wiping his hands on his apron and sliding across table three's order.

"Me and Mel are having boyfriend trouble," Katie answered for me, sounding thoroughly entertained.

Rogan started shaking his head profusely. "No, no, no." He waggled a grubby, sausage-like finger between the two of us. "I do not need another one of you coming into my kitchen and crying about their fella. No, no, no. It's not happening. Since Katie started seeing her new fella, I've had *more* than enough. One of you I can cope with, I draw the line at both."

"Like you can talk," Katie remarked with a flick of her blonde hair. "Only last week I found you in here prepping and having a blub-session because Pat had spray-painted your motorbike helmet pink."

"Doesn't count. That was a private moment, no one was meant to see it," Rogan rolled his shoulders back. "You two might as well be washing your knickers out in the street. Table three's order is ready, Cheese-*melt*."

"But we haven't finished bad mouthing our fellas!" Katie protested, blocking the doorway. "I still have to bitch about mine!"

I picked up the plates and side-stepped her with ease. "The couple at table three are probably hungry, Katie."

A distant two-pitch whirl of a siren started to ring in my ears as I stepped towards the bar. Outside, the street had suddenly started flickering blue. Cars were pulling up onto the pavement and within seconds an ambulance went whizzing past.

Goosebumps spread across my skin causing me to nearly drop my service. Without a coherent thought, I thrust both plates at Katie ungraciously and started to bolt for the door.

"Where are you going?" Katie called after me, but I was already outside and heading up Main Street. The sharp wind whipped my face, threw about my hair and pushed me towards the siren. As cars started to rejoin the road and go about their journeys, the ambulance came back into view. It was speeding towards Brigate Road.

Don't turn up the hill! I internally screamed. *Don't turn—*

The ambulance swerved the corner in front of me and started to speed up the lane towards Mum and Dad's house. I had no way of knowing, but every fibre of my being told me that the ambulance was for Mum.

I never ran so fast in my life. The whole way home, three words circled around my tortured head, *I'm not ready.*

— Seventeen —

30th August

Will practically dragged me away from his brother the first moment he could. Took me out the fire exit and into the alleyway behind the back of the theatre.

"Are you *mental*?" he barked at me, practically throwing me against the red-brick wall. "Jordan's twenty three!"

"So?" I stubbornly replied, enjoying the undeniable jealousy in Will's eyes.

"You're sixteen, Mel. He's older than you!"

"So are you! Doesn't stop you from flirting with me."

Will went to protest but I raised an accusing finger at him.

"Don't even. All you've done these last two weeks is flirt with me. You can't start losing your nut now because someone else is having a go."

Will's lips went thin and suddenly all of the air evaporated from my lungs as he stepped towards me and closed up what little space there was between us.

"You make it so hard not to flirt with you," Will growled hungrily. "Nah, scratch that, you just made it *hard*."

I gasped as I felt him against me.

What's happening? I thought manically. *This kind of thing doesn't happen to me. I don't think this kind of thing happens to anyone!*

"I really want to kiss you..." he whispered in my ear, his hand running down my side. "Do you want me to kiss you?"

Every inch of me felt like it was on fire as I let out a quivering "...Yes."

We both heard the clunk of the fire exit door and jumped away from each other.

"There you are, Mel!" Pippa cheered, throwing her thumb over her shoulder. "Someone's looking for you."

I tried to find words, my tongue feeling as though it was five times too large for my mouth. "What?"

"Yeah, some old bloke is at the box office."

My stomach dropped. "What does he look like?"

"Well... Like—" Pippa gestured to all of me, "Like you, to be honest, but a bloke, and old."

"Great," I groaned, walking towards her, my mind reeling for a million reasons, all of them so different compared with how I'd been feeling five seconds ago. "My Dad's here!"

— *Melissa Bishop, aged 16, concluding that the universe must have it in for her.*

***

The paramedics had obviously gotten to the house faster than me. What an absolute circus it must have looked to Christine next door, who I could see behind her front net curtain as Mum was being escorted into the back of the ambulance.

I pelted down the drive, breathless, and panicked, completely taken aback with the sight of Mum in a wheelchair. Her face looked like a deflated water balloon, as though her skin was unsure whether to have wrinkles or curves. Swollen in places, and sunken in others, but ultimately telling all that she was in the midst of a severe allergic reaction.

"What did you give her for her tea?" I asked Dad, pelting down the drive, ice cold beads of sweat dripping down my forehead. "Peanuts? Shellfish? She threw up when we had oysters in Jersey that one time—"

"In what world would I be giving your Mum oysters for her tea?" Dad replied with eyes bulging and an '*Are you mad?*' look on his face. Then he *really* saw me and his face fell. "What are you doing here? I thought you were at work."

"Saw the ambulance," I panted, doubled over and squeezing a throbbing stitch in my side. "Came as fast as I could."

"How'd you kn—"

One of the paramedics waved Dad over, pulling his attention. "Mr Bishop, would you like to come with us?" the woman in dark green overalls asked with a calm and pleasant smile.

Without so much as a 'goodbye' to me or a 'yes' to her, Dad was climbing into the back of the ambulance, his phone almost falling out of the back pocket of his jeans.

The doors shut and the blues and twos started to whirl. I could still hear the siren even after the ambulance had vanished at the bottom of the hill.

I blinked, standing on the driveway with all the commotion, panic, and rush of the last ten minutes still swirling around me, my mind fixated solely on the image of Mum's blown-up face.

My phone rang. It was Rogan. I switched it off without a second thought. With the image of Mum playing on a continuous toxic loop, there wasn't room to think about work, or the consequences of bolting out of the door mid-shift with no context.

Not knowing what to do with myself, running on adrenaline and shock, I stood statue-still on the drive and waited for everything around me to go silent.

That could be the last time I see her, I thought pessimistically. *That could be the last time I see her and I didn't even say goodbye.*

I had to do something to stop myself from spiralling further, so headed into the house and mindlessly started to clean.

With every item I took out of the dishwasher, or surface I wiped down, I was forced to suppress any sinister thoughts that popped into my mind. The reeling 'what ifs', the dangerous, 'could have beens' or nightmarish 'might bes'.

What if Dad hadn't been home either? Or gone to bed early?

I could have come home from work and found Mum having suffocated on her own tongue.

This might be it... And all I can do is put cutlery in the drawer and wipe toast crumbs off a chopping board!

"You're being a right unfair dick, you know?" I cursed quietly under my breath before looking up at nothing in particular. "You could at least be righteous enough to take care of your own."

I knew enough about what Mum called 'The Book' to know that the big man upstairs often put his most devout followers through hell to prove their faith. I never really got it, and at that moment I wasn't having any of it. *Not even God is allowed to be mean to my mum.*

"You fix it," I warned the ceiling, a spatula raised towards the kitchen light above me. "You fix whatever needs fixing to make her better. You have no right to do this to her. I don't care who you think you are, you have *no right*. Not when she's prayed, and worshipped you her whole life. She deserves so much better than a death like this. I'm not having it, old man! You hear me?" I spat at the space above my head, aiming my words at whatever possible entity was in control of the fates of the world. "You save her or I swear when I get up there one day I'll make *you* choke on your own tongue!"

The house phone started to ring, and I scrambled across the spotless kitchen table to grab it. "Hello? Hello?" I jumped in, desperate to hear Mum's voice come chiming down the line.

"Hello, Freckles," Dad croaked.

I'm not ready, my brain whispered while I pulled out one of the kitchen chairs to sit down.

"I've got a bit of an update."

I'm not ready.

"Is she...?" I held my breath.

"Your mum is fine, Freckles. Although, understandably, she's a bit shook up." Dad and I seemed to both let out a breath of relief simultaneously. "It was like you said, she'd had an allergic reaction. Well, it was actually anaphylactic shock, but the steroids she's on managed to slow down the reaction so it wasn't as immediate as it could have been."

"Right," I swallowed, the image of Mum dead in her study chair with a face like a watermelon playing like a poisonous broken record in my head. I ran my free hand down my face and inhaled a crackling sniff, trying to rid the image. "That's... good, I guess? Have they got any idea what triggered it?"

"You mother says that the only new thing she's tried today is some antibacterial mouthwash."

"The *mouthwash*?" I thought of the sachets upstairs. "You can get anaphylactic shock from mouthwash?"

"Apparently so," Dad trailed off, "but the paramedics managed to sort her out and she'll be fine after a bit of rest."

"Will she be staying in the hospital overnight?"

"I think so. They're letting me stay with her. We should be free to come home in the morning."

"Do you want me to come and get you both?"

"Yes, please. Or else it'll be a bloody long walk back."

My heart lurched knowing Dad was trying his best to make a joke, but falling short as his tone sounded more broken than comedic.

"I'll ring you when we know more, or if there's any other update."

"Okay. Thanks, Dad."

There was an awkward moment of silence and I didn't know how to make it end. Dad clearly felt it too, breaking it off with a cough to clear his throat.

"Talk to you later."

He hung up and I found myself glaring at the ceiling again. If God was looking back at me it would have been one hell of a staring competition.

"Thank you," I grumbled begrudgingly, "but this doesn't mean I'm happy with you."

— Eighteen —

31st August

Dad didn't even give me a chance to say goodbye! He wanted to get me, Boris, the rest of my things from back at the dorm and speed home ASAP. He's also in a right foul mood! Don't know why he's upset, I'm the one whose life is being ruined!

Why has he come to get me when he clearly doesn't want to? I moaned to myself in the front seat.

"Thought Mum was coming to get me tomorrow," I grumbled as he tried to force Boris's case into the boot of his Mini. "Why are you here today?"

"Because I am," Dad ground out, in a tone that caused me to shrivel up. Most of the time I don't think Dad is even capable of being in a bad mood, but then he snaps and it freaks me out.

I didn't feel like asking what had got his pants in a twist because I was too busy feeling sorry for myself.

Both of us were silent, grumpy, tired and cold for nearly five hours. The only time we stopped was to go for a wee and get some food at a service station.

What a joke. Instead of snogging the face off the sexiest guy I've ever met, I'm spending my night eating cold fries and a greasy burger with my dad somewhere on the M1. Brilliant.

— *Melissa Bishop, aged 16, hating her life and everyone in it.*

***

The next morning, when I eventually turned my phone back on, I found five missed calls, several torrid messages, and one baffled and heated voicemail from Rogan. Despite the ramblings, and the ranting, they all boiled down to one question: *What the hell happened?*

I didn't need to be lectured about how leaving mid-shift was unacceptable, nor did I need to be told the possible consequences of my actions if I didn't return his calls ASAP. So I turned my phone off again and sat in my bed, staring at the ceiling.

With my quilt up to my chin, I thought of very little, waiting for Dad's inevitable call on the house phone. Shortly after sunlight had broken through the curtains, it came. He explained that Mum was being dispatched and they'd like their 'taxi' to collect them from outpatients as soon as possible. Before I knew it, I'd pulled one of Mum's throwaway jumpers over my head, my trainers straight onto my feet, and was out the door with a jingle of the car keys.

The whole drive to the hospital I feared that I'd be about to experience a repeat of the other day. Mum, wracked with pain, crying uncontrollably, completely inconsolable. But as I manoeuvred through the packed car park I caught a glimpse of Mum's fluffy slippers, her chocolate brown dressing gown... and a giant smile plastered across her face.

I pulled onto the pavement and watched as Dad walked Mum towards the car. He was holding her hand, their arms swinging back and forth. It looked as though he were a parent, walking their excitable child out of the school gates. Mum was on the verge of skipping.

"Jelly-Melly!" Mum cheered as I popped up from the other side of the car. "Fancy seeing you here!"

Dad rolled his eyes, despite discreetly laughing.

"Is she okay?" I asked Dad subtly, as we both watched Mum wobble, as if inordinately pissed, towards the car.

"She's a bit... How do I say this?" Dad considered. "Off her tits."

"Oh," I blinked, watching Mum clamber into the back seat before proceeding to sign *cat*, by miming whiskers either side of her nose. I'd never seen someone so stoned — not even Freddie.

"The doctors say it's normal," Dad explained, "considering all the medication she's had pumped into her."

"*Meow...*" Mum purred from the back seat, still signing away. "What's that song about having a pencil full of lead called?"

"*Pencil full of lead*," Dad answered with an amused shake of his head.

"That's handy isn't it?" Mum giggled childishly, before placing her palm flat up against the back window. "So's this. A hand. Do you get it? A hand is always handy." She waved at us both and I felt myself actually start to lighten up a bit. It was quite refreshing to see the reverse of the norm.

Me and Dad being somewhat serious, while Mum revelled in silly jokes and her usually suppressed immaturity .

"Shall we get off?" Dad suggested, jutting his chin back towards reception. "Before they do you for parking on the curb."

"Better had," I agreed, despite wanting to stay in that weird and wonderful moment for a few more blissful seconds.

"*Meow...*"

I found Dad at the kitchen table, his glasses beside an untouched bowl of cereal, once I'd got Mum settled in bed. He looked up at me, startled, deep circles under his blood-shot eyes.

"She asleep?" he rasped, patting down the table blindly for his glasses. I rarely saw him without them, and every time I did it made me realise how small his eyes actually were.

"I think so. She had her eyes closed, but she was singing under her breath when I shut the door." I plucked an orange from the fruit basket on top of the microwave. "Did you manage to get any sleep at the hospital?"

"Two minutes. Three tops, I reckon." Dad rubbed his eyes then pushed his lenses up his nose, his eyes returning to their usual magnified state. "Did *you* manage to get any sleep?"

"Doesn't feel like it," I shrugged, aimlessly peeling the orange in my hands. "But I must have done, since I technically 'woke up'," I breathed, before asking hesitantly, "So, what happened?"

Dad leaned back in his chair and blinked, staring at the ceiling. "I don't even know, to be honest with you, love. We'd gone and got her jam sugar, had quite a nice time out, actually. Then we ate dinner. She tried to start on her jam but decided to go early to bed instead... And the next thing I knew she was coming out of the bathroom, clawing at her neck and making this God awful noise like she was choking. Choking on air," Dad removed his glasses again and pinched the bridge of his nose. "I rang an ambulance and the rest, as they say, is history."

"All because of some bloody mouthwash," I said before shoving a segment of orange into my mouth and sitting in the chair beside him. "Only Mum," I tried to joke but felt my eyes start to sting as I joked. "Only Mum could almost kill herself with mouthwash."

"Doctors said the steroids saved her life," Dad sighed. "They also informed me that she's signed a DNR, so—"

"DNR? What's a DNR?"

"A do not resuscitate order."

"Meaning what?"

Dad sniffed, "Meaning if a time comes when she needs CPR, they won't administer it. They'll make her comfortable but they won't attempt resuscitation on her."

I sat bolt upright, my brain feeling as though it was throbbing. "Why would she sign something like that?" I blinked rapidly, wanting nothing more than to march upstairs and ask the lunatic herself. "Why would the doctors let her sign something like that?"

Dad lowered his hand and shot me a sorrowful look. He went to speak but a bellowing voice came through the letterbox and rendered him silent.

"Where is she?!" the voice shouted loud enough to actually rattle the metal flap. "It's brass monkey weather out here! Can someone open this bloody door?!"

Of all the people to turn up right now.

I unlocked the front door and it burst open with such force that it almost knocked me clean off my feet.

"Mel?" Grandpa Barry's steel grey eyes narrowed as he took in the sight of me. I thought he might comment on my worn pyjamas, or unbrushed hair, but instead he stepped past me, grunting. "Yer Mum in her room?"

Gramps stomped up the stairs like an elephant on a mission, giving Dad a curt nod as he passed the open kitchen door. When outside Mum's bedroom door, he rapped his thick knuckles indelicately against the wood. "Terra, you decent?"

"Dad?" Mum groggily asked from the other side of the door, half-asleep. "Thought you were golfing in Portugal this week."

"I was. Now are you decent or not?" Gramps threw me a look over his shoulder, "I know I've wiped that arse but I don't fancy seeing it. I've only just had me breakfast."

"I'm decent," Mum finally answered and Gramps took no time in throwing the door open.

"Right, what's this I hear about you havin' a glorified headache?" he stated, standing beside her bed, looking like a steroid-filled bouncer.

Mum laughed before retorting, "That Kenneth needs his mouth glueing shut."

"You're telling me! He told the whole golf club that I had piles last month!" Gramps turned to me again, leaning forward and pushing his bulbous nose right into my face. "I'm all good now, just in case you were wondering, love."

"I wasn't, but thanks, Gramps," I grimaced, desperate to change the subject. "Do you want a brew?"

"Love one."

"Already on it, Barry!" Dad called from downstairs.

"*Normal* coffee, Ted. None of that fancy foreign rubbish!" Gramps clamoured back before turning back to me. "Your cousin Willow's got a new coffee machine. *Crap*puccino-rubbish, I tell ya'."

"Seat, Dad?" Mum pointed towards the decorative chair in the corner of the room beside her wardrobe.

Gramps pulled a face, clearly not keen, but went about putting the miniscule thing by her bedside nonetheless.

Watching him try to sit in it was like watching a gorilla try and fit into a shoebox.

When he was finally somewhat comfortable he looked at Mum with a gruff pout. "Now that Kenneth's taken the cat out of the bag, I think you better catch me up on what's going on with you, poppet."

"There's nothing going on with me, Dad," Mum sighed, trying her best, but not even having the strength to fake a smile.

"Try telling your mother that."

I rolled my eyes. "We've *all* tried telling Nana that," I grumbled under my breath.

"Only problem with going away and switching your phone off is you have to face whatever shit-storm yer Nana has been brewing in the meantime. You should have seen her when I got home from the airport this morning," Gramps shook his head, baffled. "Had the whole lot of them round. Patrice, Irine, Amanda, Gladdis — who, by the way, has had to find a new window cleaner."

"What's wrong with Eddie Squeaky Clean?" Mum asked, taking great effort to sit up.

"He got caught on the CCTV taking a leak in the compost bin while doing his rounds. Gladdis didn't fancy a lad like that looking through her windows twice a month, so she kicked him to the curb, bucket and all."

"At least he had the brains to do it on the compost and not directly onto the plants," Mum considered, trying to get comfortable by fluffing up her pillows behind her back. I could see her fists weren't clenching fully, her grip on the cushions barley making an indent into the soft fabric.

Without waiting for her to ask for help, as I knew she never would, I leaned across and started to rearrange the pillows for her. All I got for an acknowledgement of thanks was a half-smile.

"So, your brain, Terra—"

"Dad, there is nothing wrong with my brain."

"You're telling people it's nothing, Kenny and your mother are telling people it's the worst case scenario." Gramps cleared his throat, and I saw him clench and relax his fists twice over before asking, "So, which is it?"

"It's *nothing*," Mum stressed again, point-blank refusing to look Gramps in the eye while she said it.

Gramps unexpectedly glanced my way and he must have read the contradiction in my face because he started to shuffle in his tiny chair.

"Right, well, err..." He cleared his throat again. "That's that then, isn't it? No more need to chin-wag about it."

Mum gave him a curt nod, and I swore I could have seen her shoulders drop as if she'd been holding her breath.

"So, what gives the invasion then, Mel?" Gramps grunted, rapidly changing subject and looking at me suspiciously. "You finally come to your senses and moved back up North?"

I shook my head and perched myself on the end of Mum's bed. "No, just home to spend a bit of time with Mum—" I heard her cough and quickly added, "—and Dad for a couple of weeks, that's all."

"Will you be popping round to ours at any point? Would be nice to actually have someone with half a brain to talk to while I'm having me tea."

"*Oh,* yes," I resigned with a sarcastic sigh. "Waiting on Nana to give me a date, as she has some hand-me-downs she wants me to take."

Gramps cracked his knuckles. "Gerry, three doors down, has a skip just outside his house, you know? You'll pass it when you head back home. Just a thought."

Noted.

"You broken up with that wet lettuce yet?"

"*Dad!*"

"What?" Gramps huffed, "I'm on about that Wallie lad."

"His name is Freddie," Mum corrected him.

"I know what his name is, Terra. I just think he's a wally." Gramps looked at me, one of his bushy eyebrows raised. "Your Nana still hasn't forgiven him for not showing up to the Christmas Clan gathering just gone. Seething, she was. Devastated she'd wasted all that time ironing his table napkin only for it to go unused."

"Serves her right for ironing her napkins to begin with, Gramps. What's wrong with a bit of kitchen roll?" I replied before noticing Mum was rubbing her temples, her good and bad eye both tightly clasped shut. "You alright, Mum?"

"Terra?"

"Think I've got a headache brewing. Lots of noise, lots of talking. All a bit much seconds after you've woken up from a two minute nap." She pulled the duvet off herself and struggled to get to her feet.

"You need me to grab you anything, Mum?"

"No, no." She shuffled towards her ensuite, taking steady, cautious steps, like someone would when wearing a tight blindfold. "I don't need any help, thank you."

The ensuite door clicked shut and I sheepishly looked at Gramps, who was, surprisingly, smiling. A daft, sort of lop-sided smile, his eyes narrow and penetrative.

"You look worried, chuck," he noted, jutting his but-cleft chin at me.

I improvised, trying to look and sound as cool and collected as possible. "Oh I'm not worried, just tired. Didn't sleep very well."

"She'll be fine," he said outright, rolling his head towards the ensuite door but still keeping his eyes fixed on me. "She's got you, she's got me, and not forgetting that daft man downstairs."

"Sorry to disappoint you, Barry but I'm here actually," Dad joked, coming into the room with a tray full of steaming mugs of tea and a plate of biscuits. "Still very much daft, mind."

"Best thing to be, lad," Gramps patted Dad hard on the back, almost causing a tsunami of tea to spill all over Mum's carpet. Thankfully, Dad regained his balance and we all grabbed a brew and a biscuit.

"A bit of cold water on the face has done the trick," Mum said, returning. Her face was still scrunched up with pain, but there was a forced smile pulling at her cracked and thinning lips.

"This one's for you, love," Dad cooed softly, passing her the finest and thinnest rimmed mug from the tray.

As the room filled with the sound of chewing, Gramps suddenly whistled through his teeth contently before announcing, "Anything can be fixed with a brew, can't it?"

I hope so, I thought, watching Mum as she idly inhaled the tea-scented steam arising from her mug. *God, I hope so.*

– **Nineteen** –

28th January

Never thought I'd say this, but I'm moving to London to become a successful actor! *Finally* saved up enough money and found somewhere to live that wasn't a dive.

Don't get me wrong, it's a studio flat with the bathroom and cooker in sneezing distance from each other, but still — it's London, and it's out of the house! Closer to drama school, when I eventually get in (still waiting to hear back from my auditions). I'm going to be in the thick of it. Anyone who wants to be an actor *has* to live in London, it's just a fact. And I *have* to be an actor. I don't know why it's taken me so long to realise *that* is my purpose. Not being a musician. Not being a chef. And definitely *not* being a midwife, no matter what Mum thinks.

I'm going to be living in Kentish *Town*? Is that an actual town? Can you even have towns in the middle of cities? Will know for sure when I get down there next month! London, baby!

— *Melissa Bishop, aged 19, ready to jump from the nest and see if she flies.*

***

Surprisingly, considering how much she struggled spending time with the rest of her family, Mum was boosted by Gramps's visit. Dad and I left them to it, once all the tea was drunk and the plate of biscuits cleared. For the rest of the morning, I could hear nothing but their laughter through the floorboards.

Eventually, after lunch, with four missed calls from Nana Tia and a Sondhiem show tune on his lips, Gramps came plodding back down the stairs.

"*Everybody ought to have a maid.* Mel, come here and give ya gramps a kiss before I go," he whistled, before wrapping me in a tight hug, smothering me. "Let me know when you're planning on coming over to see yer nana, and I'll try and work out an early escape for us."

I laughed, pulling away and giving him a quick peck on the cheek. "Will do, Gramps."

"Good to have you home," he beamed, throwing a look towards the living room, where we could hear Dad watching the telly. "Say goodbye to your old man for me, ey?"

With that, Gramps left, and I felt my momentary smile slowly slip away.

Turning, I headed upstairs, where I found Mum, probably from pure exhaustion, still sat up but fast asleep. Her head was lolled against her shoulder, her arms limp by her sides.

That can't be comfy, I thought, instinctively going to her side and slowly moving the mountain of pillows behind her back into a flatter formation, easing her down as I went.

She murmured in her sleep just as I was trying to fight the last pillow out from under her right arm. "Mel?"

"Yeah, it's me," I whispered back, trying not to wake her further.

"I'm not going in," she weakly mumbled, her closed eyelids twitching, "just having a look."

My body felt as though it had momentarily frozen in time as I watched her eyes dart about, like moles under sand. "What do you mean?" I asked gently, reaching back and pulling the chair Gramps had nearly broken closer to the bed.

"I'm having a look but I'm not going in..."

I sat down slowly, taking Mum's limp hand gingerly. "What can you see?" I found myself asking, despite still not knowing what she was fully on about.

"There's so many more children than I was expecting," she sighed sorrowfully, causing my breath to hitch with raw emotion. "They're all so happy..."

I'm not ready.

Mum then went still and I felt my stomach rise up into my mouth. I squeezed her hand tighter as her mouth dropped open slightly. A snore rattled out of her nose and I almost swore.

"You absolute..." I cursed under my breath, barely able to see due to the fact my eyes had filled with pre-emptive tears. "You nearly had me there," I laughed, placing my lips against the back of her bruised hand and kissing it gently. "Get some sleep, you daft bint."

I couldn't avoid Rogan any longer, so I headed to work early, hoping that by offering a few free hours of labour - or rather, compensation for the hours I would have worked last night - Rogan might not sack me for my vanishing act.

Losing my job was not an option in my mind, for two reasons. One, I still needed the money. And two, I couldn't bear the thought of ringing Freddie and him relishing in the hypocrisy of it all. He was finally showing some promise, and me getting sacked would most likely give him the perfect excuse to revert to his usual ways. No doubt with the thought process of, *Well, if Mel can't be arsed to keep her job, then why should I?*

I held my breath and stepped into *Rogan's* with as much false energy as I could muster. It took less than a second before Katie was at my side, clucking like a hen and hanging on my back like a worried monkey.

"You didn't half give us all a fright last night, Mel. What the hell happened? You shot outta here like a bullet out of a cannon, and Rogan's said he's not been able to get a hold of you since."

"I had a family emergency," I explained, trying to get to the back room before she asked any more questions so I wouldn't have to repeat myself, and essentially beg for my job twice over.

My jaw instinctively clenched when Rogan turned around and his face immediately dropped as his eyes locked with mine.

"Someone better be dying," Rogan yapped before I'd even had a chance to take a breath, "because that is the only thing that's going to make me let what happened last night slide."

"Guess I'm in luck then, ey?" I grumbled, hanging up my coat.

Rogan's eyebrows nearly flew off the top of his forehead. "Ye' what?"

Katie's face drained of colour, clearly the sharper of the two. "Oh my God, who's dying?" Her sparkling eyes looked me up and down, mortified. "Is it you? Tell me it's not you, Mel."

"It's not me."

Katie clutched her chest, "Oh, thank God."

You've only known me for two weeks, calm down, I thought, not knowing whether to be flattered or concerned.

"Someone's dying?" Rogan asked, finally catching up with the waves of the conversation. "Are you having me on?"

I shook my head solemnly before forcing a smile. "So, now that we're all caught up, can I keep my job, like you said?"

Rogan scratched his bald head, clearly thrown. Whatever reprimanding speech he'd rehearsed was obviously in tatters, and now he was in a position where he was required to improvise, he was essentially buffering. "Well, I, err... Hang on a sec. I need to think about this for a minute."

There was nothing else for it, I might as well say exactly what was on my mind, because... *Why the hell not?*

"What is there to think about, Rogan?" I inhaled deeply, and leaned back against the counter. "I work for cash in hand, off the books, with no actual contract in place. I'm here early because I plan on working for free till eight, making up for the hours I skipped out on last night. That's what I can offer to you, but if that's not good enough, I'll walk out. No hard feelings. But what I will say is, I do need this job, and yes, sacking me off when someone in my life is on the cusp of dying would make you a bit of a dick."

Rogan waited an agonisingly long minute before breaking out into a smirk. "Well, I guess table six needs their order taking, then."

I grabbed a spare pad and pen from the top shelf. "Cheers, Rogan."

He gave me a curt nod before turning back to the cooker, appearing almost like a proud parent.

Katie's arm slinked around mine as I left. "That was a close trim, would've been a shame to lose you." She squeezed my arm and looked up at me, her eyes glistening. "Not to blow shit up your arse, but I would have missed you if you hadn't been allowed back."

"You've cheered up since yesterday," I noted, trying to make her let go of me before table six came into sight. "Fella no longer causing you trouble?"

She clicked her tongue at me. "He's been trying to drag me out to a party all week." She let go and did a twirl, pirouetting towards the bar. "Do I look the party type to you? A roaring fire and a good book for me, Mel," she curtsied. "I'm on my feet enough as it is for work, last thing I want to do is bust a hip on a sticky dance floor with his lordship and all his friends. Do you know what I mean?"

Not in the slightest, I thought again with a smile.

— Twenty —

15th March

Drama school auditions didn't exactly go the way I was hoping they would. I've not heard anything from any of them! But as the saying goes, 'no news is good news'.

To cheer myself up, and so I actually feel like I'm doing something to help my budding career, I've booked myself into a weekly acting class.

First couple of weeks went alright, I've made a couple of friends. There's Tilly, who is a character and a half. She's confident, that's for sure, and really pretty. Plus she likes to do things, you know? She's one of those people who's always doing something. Meeting so-and-so for coffee. Going here and there — mainly the theatre. Talking of which, she's actually invited me to go see this one-woman play with her tonight.

Don't know if I'm actually going to go yet or not. On the one hand, I don't fancy sitting next to Tilly for two and a half hours, no doubt hearing her chunter to me every other second about how she could do a better job... But on the other hand, I'm bored out of my mind. And to be honest, a bit lonely.

— *Melissa Bishop, aged 19, thinking better to sit with the devil you know than be on your own and a saddo.*

***

Everyone was out of *Rogan's* by half nine so it wasn't a surprise that the decision was made to send Katie home early, and for me to lock up once it was obvious no walk-ins were going to miraculously appear.

As I was bringing the shutter down my phone started to buzz away in my back pocket. I almost didn't want to look, fearful I was about to have a repeat of the previous evening. *Can I have a night off?* I thought, the shutter coming to a stuttering halt.

"Hello," I answered, grated. Knowing it was highly probable that my Dad was going to be on the other end of the line waiting to tell me that Mum had slipped on some spilled crabapple jelly, knocked herself unconscious, and was now splayed out across the kitchen tiles. *What an image.*

"You sound cheery," an all too familiar voice chuckled against my ear. "Is this a bad time?"

"No, you're good, Will," I exhaled. Suddenly, I was no longer outside *Rogan's,* wound tighter than a hangman's knot, but transported back to Will's living room, sipping wine and being made to blush and laugh in sweet succession. "How can I help you?"

"Ooo..." he pondered wickedly, "I could think of a number of ways."

My ears pricked up at the slight slur in his voice. *He's either drunk or having a stroke*, I thought, adding the padlock to the shutter. "You having a good night?"

"It could be better," he chuckled again, this time a hiccup bookending his joy.

"How much have you had?" I laughed.

"Enough to know I want to see your beautiful face before I go to bed tonight," Will flirted, shamelessly. "Don't suppose you're free?"

My chest tightened. *You did ask for a night off*, I thought, looking at the dark sky, sprinkled with stars, and thinking whatever creator up there had one sick sense of humour.

"I am, as it happens. Why, what were you thinking?"

Will hummed suggestively. "Do you know where *Alcool* is?"

I craned my head back, catching a glimpse of the fluorescent neon sign of *Alcool*'s from the other end of the high street.

"I do, yeah."

Will rapped his orange-peel-filled tumbler against the wiped-down bar and hiccuped. "Was that my second or third?" he asked, lifting the tumbler to his eye as if he was appraising it.

"*Fourth*," I answered, nursing what little remnants I had left of my lime and soda. "And your last, since they called last orders well over half an hour ago."

"Boo," he drunkenly jeered, watching me as I passed my glass to the understandably irked bartender. "Why call last orders when people still want to drink?"

I gestured to the barren bar, "What people, Will? We're the only one's left."

Will swivelled on his bar stool and let out a childish laugh. "Well, that's fun." He turned back to me, his smile lop-sided. "Could have sworn the place was full."

"It was," I giggled, girlishly. "But everyone left."

"Except us," he hiccuped again.

"Except us," I repeated, unable to suppress the smile he was bringing to my face.

"Are you planning on paying up anytime soon, mate?" the bartender asked, making a point of putting the card reader in front of Will and presenting him with his tab.

"Yep. On it," Will replied, taking out his wallet. "Unless you want another one, Mel?"

The bartender rolled his eyes and let out a derivative snort, before turning my way. "How's he getting home? Do you need me to call him a taxi?"

I shook my head, Will paying up. "I'll sort it."

"Right," Will puffed out his chest, finally getting to his feet and stretching his legs. After pulling on his coat, he sniggered drunkenly into my ear. "Your place or mine?" he whispered. My whole body was momentarily overcome with nostalgia. For a split second I was nineteen again, whirling with all the ecstasy and excitement I'd felt that night beside the Thames — and then I wasn't. I was twenty-three, my mum dying, and thinking of Freddie hating me if he ever found out I was having drinks with an 'old friend'.

I gulped. "Jokes aside, Will—"

"Who said I was joking?" he wiggled his eyebrows at me and I felt my stomach turn on itself, my insides constricting.

"Do you need me to drive you home?"

Ashamedly, I didn't need to hear his answer. I'd already made up my mind that I would. I had Dad's car keys in my pocket, his Mini only a ten minute walk up the hill. "Come on."

Dad's Mini looked sorely out of place as I pulled up onto Will's majestic drive. Like a beaten-up yellow turd being dropped in the middle of a perfectly pruned flower bed.

"Best looking taxi driver I've ever had, I can tell you," Will joked, undoing his seatbelt and rolling his head to take a better look at me. "You coming in?"

I shook my head despite wanting to blurt out 'YES'. Going into his house the other day when we were both sober and I was in a great need of an escape was one thing; entering Will's house when he was his drunk, flirty, intoxicating self was another. Sober Will I could keep at an arm's length because he knew where the line was. Drunk Will danced on the line and made me feel alive.

"There's something going on with you," Will suddenly sighed, ruffling his hair with his left hand and tugging on the dark strands slightly. "You avoided telling me about it the other night, and I'm not gonna lie, I've been racking my brain all week trying to work out what it is."

"Any luck?" I teased, hoping he'd entertain me for a few more minutes by listing off a series of inaccurate but hilarious guesses.

Will shrugged instead. "Thought tonight might loosen you up a bit and get you to let something slip, but it didn't work," he slurred, smiling dopily at me. "All I know is something's up. You're *different* to when I last saw you."

"Maybe that's a good thing," I said, thinking back on the woman I was when Will last *really* knew me. She was young, innocent, and fuelled by naivety and ignorant fire. A big leap from the twenty-three-year-old, exhausted and confused girl sitting beside him in her daft Dad's car.

"Is it your fella?" Will clicked his tongue, "Freddie, right?"

I scoffed, my head falling back against the headrest. "It's definitely *not* Freddie."

"You sure? Doesn't sound like it."

"Freddie and I..." I sucked in some of the thick air that was slowly filling up the small car. "We're fine."

"Relationships should be more than just *fine*, Mel."

I tilted my head, my tone patronising and droll. "You're not exactly the best person to be dishing out relationship advice, Will."

"What's that supposed to mean?" Will asked bluntly, his eyes narrowing, mutating into piercing daggers. "I'm in a great relationship."

And yet you're in a car with me, and not with your girlfriend? I thought, dolefully.

Will crossed his arms over his chest and wriggled into his chair with a drunk grumble. "I've got no complaints. We're good. She wanted to be in her own bed tonight, we had a fight about it, we kissed, made up, shagged—"

My stomach churned.

"—and we're fine now."

"Relationships should be more than just *fine*, Will," I repeated back to him, bile in my mouth.

"Touché," Will replied, before scrubbing his face with both hands. "So, when are you next seeing Freddie?"

I tried to work out the dates in my head, but when that failed, I ended up counting the past weeks on my fingertips. "Promised him when I left that I'd see him every third weekend. So that would mean I'm seeing him.." *Middle finger, index finger, thumb,* "...Bollocks, it'll be this Saturday."

"Lucky bastard," Will grunted to himself, momentarily lost in reverie.

"What do you mean?"

"I *know* you," Will purred, smugly. "You're going to eat him alive if it's been three weeks since you last saw him."

"Are you joking?" I practically laughed, "Me and Freddie haven't had sex in *months*." I found myself laughing bitterly. "It's been that long I can't even bloody remember when the last time we did it was."

Will bit his top lip, desperately trying not to laugh. If he were sober, he might have managed it. "That...That makes me sad," he half-choked, half-sniggered.

"Does it?" I sneered. "You seem to be enjoying yourself."

Will straightened up then reached across the gear-stick, taking my hand and squeezing it supportively. "I'm sorry," he slurred. "Is that it, though? Is that what's going on with you?" His eyeline dropped to my collarbone and I suddenly became very aware of how alone we were. "You're not yourself because you're not getting any?"

I burst out laughing, killing whatever putatively heated moment was happening between us. "God, I wish!" I joked, my chest filled with hot air.

"Then what is it?" Will frowned.

Don't say it. I told myself, the joy in me deflating along with my mood. "Maybe I'll tell you when you're sober, ey?"

"That a promise?" Will pouted, batting his short, charcoal eyelashes at me, a lopsided merry grin stretched across his face.

"It's a promise," I swore, knowing full well he wouldn't remember any of this in the morning, let alone when he next saw me.

— Twenty One —

15th March

I could kiss Tilly! Not like that, but like, oh my God! Right, so we were watching the play, and it was going okay, but then it ended and the best bloody universe-aligning thing happened. I saw *him*. *Will*. Right at the back of the stalls, helping a woman put on her coat. I thought I was hallucinating!

I quickly worked out which exit he'd be coming out of and scrambled for the opposite. I clambered over chairs and shimmied through the crowd, making my way to the theatre's entrance. There, miraculously timed and perfectly executed, I *'accidentally'* bumped into Will's shoulder.

"Oh, sorry, I—"

His face lit up, *thank God*. His dark brown eyes were so deep and so wide I could have lost myself in them a million times over.

"Mel!" he cheered, wrapping his strong arms around me. "Bloody hell!"

"Hiya," I gasped, trying to play it cool. My heart was beating so hard and fast I could feel it in my ears. I couldn't believe he was in front of me, hugging me, breathing me in. It had been so long, I swore he was just a fragment of my sixteen-year-old-self's imagination.

There was a cough of desired acknowledgement and Will released me, turning to the small, ashy blonde woman beside him. "Sorry, Mum, this is Mel. Mel, this is my Mum, Harriet."

I gave her my full attention, hoping I wasn't too pink in the face from just being pressed up against her son.

"Nice to meet you, Mel," she said, her voice and eyes inexplicably kind.

"Nice to meet you too, Mrs Green."

"*Oooo*, don't call me that," she beamed, swatting my arm playfully. "Makes me feel old." She looked between Will and I and a knowing sort of twinkle appeared in the corner of her eye. "I'll see you outside, Will," she said, tightening her coat around herself and starting to move with the rest of the crowd out onto the street.

Will beamed at me. "God, how have you been?"

"Good. Yeah, I live here now," I replied, hoping that he would say—

"Me too!"

My heart leapt. "*Really?*"

"Yeah, I got onto a one-year foundation course back in September. Been sleeping on my brother's sofa for the last couple of months, but — what about you?"

"Working. Got a studio flat in Kentish Town for now."

"That's awesome, Mel," he continued to grin, then threw a look towards the exit. Suddenly, he blurted out, "Don't suppose you're free tomorrow night, are you?"

I didn't need to say yes, he could tell from the smile on my face that I was one hundred percent, completely and utterly free.

— *Melissa Bishop, aged 19, feeling like the universe has forgiven her and finally started treating her right.*

***

The image of Will's face seemed to have burned itself onto my eyeballs. It was there when I rested my head against my cold pillow when I eventually got home, and remained in my mind for all the hours I managed to sleep.

His sharp, clean shaven jaw-line, his black coiffed hair, and his olivey skin, reddened by the warm scotch swimming around his system. It was all so familiar.

What are you doing? I asked myself the following morning, after lying in the dark thinking of nothing but Will for well over an hour. *You have a boyfriend.*

"Who hasn't bothered to check in on me in two days," I argued with myself aloud, feeling my head sink into my pillow.

Freddie knows what you're going through with your mum, he's just trying to give you space.

"I don't need space," I groaned, rolling onto my side and pulling my quilt up and over my head. "I need a boyfriend who actually cares about me."

That's not Will. You know that, right?

"Well, it certainly isn't Freddie either."

Freddie cares. He let you come up and live with Mum even though he clearly wanted you at home. He got a job, even though he's basically allergic to employment. He even said it himself, he's trying to do his bit. Give him a chance, Mel. Jesus.

"Oh my God, just shut up—" I squeezed my skull in my hands, my hair entangling itself between my fingers. "I can't do this."

You can't try to leave him again...

"I said, shut up!" I hissed, burying my face into my pillow before proceeding to scream into the fabric.

"Everything alright in here, love?" I heard my Mum ask, the sound of my bedroom door squeaking open filling the room.

I revealed myself, sheepishly pulling my quilt off my head. The static from the cover caused my hair to slowly rise, sticking out in all directions as though I'd just been struck by lightning.

"Morning, Mum," I bleated, trying to flatten down the frazzled strands as best I could. "You okay?"

"Heard you talking to someone," she glanced around the room with her good eye, the other now completely swollen shut. Her inspection stopped when she spotted my mobile on the cluttered nightstand. "I assumed you were on the phone."

"No, no," I laughed nervously, "I was... talking to myself."

"Anything I can help with?" Mum asked, letting herself fully into the room and clearly wishing she hadn't. She took in the bombsite of clothes around her, her top lip curling disapprovingly. "You sounded rather put out."

"I'm fine, Mum. Honest," I lied, pressing my back against the headboard and bringing my knees up to my chin.

"Is it Freddie?" she asked bluntly, her arms momentarily crossing over her chest.

"What makes you think that?" I asked, hoping that she hadn't heard the exact words I'd been grumbling into my pillow.

"It's *always* Freddie, love," Mum sighed, picking up a lonely sock and dropping it into the empty hamper by the door.

Not always, I thought callously, knowing that Mum would be the last person to admit she was ever a problem in my life — she wasn't even willing to admit she had cancer.

"I think we're going through a rough patch," I confessed, watching as she bristled with every word I uttered. "We've both been so busy, him with his new job, me with..." I bit my tongue. "Everything that's going on around here. We haven't exactly had any time for each other."

"People *make* time," Mum said, pursing her lips before proceeding to pick up a jumper from the end of my bed and fold it neatly.

"Exactly. Which is why I promised I'd go and see him this weekend. But if you want me here, I completely understand—"

"It's not about what I want, dear," Mum cut me off. "Don't stay here on my account."

"I'm not," my nose wrinkled as I held back my lie. Of course Mum was the reason I was home. If it weren't for Mum, I'd still be in London. I might still be in drama school. "Do you want me here?"

"I want you to be happy," Mum resigned, perching herself on the end of my bed. As she sat, a visible twinge of pain flickered across her features, distorting them momentarily. It took me back to the moment she was curled up in the back of Dad's Mini, writhing with pain. *Dad can't go through that on his own.*

"When's your next treatment?"

"There isn't going to be a next treatment, love," Mum's good eye fluttered, innocently. "I had a phone call with the consultant after the first treatment and we both decided that it would be best to formulate a different strategy."

"Meaning what?"

"Exactly what I say, Melissa," Mum rebuffed. "I've stopped my treatment, and am now looking into other alternatives."

There are no other alternatives, I thought manically before blurting out, "Does Dad know?" I blinked, wanting nothing more than to go and find him and drag him into the conversation by his stained woolly jumper.

"I told him last night while you were at work."

"And what did he say?"

"What *can* he say?" Mum sat back, affronted. "It doesn't really concern him. It's *my* treatment."

I ran my fingers through my hair and pulled on the mass of frizz till my scalp hurt. Anything to distract myself from what I was hearing.

I wasn't surprised she hadn't consulted Dad about stopping her chemo treatment, why should I have been? Mum didn't consult him about anything, she never had done. It never really bothered me as it only really came down to what she stocked the fridge with, what she made for tea, or what she spent her wage on. But this was different, this was her *life*.

"So, what does this mean?" I asked, biting the inside of my cheek, trying not to raise my voice. "They can't operate, and you already said that radiotherapy was off the cards. What alternatives do you *think* you have?"

"Well, since the CT showed that the mass has spread to my spine—"

"*What*?" my head shot up, my brain feeling as though it was dissolving inside of my skull. "You went for a CT scan?"

"While I was in hospital the other day," Mum shrugged. She might as well have been telling me she went for a Full English on the maternity ward. "Why are you pulling such a face?"

I groaned into my palms. "God, you don't half know how to make a crappy situation more difficult, don't you?"

"You're speaking in negatives, dear," Mum pouted. "I don't know whether to be flattered or insulted—"

Mum's face then dropped — literally dropped. Pale yellow vomit suddenly came spewing out of her mouth, spraying up the bed.

I let out a noise that barely sounded human, before I was forced to lunge forward and catch her body as it slumped. I tried my best to hold her upright in my sick-smeared arms. I gripped her tight as if she were a broken babe and screamed for Dad to call an ambulance.

— Twenty Two —

16th March

I've never been such a nervous wreck in all my life. I waited for Will outside of The National's main entrance, like he asked, for what felt like an hour. My legs were shaking, my hands trembling, and my stomach tying itself into knots. Though, when I saw him finally walking towards me, a wave of calm washed over me.

He kissed my cheek and told me I looked fit. I could've died — I'd tried so hard to look good. Hours spent straightening my hair, and even longer trying to pick out the perfect outfit. In the end, I'd gone with my only skirt, a pair of boots, and a thick woolly jumper. (Was seriously starting to regret the jumper, though, as just being in Will's presence was making me sweat!)

We started to walk along the side of the Thames, Will making sure to hold my hand and interlock his fingers with mine.

"There's a couple of food trucks up here that we can grab something at," he said, pointing ahead. "If that's okay?"

Anything was okay. Food truck, Michelin star restaurant, kebab shop, I would have done whatever.

We talked, we caught up, flirted and laughed, Will never taking his eyes off me. Every now and then I thought he was going to kiss me, but something was holding him back.

A nostalgic worry piped up a reason in the back of my mind, and before I could stop myself I ended up asking, "So, how's Lucy?"

"Who?"

"Lucy, she was—" I started to laugh, at myself or him, I wasn't sure. "She was your girlfriend back during that summer course thing we did."

"Oh, Lucy!" Will shook his head. "Jesus, what a throwback. Err — Yeah, no, she's not my girlfriend anymore. We broke up a couple of weeks after I got back home."

My heart started to skip, swelling with joyous anticipation and hope as I asked, "So, you don't have a girlfriend?"

Will took a moment to look at me intensely, subtly licking his lips before shaking his head slowly. "No, I don't have a girlfriend."

"Oh–" Before I could finish my sentence, not that I even knew what I was going to say next, Will's lips were on me. He kissed me hungrily, pulling me closer and pressing my body against him. Thank God, it was dark! We were in public!

It all felt so deliciously familiar... Only this time we wouldn't get ripped apart from one another. This time, I was in control of things.

"Your place or mine?" I panted, as soon as he gave me a second to breathe.

— *Melissa Bishop, aged 19, with her sixteen-year-old self cheering her on from the back of her mind.*

***

The hospital felt more like Kings Cross Station concourse than a ward. People were whizzing past, in their own worlds, eyes forward, ignoring everything and anything that wasn't their destination.

Every nurse that I tried to speak to, every doctor whose attention I tried to grab, essentially blanked me. The only thing Dad and I had been told since the moment we arrived was, "We'll update you when we know more."

That left us in a waiting room not even knowing where Mum was, or if she was even still alive. Dad drank bitter cheap coffee out of a tiny plastic cup and I tried to sip a tea that had bits floating in the top.

Finally, after the third hour of silence, a doctor approached Dad, clipboard in hand. I could tell from their solemn expression that it wouldn't be good news. I held my breath.

I'm not ready.

"Mr Bishop?" the doctor asked, tilting their head in Dad's direction. "My name's Doctor Collins—"

"Hello," Dad croaked, before shoving his fingers under the bridge of his glasses and pinching his nose. "How is she?" he asked with a quiver underlying his voice.

"She's stable."

Dad and I both exhaled simultaneously, like two inflatable lilos being punctured by the same pin.

"We believe her to have had a minor stroke," Doctor Collins continued after giving us a moment to breathe again. "The tumours in her brain seem to be preventing blood flow, so we're going to keep her in for a while so we can monitor her."

"How long are you keeping her for?" I hated hearing myself ask. I sounded like a desperate child who'd had their toy taken away.

"As long as we need to."

Translation: *We haven't a sodding clue.*

"So, she could never come out?" I felt my fists instinctively clench. Dad wrapped his arm around my shoulder. *What a joke*, I cursed to myself. *I give up drama school. I ruin my already fragile relationship with Freddie. I move back home and I go through hell to be by Mum's side, all for her to go and get herself locked into a hospital for the rest of her days? What an absolute PISSING joke.*

I tuned out for the rest of the conversation as Doctor Collins and Dad started to use medical jargon and discuss things I didn't understand.

But then I heard, "hospice" and all of a sudden my ears pricked up. "Ye' what now?" I stepped towards them both.

"We were just discussing possible plan Bs, Freckles... In case your mum deteriorates."

"We're not putting her in a home," I snapped, glaring at Doctor Collins as I spoke, assuming this was their suggestion. "She's only forty nine!"

"A hospice isn't anything like a nursing home," Doctor Collins began, clearly not appreciating the unforgiving side-eye they were receiving. "It's a place where people of all ages are given end-of-life care, physically, emotionally and spiritually."

"You sound like a brochure," I ground out before biting my tongue and remembering this poor sod in front of me was probably at the end of a twenty-hour shift, with aching feet and no coffee in their system.

"Sorry..." I breathed, scrunching up my face to stop myself from even thinking about crying. "Is that— Is sending Mum to a hospice something we *need* to be discussing?"

Doctor Collins's eyes fell to their pale blue slip-on shoes momentarily, before they steeled themselves and answered, very diplomatically, "It's always good to know what options are available should the decision need to be made quickly. I wouldn't necessarily say that your mother needs to be in a hospice at this time, but with her treatment no longer in motion, and the repercussions of this minor stroke not yet known, I would recommend that you and your father think about the support you would like for Theresa and yourselves moving forward."

Before I knew it, Dad had taken my arm and was leading me out into the car park. I wanted to dig my heels into the bleach-cleaned floor and express that I wasn't leaving until I'd seen Mum. *Just in case.* But I didn't have the energy or the heart to drag Dad back into the building.

The drive home was sombre and silent. It was almost becoming the natural order of things, to sit in a car with Dad and feel like pure and utter crap.

I thought back to when I was little; Mum picking me up from school with a packet of soft mints in her pocket and a buttercup she'd picked from the side of the road in her hand.

"Good day at school, Jelly Melly?" she'd ask, passing me the tiny yellow flower, before taking my hand and encouraging me to skip back to Dad's then not-so-beaten up Mini.

"Yeah! Ms Atkins taught us our three tables times," I cheered, hopping into the passenger seat.

"It's sausages and mashed potato for tea," she informed me with a preemptive grin, knowing it was my favourite.

I remember wanting to lean over the handbrake and squeeze the breath out of her. So much joy over something so small like bangers and mash.

It's weird, really, thinking back on your childhood and feeling nothing but resentment for your own innocence.

Mum had been a guarantee to that little girl, an immortal being who would always be there when she needed her. Now Mum was as good as gone. She was in a hospital bed somewhere, unconscious, and no longer someone who I fully believed would be with me forever.

Ah, to be young again. Not because you're young, but because you're stupid and naive... And full of nothing but wonder without an ounce of worry of what's to come.

— Twenty Three —

16th March

We'd decided, even though it was closer, that his brother's flat was a stupid idea. Will didn't even know whether Jordan would be home, whereas at mine there was no one we needed to worry about.

"We can be as loud as we want here," Will whispered into my ear as I was putting my keys into the apartment door.

I gulped, feeling suddenly six feet out of my depth. I couldn't help but wonder what my sixteen-year-old self would think about all this. I was about to have *sex* with *Will*.

That reality slapped me round the face, sending me into an internal blind panic. I had no idea what I was doing!

Will clearly did. He'd done nothing but make me wriggle and moan the whole way home. Finding the perfect moments when no one was around to steal a kiss, or nibble at my ear.

My mind was reeling uncontrollably, but thankfully Will was none the wiser as he pulled me into the blacked-out flat.

I didn't want him to know how nervous I was, or how clueless I was. *Oh God, what if he thinks I'm awful?* I panicked.

We fell onto my bed, Will pushing all his delectable body weight into me. "Oh God," he moaned against my neck, kissing my skin with feverish anticipation. "I've been waiting years to do this..."

"Will," I breathed, my hands frozen by my sides. I didn't know where to touch him. I mean, I could have had a good guess, but I didn't want to get it wrong!

"Yes?" he replied, his hands expertly roaming my body. "Something wrong?"

"Can we slow down?" I panted, "It's just going a bit fast."

"Sorry," he whispered, running his thumb slowly over my bottom lip. "I can go slow if you want."

I managed a nod, my brain not really fully working. "Yes, please." I shivered as his hands started to roam my body much, *much* slower than before.

It's going to be fine, I told myself, taking a deep breath in through my nose. He'll, "...Be gentle."

The last two words passed my lips as I exhaled and I couldn't help but notice Will momentarily freeze. It was only a split second but long enough for me to know he'd heard me.

"Don't worry, Mel," he cooed, kissing my collarbone and working his lips down towards my navel. "I'll be gentle with you."

– *Melissa Bishop, aged 19, in absolute ecstasy and bliss.*

***

With Mum seemingly not coming out of hospital for a couple of days, Dad eventually convinced me to go home and see Freddie as promised. "Your mum's in the best place, Freckles. If something does happen, they'll be able to fix it instantly. She's in good hands, love. Better off than if she was still at home."

I wasn't so sure, but knew I needed to go home. Freddie's texts had become sparse and short, never consisting of anything more than, 'Just got home from work', 'I'm chilling', and 'Talk later'.

Not that it was at all possible, but a tiny piece of me believed he was being so distant because he knew about Will. Freddie, somehow, via hidden spy camera or crystal ball, knew I'd spent yet another night giggling and wantonly flirting with another man.

Nothing has actually happened between you and Will. It is literally all in your own head, I reminded myself while being pressed up against strangers, like oily sardines in a tin, on the Tube.

"This Northern Line rail service is to *Morden*. The next stop is *Oval*—"

I weaved my way towards the exit, narrowly missing the armpit of someone who clearly wasn't wearing any deodorant. *Mum wears deodorant*, I thought, patiently waiting for the doors to hiss open.

You're supposed to be taking a mental break! I scolded myself, stepping off the tube and onto the bustling platform. *Stop thinking about Mum!*

That thought process seemed to make everything worse. It was only when I walked into the flat and saw Freddie comically at the kitchen sink wearing an apron and yellow rubber gloves that Mum eventually flew out of my head.

The flat was spotless. Pristine from skirting board to ceiling. The coffee table was sparking clean, and I could have sworn the carpet was in a better condition than when we'd originally moved in.

"Bloody hell, Fred," I laughed, completely taken aback. "Were you expecting the royal family or what?"

"Nah, just my princess," Freddie flirted, adding to my bafflement by coming out of the kitchen to greet me with a kiss and a squeeze. "Are you wanting a shower before we eat? Get all that travel smell off yourself?"

"I can do," I smiled weakly, before being rendered speechless by a bunch of flowers being thrust into my face.

"Got you these," Freddie beamed, taking my bag out of my hands so I could take the bouquet from him.

"Wow, Freddie, this is..." I trailed off, stiffening slightly because everything was *so* different. "Why have you got me flowers?"

"Thought you might like them," he shrugged, before dipping his head and scuttling back into the kitchen. "Pasta with cheese alright for tea?"

I rolled my eyes, smiling through the sarcasm. "Wouldn't expect anything else."

"It'll be ready in fifteen so if you're going to jump in the shower, you'd be better off doing it now."

Tea was pleasant. *Weirdly* pleasant. Freddie was attentive and considerate, asking about Mum and Dad, about work and how I was feeling about everything life was throwing at me. If it weren't so out of character for him, I would have thought myself the luckiest girlfriend in the world.

"What's with you?" I asked abruptly as Freddie poured me a second glass of wine.

"What do you mean?" he said, throwing me a look like a wounded pup.

"You're being weird."

"No, I'm not," he snorted, collapsing onto the sofa beside me and giving my shoulder a quick peck. "I'm trying something new."

New? I thought. *New is dying your hair, or shaving off your secondary school moustache — this is a personality transplant.*

A warmth started to spread across my chest suddenly. Slowly but surely, it spread across my body before nestling, and humming between my thighs.

A new Freddie...? I thought wickedly, sipping my wine. *Maybe it's time for the old Mel.*

I made some dumb excuse about needing the toilet and scurried to the bedroom. There, I pulled open the top drawer of my dresser and dug my way to the bottom. Beside a stocking filled with lavender was a red lace babydoll. I'd bought it for our first Valentine's together, only Freddie got so out of it with his mates that it completely slipped his smoke-fogged mind that we'd made plans. The lingerie had been relegated to the bottom of my drawer ever since.

With trembling hands, I changed into the babydoll and tied my hair up in a matching scrunchie. "It'll do," I joked to myself, assessing my figure in the wardrobe mirror.

I tried to ignore the fact my hands were shaking uncontrollably as I made my way back into the living room. My whole body was fizzing with anticipation and adrenaline. I cast my mind back to hotter and more exciting times, trying desperately to channel my nineteen-year-old self. *Eat him alive*, I breathed deeply, approaching the sofa.

"...Freddie?" I asked, my voice a quivering mess. "Do you—"

I froze. Freddie was looking at me like he'd seen a ghost. Agonisingly, he wasn't saying or *doing* anything.

"What do you think?" I did a little twirl for him and was mortified to see him not even blink.

Finally, after what felt like an eternity, he grumbled, "Are you—" he coughed. "Are you not cold in that?"

A bereft laugh fell out of my mouth. "No..." I swallowed the hard lump in my throat. "I was kind of hoping we could... *You know*."

Freddie finally blinked. "We've just eaten."

"It's not like swimming, Fred," I snapped, biting my bottom lip to stop myself from crying. "You don't need to wait twenty minutes."

"Yeah, but like—" Freddie scratched the back of his head, his cheeks reddening. "I'm properly bloated... And I was just about to head out onto the balcony for a smoke."

"Right." I forced a smile, my eyes filling. "Never mind then." I turned on my heel and practically fled back to the bedroom.

— Twenty Four —

17th March

We lay together for ages, Will holding me in his arms while he got his breath back. "Was that *gentle* enough for you?" he grinned, burying his face into my hair and kissing the top of my head.

"Yeah..." I could hear in my own voice that I was distant, so I wasn't surprised that Will asked if something was wrong. "I'm fine, I've just..." I pulled my quilt a little higher, embarrassed, "I'd never..."

Will went stock-still, then pulled away from me so we were positioned at opposite ends of the bed. "Tell me that wasn't your first time, Mel," he said, his mood and tone flat, but his eyes painfully wide and panicked. "*Please* tell me that wasn't your first time."

I shook my head. "It wasn't."

He exhaled immediately with relief, his whole body relaxing. "Oh, thank fu–"

"It was my second," I cut him off and watched his jaw clench.

"Second?" he repeated, shuffling not so subtly to the very edge of the bed. "You've only had sex *once* before?"

I clearly wasn't as bad as I thought if he wasn't able to tell that from the shag, I mused to myself before nodding.

"Yeah. It was right before I moved. My mates had thrown me a bon voyage party and we all got really drunk. My mate – well, I thought he was my mate – he wanted to fool around a bit. I was having a good time so I thought, why not? Not like I'd not done *other stuff* before. We went up to my best friend Miriam's bedroom and then it all kind of got a bit out of hand." I breathed, not sure why I was telling Will any of this, not like he would have ever found out.

"My mate said he wanted to shag. I said no. He dropped it. Then he asked again a couple of minutes later... I said no, and I thought he'd dropped it for good. But then he was all over me, asking me over and over again to have sex."

I blinked, trying not to picture my friend's face as he pressed himself against me; not when I had Will's perfect face, literally right in front of me.

"I don't remember saying yes, but I must have done, because then he was on top of me, saying how grateful he was. He was drunk, so he didn't last long. I was drunk, so I don't really remember it. Just remember that it hurt like hell, and that I couldn't pee without it stinging for three days after."

Will blinked at me before managing a somewhat forced smile. "Right... So, this *was* your first time."

"Not technically—"

"Not *technically*, but you can pretend it was if you want." Will then wrapped me up in his arms again, so tightly I could feel his heart beating fast against my bare skin. "When people ask how you lost your virginity, you can tell them about this. About me. Say your first time was to a really sexy guy who rocked your world and even cuddled you after, because he's a legend."

I laughed.

"That way you never have to think of that shitty mate or that crappy first time ever again."

– Melissa Bishop, aged 19, wanting that moment, being held by Will, to last forever.

***

I've never pulled on clothes so quickly. A million vomit-inducing thoughts came skimming through my head. I wanted to grab my scissors and cut the babydoll into a thousand little pieces, then bury the ash.

Just when I thought things couldn't get any worse, the most poorly-timed text came through, causing my pitch-black bedroom to light up momentarily. My heart lurched, thinking it was going to be the inevitable text from Dad telling me that Mum had died — to really put the cherry on the cake of an absolute horror of a night.

Dad would never text me that.

I reached for my phone, curiosity pitching self-loathing to the post. It was Will, inviting me around to his for another night of chips and dips. I text back,

Can't. I'm in London. X

The reply came almost straight away.

Showing Freddie what he's been missing?? Oi oi x

God, it was mortifyingly embarrassing. How could I even type out... 'Tried to, didn't work. Freddie wanted a joint more than me.'

My eyes burned as I reread Will's message over and over again, forcing myself to keep the awaiting flood of tears at bay.

Eventually, I decided it best not to reply at all. I couldn't bring myself to tell Will the truth, or worse still, lie to him about my boyfriend's interest in me.

Another message buzzed through, lighting up my phone and therefore the blacked out bedroom.

Leaving me on read? You must already be having fun!...
Lucky guy x

My thumbs hovered over the keypad. Will being nice to me was the last thing I needed, so I decided to bite the bullet.

Tried. He wasn't interested x

Before I'd even registered what I'd done, I'd thrown my phone onto the bedside table. I couldn't think of a time I'd felt worse about myself.

Less than thirty seconds passed before the room lit up again, Will trying to call me.

After his third missed call, I finally answered and held the phone to my ear.

"Are you *kidding* me?" Will started to rant down the line. I couldn't help it, but hearing the soft rasp of his voice, clearly mid-rage and wild tirade, brought the smallest of heartbroken smiles to my face. "Like, what happened? Did he just go, 'Nah, I'm good, thanks'. Like, is he for real? What the hell did he say?"

"I'd rather not go into it," I confessed quietly, my voice hiding in my throat.

"No, I'm not having this," he interjected passionately. "I'm coming down there to give his head a shake, he clearly doesn't have it screwed on right."

A snively laugh bubbled up from my chest. The image of Will bursting through the front door and rattling Freddie senseless demanding he sleep with me was utterly ridiculous and mortifyingly tragic. The laugh turned to a sob, and within seconds I was suddenly crying violently down the phone to the one person I really didn't want to hear me cry.

"Jesus, Mel," Will steadied his tone before continuing. "Talk to me. What happened?"

I wiped my face with the back of my hand and blubbed. "I tried getting dressed up for him and he... wasn't interested. Said he was full from dinner, and about to have a smoke." It hurt to say it out loud, hurt to hear it, hurt to admit how unattractive my boyfriend must've found me to not even attempt to show an interest.

"Did he even look at you? What were you wearing?"

"I—" I couldn't bring myself to say any more, my body was already at its peak of embarrassment.

Suddenly my phone started to bleep. I looked at the screen and saw Will had hung up. *Great, I'm that horrendous that even Will doesn't want to speak to me.* My thought was cut short by Will's face appearing on the screen, alongside a request to video chat.

I didn't want him to see me. Not when my face was no doubt going to be covered in snot, salty tears, and shame, but I couldn't help myself.

I answered and hoped that my room being so dark would hide my tear-stained face. Two seconds hadn't passed before Will was demanding I turn a light on.

"Seriously, Mel, let me see you." His face beamed from the other end, his eyes glistening with support and a twinge of, no doubt, pity.

I reluctantly flicked on the bedside lamp, the room, and me lighting up. Even in my pixelated reflection I could see I was a mess. My straightened hair had already started to frizz, my make-up smeared to hell.

"You're wearing a hoodie?" Will's eyebrows furrowed, a line appearing between them.

I looked down at myself, dumbfounded. *What else was he expecting?* I live in hoodies. If I was at all fashion-inclined, I would no doubt say they were my signature look when paired with leggings and slipper socks.

"I want to see what dressed-up Mel looks like."

"What do you—"

I almost choked on my own tongue as I suddenly realised what he was suggesting. My eyes locked onto the cast-away babydoll lying dishevelled in the corner of the room. *He can't be serious.*

"It's purely for scientific reasons, if that makes you feel better about it," Will teased. "I'm not being pervy just trying to work out how thick your boyfriend actually is."

"He's not thick," I grumbled, with a lump in my throat. "He's clearly not interested in me."

"Show me?" Will's voice was firm, but caring. He wasn't demanding, or ordering, he was simply asking.

I'm still unsure what compelled me to oblige but without another thought about it, I was sliding slowly out from under my bed covers and grabbing the babydoll off of the floor. With a skillful manoeuvre of my hoodie I was able to slip it back on underneath, without ever becoming fully naked.

As I went to pull the hem of my hoodie up over my head I realised my hands were trembling. I cast aside a small nagging voice in my head that was telling me this was a line — a line I shouldn't be crossing.

But why not? I thought, battling myself. This was nothing, Will simply wanted to see what Freddie had turned down. *God, what if he agrees with Freddie? What if Will looks at me in this damn stupid thing and goes, 'Yeah, your fella's right, you look horrendous. Better return it, or better yet, burn it'.*

"Mel, you're still wearing your hoodie," Will stated, regaining my attention, "Are you trying to build up the suspense or...?"

I shook my head, suppressing a nervous laugh. After propping my phone up on the bedside table, I took a few steps back, Will grinning like a cheshire on the tiny screen.

"This is so stupid," I half-blubbed, half-sobbed, scrunching the cuffs of my sleeves into my fists. "You don't want to see this, I look like a right mess."

Will shook his head enthusiastically. "I hate to disagree with you, but I most definitely *do* want to see this. Now take the hoodie off, Miss Bishop, before I get on my knees and beg."

I rolled my eyes, laughing at his constant need for the dramatics. Clearly, despite conforming to working in an office, he was still very much an actor at heart. "You wouldn't get on your—"

Before I'd even finished my sentence, Will's camera was jostling about, making me practically motion-sick. After a blurry image of his bedroom ceiling, then his wall, then his bedside table, I saw Will again, on his knees, hands together, as if deep in prayer.

"I'm begging you, Mel. *Please. Take. Off. The. Hoodie.*"

My breath caught in my throat, proceeded by a second of doubt, and then I was pulling my hoodie slowly up and over my head. My hair covered my face, frizzing from the static of the fabric. I patted it down, tucked it behind my ears, and finally looked back at the phone, apprehensive as to what I would see.

Will was still on his knees, his eyes wide. *God, he must be in shock*, I thought, my insecurity building. He wasn't saying anything, which made every second stretch out, and allowed room for my guilt, shame, and self-loathing to retake its place in my chest. *Do I really look that bad?*

Suddenly Will was biting his right fist so hard I could see the skin of his knuckles puckering white. "Holy sh—" He fell a little forward, never taking his eyes off the screen. "Mel, hold on, I'm going to have to change the camera angle before I end up shaming myself."

Shaming himself? I blinked dumbly, Will taking his phone back to his own bed, his face filling the screen.

"You look—"

"That bad?" I scrunched up my face, feeling my nose wrinkle, stopping the fresh set of tears from falling.

"Shit-hot," Will breathed. "I'm not exaggerating here, you look *fucking stunning*, Mel."

I blinked rapidly, feeling myself ready to burst into tears for a completely new set of unexpected reasons.

"What?" was all I could muster. *He's just being nice,* I told myself before looking back at him. *He's just saying that to make you feel better.*

But from the look on his face I suddenly knew that wasn't the case. Will was staring at me as if he was trying to memorise the image, trying to drink it in, and make it last.

Will scrubbed his face with his hands vigorously. "Oh God, I don't know what your fella is on..." he grumbled. "I mean look at you. *Look at you.*"

I couldn't help but bite my bottom lip to try and stop the biggest, widest grin from sweeping across my face.

"How could he not want you?" Will shook his head, dumbfounded. "How could he have something that hot in front of him and not do anything about it?"

I laughed, "Well, he didn't, so I'm chucking this." I tugged at the silky fabric of the babydoll.

Will's eyebrows raised mischievously. "Are you chucking it now? Like, right now? I mean, not that I support that because I think it suits you, but if you want to tear it off, and throw it out the window right this second, then I will support that."

I rolled my eyes, shuffling forward and retrieving my hoodie from the floor. *Now that would be crossing a line*, I thought, bristling slightly. I pulled out the sleeves, and watched as Will's face fell.

"You aren't seriously getting dressed again?" He pouted, "At least let me take a screen-shot!"

Without giving him another second I pulled the hoodie back on over my head and took my phone back to the bed. "Knowing you, you would've already taken two screen-shots by now."

"I've actually been screen recording this entire time, if you must know," he joked before asking sincerely, "Do you feel better?"

"Yeah," I whispered, "Thank you."

"You've got nothing to thank me for, Mel," Will sighed, ruffling his hair. "Trust me, I should be the one thanking you."

— Twenty Five —

17th March

I'm not going to text Will right away, he only just left and won't have any signal as he's on the Tube.

It was a really cute goodbye, actually. He gave me a peck on the cheek and squeezed my hand, before whispering, "This was fun."

I think *fun* is a bit of an understatement. It was bloody perfect.

— *Melissa Bishop, aged 19, her faith in sex restored.*

***

Freddie, thankfully, had fallen asleep on the sofa so I spent the rest of the night on my own. He'd no doubt crashed in a state of blissful ignorance, probably completely unaware I was literally and metaphorically halfway out of the door.

I had convinced myself to leave without waking him, then I wouldn't have to speak to him. Or worse, look him in the eye with the knowledge that he didn't find me attractive and someone two hundred miles away did.

It was only when I couldn't find my keys that I had to somewhat stir Freddie awake, adamant they were somewhere under him amongst the sofa cushions.

"Freddie, have you seen my keys?" I asked softly, hoping that by keeping my voice low and flat he wouldn't fully wake and I could still leave without being further mortified.

"Are you going?" he grumbled, sitting up and rubbing his blood shot eyes.

I ran my hand under the newly available hiding place, disappointed when I found nothing but the TV remote and some long-forgotten bobby pins.

"Yeah," I trailed off looking under the joint-stub-laden coffee table again. "My train back is in an hour."

"Oh," Freddie stretched, still coming to. "I thought you were home for two nights?"

"I hadn't really decided, to be honest, Fred," I grumbled, motioning for him to move off the sofa so I could check the last feasible place my keys could be hiding. "But after last night, I got the feeling that you didn't really want me..." I swallowed before adding, "...*around*."

"Are you joking?" Freddie retorted, suddenly very awake. "I've been on my own for three weeks. Was looking forward to you being home so much that I cleaned the whole bloody flat. *Or* didn't you notice?"

"Course I did."

"Funny, because I never got so much as a thank-you last night," he retorted. "You didn't say thanks for cleaning, or for cooking. Not even a 'cheers for the flower. *No,* all I got was a '*Why have you got me flowers?*'" he twisted his face and made his voice three pitches higher in an attempt to imitate me.

"But you've *never* bought me flowers."

"*So?* I have now, haven't I?" Freddie got to his feet and started pulling at his hair so harshly I thought he was going to scalp himself. "First time for everything," he groaned, "and a last, because fat chance if you think I'm going to buy you flowers again, since this is the reaction I get."

"I'm not reacting to you getting me flowers, Fred," I rolled my eyes and felt my stomach churn. Every fibre of my being was at war with itself. Some of me wanted to cry, parts of me wanted to scream, the rest wanted to run and hide. "I think we need to talk about last night," I finally said, the part of me that was the most reasonable and level-headed winning the raging mental war.

"What do you mean?"

I couldn't help but give him a look. One of those side-eye glances, with the words '*Are you joking?*' written across my forehead. "You didn't *want* me..."

Freddie's face dropped, his eyes drooped, and all of a sudden he was looking at me like I'd just wet myself. "Mel," he breathed deeply, his fists clenching at his sides. "You've been gone for weeks. We've barely spoken, and you threw last night on me with no warning. I panicked."

"Panicked about *what*?" I choked. "It's sex, Fred. Not like we haven't done it before. Fair enough, it's been a while - hell, it's been longer than a while - but Jesus Christ, it's not like it's hard to pick up where you left off."

"For you, maybe," Freddie grumbled, swiping up his tin of buds from the coffee table with one hand and his grinder with the other. "Some of us aren't exactly feeling good enough about themselves right now to jump right back into it, you know?"

I swallowed the hard, sticky, concentrated ball of saliva that had appeared in my throat. *Does he know about Will?* My brain fretted, my face probably draining of all colour. *Had he heard me on the phone with him last night?*

"What's that supposed to mean?" I asked, trying to keep my voice steady and not let any of my internal panic show.

"It *means* that you emasculate me, Mel. How am I supposed to feel good about myself, feel like a man, and like, get hard, when all you do is make me feel about *this big*?" he pinched his forefinger and thumb together before opening his tin and dropping a fresh bud into the grinder. "I'm working so hard on bettering myself. I got the job, like you asked. I cleaned the flat, like you've been banging on about me doing for ages. I cooked you tea, I did the washing up. Like... Jesus, what more do you want from me?"

I took a deep breath and sat on the sofa, my coat and backpack on my lap. "It's not unreasonable to want sex in a relationship, Freddie," I blinked, hating that I was even considering asking him this question, let alone that I was in a position where I needed to. "Are you not attracted to me anymore?"

Freddie did the worst possible thing he probably could have done in that moment. There wasn't an immediate 'no', or even a sorry 'yes'. Just a half-arsed, not-really-bothered shrug.

"Not really attracted to anyone or anything at the moment," Freddie then said, clearly feeling the tension in the room. He twisted the lid and base of his grinder in opposite directions, the gritty noise making the hair on the back of my neck stand up on end. "Not really feeling much at all, to be honest. Suppose that's what comes from being on your own all the time."

"And that stuff?" I asked, already feeling the sickly scent of it tickle my nostrils. "Do you seriously think that's helping matters?"

"It's no different to you writing in that bloody diary all the time. This keeps me sane," he replied. "It takes me out of life for a bit. Same as what writing, or your folks, do for you."

Or Will, I thought, with a painful twinge settling in behind my left eye. There were so many more things to be thinking about, *why is Will top of the pile?*

"Well, like, I mean your folks before, not your folks at the moment, obviously," Freddie let out a laugh and rubbed his finger under his nose. "Sorry, that was a dumb thing to say."

"Yeah, it was..." I trailed off.

"Alright, no need to get arsey about it."

"I wasn't, I was actually agreeing with you," I fired back before letting out an exhausted sigh and pulling my bag onto my shoulder. "Mum *is* my life at the minute. She's in hospital right now—"

"I'm aware," Freddie rolled his eyes as though he was bored of hearing about it.

I stood up and stared at him, my mind no longer on our crumbling relationship, or my Mum, or Will, but on the scrawny boy standing in front of me. He looked nothing like he had done when we'd met. His hair had grown in excess, now hanging off his head like a ragged mop. I didn't fixate on how cool he dressed, simply locked in on the fact that everything he wore didn't fit him. It hung off of his body, baggy and sad. His eyes didn't sparkle, and his voice didn't make me feel warm and fuzzy anymore. Freddie made me feel tired.

"I'm going to miss my train," I said, before turning and heading for the door.

"What about your keys?"

I don't think I'll need them anymore, I thought with a sad weight growing in my chest. "I'll work something out," I improvised, reaching for the door handle and feeling Freddie's eyes boring into the back of my skull.

"Mel...?"

I looked over my shoulder and saw Freddie's eyes were wide, but not with fear, or panic, or pain, but confusion.

"What?"

Freddie inhaled, his nostrils flaring, and his left hand flexing by his side. "You are going to come back, right?"

I couldn't help but glance at the wall beside me. The paint still chipped, the plasterboard still bearing the scars of the one and only time I'd ever tried to break up with him.

"Well, *are* you?" he pushed, his dark eyebrows pulling together, and his eyes narrowing.

"Course..." I replied, casting the memory aside, before stepping out into the dingy hallway and hating myself just that little bit more.

— **Twenty Six** —

21st March

Managed to control myself long enough to last four days before texting Will. Asked if he wanted to go for another drink. I'm waiting for his reply, it's been a couple of hours.

...He's probably at work.

— *Melissa Bishop, aged 19, naively unaware she's in the midst of her first ever ghosting.*

***

It felt strange to push open the front door and not have either Mum or Dad cheer a 'hello' at me. *Something you're going to have to get used to*, I thought morbidly, before taking off my coat and hanging it up on the bannister.

I'd ignorantly assumed that Dad would be sitting at home waiting for me to come back. Thought he'd be hovering by the kettle eagerly awaiting to make me a brew. He was instead at the hospital, attempting to see Mum during the strict visiting hours.

"I'll be home in an hour or so," he told me after updating me on her current positive recovery. "Or when they kick me out."

I popped my head around the kitchen door and saw piles of crockery beside the sink. Butter and crumbs smeared across the chopping board, and a few pans stacked atop of the cooker.

"What the hell has he been cooking?" I asked aloud, before turning and seeing an abandoned load of washing hanging half-in, half-out of the washing machine drum. "I've only been gone a day," I grumbled, preemptively cringing before I headed into the living room to witness an even sorrier sight.

Blankets and Dad's work papers thrown about, mugs of tea abandoned, and a stain of something orange on the carpet. "Did he get robbed, or throw a house party?"

While in the very pits of cleaning, elbow-deep in washing up bubbles, I felt my phone start to buzz in my back pocket. My stomach churned as the first person to pop into my head was Freddie. I'd thought about him constantly for the entire journey home, trying to work out what we were. Still together? Not together? Together, but him not attracted to me? Or, if I was perfectly honest with myself, together, but neither of us attracted to each other? What *were* we?

I read the caller ID and almost dropped my phone into the sink — I *so* didn't need to talk to Will. Not after the previous night.

I let it ring out, hoping Will would only need one failed call to take the hint. He didn't.

He rang again after about five minutes.

"Hello," I answered, hating the way I felt my cheeks grew hot when I heard his voice.

"Afternoon, beautiful, you okay?"

"Fine," I replied, trying not to immediately start off the conversation in dodgy territory. "How are you?"

"What's with the tone? I feel like I'm in trouble. You sound so serious."

"I'm just tired," I rubbed my brow and leaned against the sink. "Only got back home an hour or so ago."

"You're back up north already?" I could feel him smiling down the line, and worked hard to ignore the fact it set off a gentle hum deep within my chest. "Do you want to do something?"

Say no, I ordered myself, even though the majority of my brain had started to fizzle with joy and anticipation as it flicked through the Rolodex of what Will could possibly mean by *'something'*.

"I've got to clean the house while my folks are out, so I'm going to have to pass today."

"Oh." There was a long pause. "What about tomorrow?"

"Not good either," I chewed, anxiously, "I..." *Think of something.* "I have to take my mum to the garden centre." *Think of something better.*

"I see..." Will trailed off, but I could have sworn I could hear a suppressed laugh. "No worries then. Talk to you later."

"Okay."

I hung up and sunk down to the kitchen floor, hitting my phone against my forehead and calling myself every possible insult I could think of.

It took an hour for Will to try again, and by that point, the house was spotless, my body aching, and every single part of me riddled with boredom.

"You forget something?" I said, answering with a huff.

"It's a technicality really," Will started. "You said you would be free tonight if you weren't cleaning your folks house."

I looked around the spotless living room. "Yeah... So?"

There was a knock at the door. I got to my feet as I told Will to wait, "Two secs—"

I swung open the front door and almost fell backwards when I came face-to-face with Will, grinning like a dopey Cheshire cat.

"If I helped you clean, would that mean you'd go for a drink with me?" I heard him ask twice over.

I hung up, my jaw practically on the front mat. "Jesus, Will," I gasped. "What the hell are you doing here? *How* are you here? How do you know where my folks live?"

Will's eyes crinkled at the corners as he let out a merry laugh. "Err... because I've been here before." He threw a thumb over his shoulder, back towards the road. "I mean, I may have been horrendously drunk at the time, but I do remember walking up a big hill. Despite not being able to remember *which* house was your folks', I hoped I'd get the right one after knocking on enough doors." Will's eyes flicked towards the next door neighbour's front garden. "Christine says hello, by the way."

My stomach did a flip. *Oh, God.* Christine the gold medalist curtain twitcher speaking to Will could only lead to disaster. If Will had knocked on her door looking for me, she would have had no restraint in telling him—

"And she also said that she hopes your Mum comes back from the hospital soon."

Christine, you utter cow bag.

Will then gave me a look; not one of anger or disappointment, just plain old, '*Care to explain?*'

"How much did the old crow tell you?" I asked, leaning against the frame and sucking my teeth. I had half a mind to take one of Mum's gardening gloves over the wall and challenge her to a duel by slapping her around the face with it.

"Enough for me to know you've had a lot more on your plate these past couple of weeks than you've been letting on," Will shrugged. "And she also told me her granddaughter is single... God knows why."

"Christine's *granddaughter* is old enough to be your Mum."

Will wiggled his eyebrows, "Oh, well that changes things. I'll go back and join them for their family Sunday roast tonight."

I heard my giggle before I'd even registered it. Will had actually managed to make me laugh, despite everything currently raging around my head. *How does he do it?* I wondered, assessing him and soaking in his cool, calm and collected image. *How does he make me forget everything, even if only for a few seconds?*

"Do you want to come in?" I asked, already stepping to the side to let him pass.

"Thought you'd never ask."

Will sat comfortably on the sofa, then stared at me with an inquisitive, lopsided smile spread across his face. "Do you want to talk about it?" he eventually asked.

"Not even a little bit," I said, before collapsing into the armchair closest to me and wanting nothing more than to curl up into the foetal position and mummify myself with Mum's weighted blanket.

"Is there anything I can do to help?"

Nothing morally acceptable.

"No," I grumbled, hiding my face with the blanket and hoping that, by not looking at Will, he would miraculously disappear.

"Can I get you a drink? Tea? Wine? Rum?"

"Bleach?" I interjected, the tension in my muscles releasing slightly, comforted by the sound of Will's laughter from the other side of the room. "Don't think my folks have had booze in this house in the last decade and a half." I pulled the blanket back down. "Do *you* want a brew though?"

Will shook his head then pursed his bottom lip when the room went silent.

"You look like you're thinking," he commented.

"I am," I puffed out my chest slightly. "I'm trying to work out why you're here."

He shrugged, then looked genuinely a bit shy and reserved, before replying, "I thought you might be mad at me." He bit his protruding bottom lip, making my cheeks flare up. "Last night, we may have... gotten ourselves into a bit of a grey area, and I basically wanted to double check that we were still good?" he raised his hands defensively. "Like, I'm not saying I regret what happened, God no, I just wanted to double check that it hadn't affected our friendship. That's all."

The word 'friendship' made my ears feel as though they were bleeding.

"Call me paranoid, or whatever, but I got the feeling when I called you earlier that we weren't great, and rather than drive myself mad worrying about it, it made sense for me to drive over and ask you straight." Will rolled his eyes and fell back into the sofa cushions. "But now, after talking to Christine—"

"Your future grandmother-in-law?" I cut in, trying to throw the conversation off track since I knew exactly where it was headed.

"That's the one," Will unfortunately persevered. "Since I'm now a little bit more aware of why you're actually here and what you're going through, I realise I've been a bit self-absorbed. Because at no point did it ever occur to me when I decided to drive over here that you might be upset about something other than me. So, I'm here to say sorry, more than anything else."

"That's very big of you, Will."

"Well, I'm a very big boy," his eyes sparkled as the corners of his mouth twitched. "Which you already know."

If it hadn't been so obvious I would have thrown the blanket back over my head to hide my magenta cheeks. All I could do was hope they felt redder than they actually were.

I swallowed. "We're fine, Will. Last night was two mates having a bit of a laugh and you cheering me up, that's all."

"Good," Will breathed deeply, before ruffling his dark hair and grinning widely. "Glad we're on the same page." He looked at me and tilted his head, the way everyone seemed to, right before they brought up the conversation of Mum. "Seriously, though, the other stuff you've got going on... Do you want to talk about it?" Will sat up straight. "I mean, are you talking to *anyone* about it?"

I shook my head. *Who have I got to talk to?* I wondered, going through the list of possible candidates.

Dad? He has enough on his plate, he doesn't need me offloading all of my baggage on top of his.

Gramps? Again, he's currently trying to wrap his head around losing his child, something no parent should ever have to go through, no matter what their age.

Nana Tia? Is clearly in denial as she hasn't so much as called Mum to check in on her since the day she found out.

Freddie? I almost laughed aloud.

"Then talk to me," Will sighed, leaning even further forward off of his chair as if tempted to forget the space between us, leap across the room, and swoop me up into a tight embrace.

"You don't really do the whole chat thing though, do you? Especially if it involves feelings and emotions, and all those things you like to pretend you don't have."

I saw Will's jaw clench, a glint of something unfamiliar in his eyes, before he broke out into his usual default smile. "That's only the case with women I'm sleeping with, and unfortunately, you're not currently in that category."

Currently?

"Don't worry, I remember the rules," I heard myself snort derivatively.

"I kind of..." Will paused, then licked his lips and fell back into the sofa, looking at me, visibly at war with his own thoughts. "If what Christine told me is true, then I kind of might be one of the best people you *could* talk to about what you're going through."

"Oh yeah, and why's that?" I hummed, wondering how much Christine could actually know, considering all of her information came from what she witnessed from behind her floral net curtains.

"My dad died when I was five," Will confessed. "So, having a dead parent, or in your case a dying parent... is something I pride myself on knowing a fair bit about."

— Twenty Seven —

3rd April

Does it make me trashy that I don't remember his name? 'Him' being the guy I hooked up with last night. I suppose it depends who I ask, doesn't it? Nana Tia would say yes, I'm now no more than a common prostitute. Whereas someone like Will, or let's be honest, Cousin Willow, would give me a pat on the back and say, 'Makes you a legend'.

All I remember was that he was a Geordie and liked snowboarding. Or was it longboarding? Might have been hoverboarding? Not that I'm even sure that's a thing.

He wasn't a good shag, that I *do* know. I'm surprised I can even make that judgement having only ever been with two (now three) people, but et's just say, Will, without me even realising, has set the bar unbelievably high.

God, why am I even holding back? This is my diary, not like anyone's going to ever read it! Will was all I could think about the whole time last night. Literally every time whatever-his-name-was did something, all I could think was, *Will did it better.*

— *Melissa Bishop, aged 19, at the starting line of her sexcapade.*

***

"I'm so sorry," I said, horror flooding my face.

Will shrugged. "No need to say sorry, Mel, not like you were the one who killed him."

"He was *killed*?"

"No," Will laughed, weirdly merry. "He got lung cancer when I was really little and he simply became one of those statistics. Someone who didn't make it. From what I can remember, it was a long time coming. He was in and out of remission for years. Jordan was about eleven when Dad died, so he remembers more of him than I do. Not that he likes talking about it."

I blinked, not knowing what else to do. There was something in the uncharacteristic softness of Will's voice that made me feel as though I was in a privileged position to hear this kind of information come out of his mouth.

"Mum was his carer for the last couple of years of his life. Don't know how she did it, to be honest," Will shook his head, humming pensively to himself. "It sets unrealistic expectations for relationships, doesn't it?"

"Tell me about it," I murmured under my breath, thinking of my Dad, heroically caring for Mum.

No matter what Mum said, no matter what she did, Dad was there when she called, and seemingly happy to be of assistance in whatever way she needed — not only since her prognosis, but for their entire marriage.

"Do you miss him?" I asked, chewing on the inside of my cheek, nervous to hear what could be my own prospective future.

"Not really," Will's eyebrows furrowed as he contemplated his answer a little longer. "I don't really remember my dad enough to miss him. It's more like I miss the idea of him."

"What do you mean?"

"You always miss the best version of someone, even if they aren't dead, they can be merely out of your life. You miss what they were to you, never who they actually were. You miss all the good stuff, but not the bad, despite the fact that's what made them *them*." Will exhaled, confessing, "I miss having *a* dad. But *my* dad? He was a bellend."

I almost choked.

Will's eyes glistened with delight that he'd caught me so off guard. "No, seriously," he laughed. "He was funny, and a brilliant piano player, but Jesus, he was a crap dad, and an even worse husband."

Will's face fell for a millisecond, and for a moment I caught a glimpse of him as a young boy. Younger than he was even when I first met him all those years ago. He looked lost, helpless, and ever so sad.

"He cheated on my mum," Will confessed suddenly, the sadness in his eyes deepening. "Multiple times, with multiple women. He was a professional musician. He worked in an industry where he met new, interesting and beautiful women with every new job. He essentially had a roster of women who he knew he'd have a designated amount of time with and then likely never see again."

Will almost sounded wistful. Like that was somehow a situation to be admired rather than repulsed by. *Maybe he does admire it,* I wondered, before asking,

"Did your Mum know?"

Will stared right at me, his eyes boring deep into my soul from across the room. He nodded. "She found out a few months before he died. He was bedridden, had lost his speech, and knowing it was close to the end, Mum had started sorting through some of his things. She found letters, photographs... Every kind of evidence a person would need to know her entire marriage had been a lie."

"Oh my God..." I found myself whisper under my breath. "What did she do?"

I half-expected him to say she killed him without any kind of irony at all. But I'd met Will's mum. I barely remembered her, but from what I could recall, she was sweet with kind eyes — she didn't strike me as a killer.

"Mum didn't do anything," Will shrugged. "She carried on caring for him, right up until his last breath."

"*Why?*" I blurted out before I could stop myself.

"I asked her the same thing," Will rubbed his hands together. "She said that was her way of getting out of it unscathed. If she'd made a big deal about it, tried to divorce him, or fend for herself, she would have done some serious damage to not only herself, but to everything around her. Me, Jordan, her whole life. By just putting all the evidence back where she found it and pretending like none of it existed, she could carry on her life as is, until he eventually died and she could start again."

"When did you find out about this?" I couldn't help but ask, eager to know if this information had come to Will early in life, as if that would somehow explain why Will behaved the way that he did. Or it might confuse me more. I was only going to find out which if I actually asked.

"Shortly after I moved out of home and in with Jordan. He... *Well*, you've met him."

"I have," I nodded, wondering if making a joke now would ease some of the tension that had built in the room or simply make it worse. "A few times."

"Enough times to know what he's like. Jordan's never been capable of being loyal to any woman he's ever dated."

Pot. Kettle. Black. Dickhead, I retorted to myself.

"Jordan had a parade of women coming in and out of the flat and I couldn't cope. One day, without realising, I ranted to my mum about it. She hit the roof. Told me he *can't* be like his dad, she raised him right," Will scowled. "Naturally, I was confused, because why *wouldn't* Mum want Jordan to be like our dad? Then it occurred to me maybe he wasn't the stand-up husband I'd been brought up to believe he was. I asked more questions, and she told me everything."

"Does Jordan know?"

Will shook his head. "Promised my mum I wouldn't tell him. Plus, it wouldn't do Jordan any good, or change who he is. He's been a womaniser ever since he hit puberty. Maybe even before that, as I remember him marrying three separate girls on our road one summer and causing a cat fight to break out amongst the eight-year-olds."

I laughed softly before something in the back of my head went off like a petty little lightbulb. "So Jordan was your father figure? That makes sense." I chewed the inside of my cheek as I felt Will's eyes suddenly fix upon my face, and narrow with each silent second that ticked by.

"And what's that supposed to mean?" Will asked, his voice low.

"Just that—" I felt like I was dipping my toes into boiling water, but couldn't resist it. This was an unnatural occurrence, Will opening up. *What if I never get this opportunity again*? I wondered, before deciding to commit to the inevitable car crash and come right out with it. "All this sort of explains why you are the way you are with women, too. You learnt from your big brother. You flirt, you seduce, and you... cheat," I exhaled, before adding, "I sometimes think you can't help it. It's just who you are."

Will was scowling at me so viciously I felt that maybe I had taken it too far. But then his face relaxed and he smiled, and ruffled his dark hair again.

"I've never *technically* cheated on anyone," Will shrugged, beaming from ear to ear.

"Just dabbled in the *grey area* from time to time," I tried to joke and earned myself a deadpan glare. "Look, all I'm saying is, would you be happy with your girlfriend knowing what happened last night?"

"Or Freddie?" Will added, bristling me.

"I don't think he'd care," I got up from my chair and headed for the back door. *I need air.*

"You and him still...?"

"Together?" I finished for him, as Will seemed unable to find the best way to complete his sentence. "God knows." I rolled my eyes, opening the back door fully and letting a relieving gush of cold October air into the room.

"Do you see it lasting with Freddie?" Will suddenly asked, joining me at the door and leaning back against the frame. "Or do you feel like you're flogging a dead horse?"

I didn't answer, only looked out into the back garden, trying to focus on something other than the fact Will was now less than five inches away from me.

"Do you want it to work with him?" Will pushed, causing my eyes to actually start to sting.

"Course I do," I bit off. "Wouldn't be working my ass off, paying the rent, and everything else if I didn't."

"You pay for everything *and* he's not sleeping with you?" Will shook his head in bewilderment.

"He said that he—" I choked on my own breath, the harsh memory of the morning spewing out of my mouth. "Freddie said, before I set off, that he felt emasculated by me. Because I paid for his half of the rent, I've made him feel less of a man... And that's why he isn't wasn't in the mood to do *stuff*."

"But he *lets* you pay for everything?"

"He has to. Like, he *asked* me to. Freddie has no money, he never has. He's not been able to hold down a job longer than a month since we've been together."

"Why are you *with* him?" Will stressed, his whole body tense. "I don't get it."

"Neither do I." I stepped outside and walked towards Mum's allotment so that I didn't have to bear being next to Will any longer. "I think it's because I can't deal with a Freddie break-up right now. Not on top of everything else."

"How's a Freddie break-up different from any other break-up?" Will asked, following me like a shadow into the garden.

"The last time I tried to leave... We'd only been living together for a few weeks but I couldn't cope. We had a massive fight about how I felt the relationship wasn't working, and Freddie got so mad he punched a hole in the wall. Nearly broke his hand." I cleared my throat, nervous to say out loud something I had never told another soul. "He then threatened to kill himself if I left. Got onto the balcony and everything..." I ran my hands through my hair with a resentful sigh. "I had to ring the police to get him down, and I've never tried to break up with him since. Because witnessing someone going through that... It's a once in a lifetime thing. Leaves me with no other option but to try and *try* to make it work."

"Do you think he would have jumped?" Will asked softly, his attention on me despite the splendour around him. There were an abundance of chrysanthemums to his left, a flourish of marigolds to his right. He didn't care, he was staring at the red-headed, red-eyed, emotional mess in front of him.

"I honestly don't know," I hummed in thought. "Freddie is unpredictable sometimes." I looked across at Mum's crabapple tree and my heart immediately started to ache. "My mum hates him."

"I'm not surprised," Will joked, finally looking away from me and sitting on Mum's cast iron bench. He stretched his legs out and placed both of his hands behind his head as though he were sunbathing under a summer sun and not freezing beneath an autumn sky. "Do you want to talk about her yet? Or are we going to stall some more and talk about your idiotic boyfriend for a bit longer?"

"Jesus, Will," I swore, joining him on the bench, not knowing whether I wanted to hug him or slap him.

"That's literally all you have going on in your life at the moment. I'm merely working with what I've got," he shrugged, draping his arm over my shoulder.

"You're an arsehole, you know that?"

"Of course. Being self-aware of my dickishness has been one of my unique selling points since I was about thirteen."

"That late?"

"Twelve-year-old me was very oblivious."

I laughed, feeling the gentle movement of his body next to mine as he enjoyed his joke along with me. Then we both went very still and I heard him whisper. "Tell me how you're feeling, Mel. I want to help."

"There's nothing *to* tell you," I confessed. "She's dying. Simple as that. Nothing anyone can do about it."

Will rested his head against mine and I found that our breathing had synchronised. His chest was rising with mine, our sighs intertwined.

"Can I give you some advice?" he eventually said, his free hand nesting itself in the hook of my elbow. He traced the delicate patch of skin with one lone finger. "Don't be too militant about it. Allow yourself to feel whatever you need to feel in order to get through this. I'm here if you ever *really* want to talk about it."

"Thank you," I whispered, my whole body growing heavy to a point where I truly believed I might fall asleep in his arms.

Will's finger continued to draw lazy circles up and down my forearm. I'd never felt so peaceful.

"I've had an idea," Will murmured after a quiet moment, nuzzling his face into the crook of my neck before placing a tender kiss on my shoulder. "Call me stupid, or an idiot, but I think I might—"

My phone suddenly started to ring in my pocket and both Will and I froze. It was as though the wind had changed direction, and an anxious chill ran down my spine.

I'm not ready.

I scrambled for my phone and ripped it from my back pocket. The caller ID read '*Dad*' and my heart sank deep into the pits of my stomach.

I'm not ready.

Will sensed my internal panic, fear and sadness leading him to take my hand and squeeze it tightly. "You got this. I'm right here with you," he whispered encouragingly, planting a soft kiss on my temple.

I answered. "Hello? Dad? Is everything al—"

Mum's blood-curdling scream came ringing down the line like the tortured wail of a banshee. I knew without Dad saying a word that another scar was about to be seared onto my soul.

— Twenty Eight —

27th April

Hugo from acting class has asked me on a date. Thankfully, he waited till everyone was occupied with putting their things away before pulling me aside and telling me about a sushi place he thought I might like.

I didn't understand him at first, so said, "Oh, thanks, I'll check it out when I crave a bit of raw fish."

He pulled a face and tried again, "No, what I mean is, do you want to go now? With me? For lunch?"

"Oh," was all I could muster. Not, 'Sorry, I'm an idiot', or even, 'Yeah, that sounds lovely'. Just, 'Oh'.

My brain was too busy spitting up its usual — *Hugo's not as tall as Will, not as burly either.* Will is also a better actor. That's why he's on a drama foundation course and not in a class like this.

"Mel?" Hugo pushed, trying to regain my attention.

"Sure, why not?"

By the look on Hugo's face I'm guessing that's not what a guy wants to hear when he's just asked someone out.

— *Melissa Bishop, aged 19, deciding she needs to book more acting classes if she's ever going to convince anyone that she's over Will Green.*

***

"Medication withdrawal," was all I understood from what jargon the nurse had offloaded onto me when I arrived onto the ward.

Even at the reception desk I could hear Mum's screams and wails come echoing down the hallway. "Your dad is already in there," the nurse said, motioning for me to walk towards the swinging doors where the spine-chilling shrieks were originating from.

My feet didn't feel as though they were attached to me, but somehow I found the strength to step forwards towards my fated trauma. Before I knew it, I was at the threshold, looking through the crack of the partially opened door and seeing what could only be described as Absolute Fucking Carnage.

Mum was being pinned down by four nurses, all of them clearly desperate to try and stop her from ripping out the copious amount of tubes protruding from her body. Without context, an onlooker might have believed they were trying to perform an exorcism.

"Mel...?" I heard Dad's hollow voice call from the corner of the room.

"They're trying to kill me!" Mum wailed, her head rolling from side to side, her hair whipping against the bright white pillow. "Help me, please!"

I instinctively stepped forward, as if some primal switch in my brain had suddenly been wrenched on by Mum's desperate plea. She begged for help again and again, despite it looking like the four nurses were the ones needing aid.

"Mum?" I asked, milliseconds before Dad's hand slipped into mine and pulled me into his little corner of the room.

"She can't hear you," he whispered to me, his voice ghost-like. "We've been trying for ages to get her to recognise me but she—" Dad clamped his mouth shut and scrunched up his face as we heard Mum let out another ear-splitting shriek.

"Do you need me to try?" I asked, not knowing whether I wanted him to say yes or no.

A doctor entered with too much cheer on his face to be ever considered genuine considering the current state of the room. "Hello, Mrs Bishop," he started, as if Mum wasn't currently being pinned down and screaming at the top of her lungs. "I'm here to give you a small injection."

Mum's right leg broke free and she kicked with every bit of strength she had left at the nurse who'd let it lose.

"They're trying to kill me!" Mum wailed again, this time her voice sounding like a terrified child. "They're trying to kill me! *Someone* help me!"

Through the bars of her hospital bed I could see her bloodshot eyes were fixed on me, and I couldn't help but reach out for her. She looked so lost, so broken, so helpless...

"They're trying to help you, Mum."

Her neck suddenly craned back, her body contorting itself, desperate to break free.

Dad's hands flew to his ears, Mum's screams becoming unbearable the moment the doctor's needle pierced her skin. I thought I was going to throw up when she suddenly jerked against the bars and smacked her face. Blood started flowing freely from her nose, her whole body trembling, losing the fight to whatever sedation was now coursing through her.

"They're trying to kill me," she repeated, her voice now weak. "I don't want to die…"

Dad was hiding in the prayer room. I found him after sitting beside a sedated Mum, in silence, for what felt like hours. I'd waited for him to return after fleeing the commotion, but didn't once consider that he might not, until it turned ten and he was still missing.

Of all the various chairs to choose from, Dad had decided to sit in the one furthest away from the door. He was curled over, his elbows resting on his knees, his head in his hands.

He looked up and I had to do a double-take — he didn't look like my dad at all.

Sad and Dad were two concepts that simply didn't make sense together. He was someone who, at one time or another, I genuinely believed couldn't feel anything other than immature bliss. Whether that was due to my ignorance or simple wishful thinking, I would never really know.

Nothing ever seemed to bother Dad. He was always the 'shrug off and carry on' type. "What's the point in letting it get to you? You could get hit by a bus tomorrow," was one of his most known phrases. And yet, in that moment, all I could think of was how defeated and heartbroken he looked.

I couldn't bear it. I focused on the fact that his eyebrows were bushier than usual, his beard was the longest I'd ever seen it, and grey hairs were sticking out of the top of his head at weird angles. His nose was red and rosy, the cuff of his fleece frayed, there was mud on his left shoe — I focused on anything that would distract me from the fact he was crying.

"That's not my wife…" he wept, removing his glasses and pinching the bridge of his nose tightly. "I don't know who that woman in there is."

"She's in there… somewhere," I tried to reassure him, taking a hesitant step further into the room.

Dad tilted his head back and let out a heartbroken sob.

I scurried to his side and sat beside him, wrapping my arm around him and trying to squeeze through his layers of woolly clothing. "We just have to wait for her to come back to us, Dad."

"I don't think she can come back from that. You saw her in there. She didn't even know who we were." Dad rested his head against my shoulder, his whole body trembling with grief. "I knew I was losing her... But I never thought I'd be losing her like this."

I could do nothing but hold him. A man too big to fit into the curve of my arms, but I held him as best as I could while he grieved a woman not yet dead, but already lost to him.

— Twenty Nine —

1st May

Soo... Drama school isn't happening. I finally found the rejection emails that've been sitting in my spam for God knows how long! The whole time I've been telling myself no news is good news, and the bad news has been there for weeks!

Was I really that bad? I thought it'd be a good idea to do something out of the ordinary – Henry V seemed like it would stand out amongst all the Juliets and Lady Macbeths.

"Once more unto the breach, dear friends, once more!"

Maybe I completely missed the mark and just looked like an absolute dickhead. Trying so hard to stand out that I ended up standing out for all the wrong reasons. I was probably written off the moment I started wailing like a banshee.

There were people there who'd been auditioning for years — I hope that's not going to be me one day.

I have to get in... Some day. Somehow. Guess I can do nothing now but work and save in the meantime. Oh, and learn Juliet's monologues!

'Romeo, doff thy name,
And for that name, which is no part of thee,
Take all myself'

Been there, babe.

— Melissa Bishop, finding she may have something in common with a fourteenth century, 13-year-old fictional character.

***

Dad and I fought long and hard to get ourselves into the car when the nurses rang to tell us that Mum had been moved to a nearby hospice the following afternoon. Apparently it all happened so fast. *No shit*. But by 3pm, she was settled in her room and asking for us.

"How can she be asking for us?" Dad and I echoed to the hospice nurse at reception. "She didn't even know who we were yesterday," headed, visibly affected by even mentioning the feral event. "She couldn't comprehend anything, let alone *ask* for someone."

The nurse gave us one of her most practised and perfected smiles. "I assure you, she's fine today, Mr Bishop. If you wouldn't mind following me."

What little bravery I had left was used to walk into Mum's room. My jaw almost hit the floor when I saw her sat up in bed, fluffy slippers on, and a steaming cup of tea in her hands.

The only scrap of evidence that the previous day had even happened was a tiny pair of steri-strip plasters over the bridge of her very bruised nose.

"Hello!" Mum cheered as Dad and I stepped into the brightly lit room, both stunned into silence. Mum splayed her left hand and waved merrily at us, before enthusiastically motioning to the two available chairs. "Sit, sit. You both look knackered."

"Theresa?" Dad blinked.

Mum grinned at him, then sipped her tea. "They make a good cuppa here, love, you should order yourself one. Hold on," Mum reached across herself for the bright orange buzzer. "Ring-a-ding-ding," she chimed before pressing the buzzer and smiling as an identical tinny tune played out in the hall. "If she's brunette, it's Kara, and if she's grey, it's Ruth," Mum reduced her voice to that of a whisper, "*and it's a wig.*"

A brunette woman, not much older than me, popped her head around the door. "Everything alright, Theresa?" she asked, nodding at both Dad and I in acknowledgment.

"Would you be able to bring in some tea for my family, Kara? It'll be an easy one for you as they both like their tea the same way. Milky with one sugar—"

"*Two* sugars," Dad and I corrected in unison automatically, before looking at one another in mirrored disbelief.

"Of course," Kara smiled, "anything else?"

Mum's eyes lit up. "I'll have some more raspberry jelly if there's any left over from lunch."

"I'll have a look for you, love." Kara left and I found myself sitting down simply to stop myself from toppling over.

What's happening? I asked myself, feeling as though I might have hit my head when leaving the hospital the previous day, and was now in some medically-induced coma.

"Are you going to sit, Teddy, love?" Mum asked, taking another sip of her tea. "You look like a statue, standing over there with a slack jaw and a stiff body."

Dad apprehensively sat down, also oblivious as to what the hell was going on. Mum was meant to be sick. Worse than sick, she was meant to be screaming, wailing, unpredictable and unstable, not sitting in bed, cheery as a child on Christmas morning.

"You learned sign language at school, Jelly-Melly, what's the sign for 'bird' again?" Mum asked randomly, turning to face me with a sweet smile. "I can see so many birds through the window but I can't for the life of me remember what the sign for bird actually is."

"I don't know, Mum," I replied quietly, my mind racing at a thousand thoughts per second. "I've never learnt sign language."

"Have you not?" Mum blinked, before curling up her left fist into a ball and seemingly drawing circles with it on the end of her nose. "Well, this means pig." She stuck out her little finger and started to draw clockwise circles on her left temple. "And this means sheep. There you go, every day is a school day."

"Okay..." I trailed off, watching her wriggle into her bed, giddy and proud of herself for delivering me a little bit more knowledge.

"Did you learn sign language at school, Teddy?" Mum asked. "Or was it German?"

Dad blinked at her before letting the smallest of bemused smiles sneak out from beneath his ever bushier beard. "French."

Mum shrugged. "Close enough. *Literally.*" She threw her head back and laughed as Kara returned.

"Managed to sneak you a spare jelly, Theresa," Kara commented, passing Dad and I our tea and pulling out a sealed pot of jelly from her pocket.

"Ooh, you're a star," Mum beamed before looking at the jelly proffered to her with a contemplative tilt of the head. "Don't suppose you've got any sprinkles... Or squirty cream?"

Kara cracked-up, passing Mum a spoon. "'Fraid not. Let me know if you need anything else, Theresa."

Mum watched Kara leave, her spoon clasped tightly between her lips as though it were a smoking pipe. "She's usually a lot more chattier than that," Mum mumbled, before scooping out some of her jelly with her pinkie. "When I arrived this morning, I couldn't get the pert lass to shut up."

The rest of the visit continued in much the same mind-boggling way. Mum was merry, laughing, and childish to a point where all of her excitement eventually exhausted her.

"We'll come and visit you again tomorrow," I whispered, pecking Mum's cheek when her left eyelid was starting to close and match her right.

"You promise?" Mum murmured, already half-asleep.

"Promise," I assured her, squeezing her hand and only then realising how much weight she'd lost. Her face was still as round as ever, but her fingers were near enough bone. Her wrists had become brittle branches, her veins clearly visible on the backs of her hands. I tried to keep my revolutionary shock to myself while I headed for the door, letting Dad say his own farewells.

In the hallway, I found Kara, flicking through some papers. She looked up at me and smiled awkwardly.

"Are you heading out?" she asked, a weird squeak to her tone. "Or does your mum need something?"

"No, we're going now."

Dad came out of the room too fast and bumped into me so hard that I almost fell over.

"You alright, Freckles?" he asked, taking grip of my arm while I regained my balance.

"Yeah," I assured him, giving his hand a squeeze. "Bit thrown, but not by you."

"Tell me about it," Dad grumbled, scratching the back of his head. "Feel like I imagined yesterday... Or I'm hallucinating today." Dad turned to Kara, "How long has she been like that?"

Kara clearly didn't understand the question. "Theresa's been the same since she arrived from the hospital this morning."

Ring-a-ding-ding.

"Excuse me," Kara smiled again, before scurrying off down the hall and disappearing into another room.

Dad took the opportunity of an empty hallway to let out an exhausted and bewildered laugh. "*Did* yesterday happen?" he asked, his voice quiet. "Or am I actually going mad?"

"It happened," I reassured him, rubbing his arm supportively. "Or we're going mad together."

— **Thirty** —

27th May

I'm not proud of myself. I knew it was a stupid thing to do, but when Hugo announced to the whole acting class that he was going to a friend's end-of-term showcase, my heart leapt. His friend was on the same course as Will!

I asked Hugo for the details — time, place, etc.,etc. He seemed to think I was fishing for a second date but after the chopstick incident? Err, *no*.

I miraculously managed to gain on-the-door entry to Will's showcase, and before I knew it, I was sitting in a rickety metal chair about to see Will for the first time in months.

It was a risk, I knew that, I'm not stupid. Will clearly didn't want to see me, or speak to me since he'd left me on read multiple times... But what harm could it do, me being there? Not like I could make things worse between us by being there.

Or so I thought.

That was until I heard a seductive whisper of, "I remember you," coupled with hot breath on my neck.

And I turned around to find Will's older brother, Jordan, sitting beside me.

— *Melissa Bishop, aged 19, with a growing sense that she may have cocked up slightly building in her stomach.*

***

Feeling a little like I'd stepped out of a regency novel the following morning, I decided to have my breakfast outside. Wrapped tightly in my duvet, my arms were bound as I tried to slurp my cereal off the spoon, milk spilling all over my chin. So, maybe less Jane Austin and more T.rex.

I sat on the same bench Will had held me on two days prior. Feeling the kiss he'd placed onto my shoulder like a burn from a red-hot poker, I brought my knees up to my chest. Why had that moment had to end? Why had it even happened to begin with? It wasn't Will.

That's what was confusing me the most. Will had never acted that way around me before, even when he didn't have a girlfriend.

He was never the talkative type, the supportive type, and never the one to do small romantic acts of affection.

I realised I was subconsciously caressing my shoulder, my mind desperate to hold onto the memory.

Will seemed to know I was thinking of him, as a supportive text came through as I was supping up the last dregs of cereal from the bottom of my bowl.

Hope you're doing okay. Wanted to check in and see how you are?? No pressure, if you're not ready to talk about any of it yet, but please know, I'm here if you change your mind. Xx

My heart ached. Why did he have to be *so* nice? Why couldn't he simply leave me alone?

Because you don't want him to, I thought with a self-deprecating snort.

"Are you birdwatching, Freckles?" I heard Dad ask, coming down the path with his hands shoved deep into the pockets of his fraying cream cardigan.

"Thought I'd try a change of scenery," I nodded towards Christine's adjacent backyard. "And give nosey-nellie something to chin wag about at her coffee morning." I attempted to mimic Christine's raspy old voice, "*Oh, you should have seen that frizzy Bishop girl this morning, Ruth. She was in the garden with her bedsheets. Things must really not be going well for her. Poor lass is clearly on the precipice of a mental breakdown.*"

My phone went off again.

Can I see you tonight? Would that help? Talking face to face rather than over the phone? Xx

And *again*.

Again, no pressure. Just want to help in whatever way I can. Xx

"You're popular this morning," Dad noted, jutting his head towards my pinging phone. "Or is that an alarm going off?"

"It's a... *friend*," I replied, hoping that the sharp October breeze hitting my face would counteract the blush I felt brewing beneath my cheeks.

"So, not Freddie?" Dad raised a suspicious eyebrow. He'd been naturally curious when I'd returned home a whole day earlier than planned. "Are you and him...?"

"Going through a rough patch," I said under my breath, feeling as though filling Dad in would be one of my poorer decisions. Dad didn't like Freddie enough as it was. If I told him all, and Freddie and I ended up staying together (which, deep down, I knew we would), I'd never be able to look Dad in the eye again.

"We haven't spoken since I left the other day, and we didn't exactly leave on the best of terms. So at the moment, I would say Freddie's..."

"A glorified house-sitter?" Dad suggested, unironically.

I felt a warmth grow in my chest, a giggle briefly tickling my throat. "Something like that."

My phone went off again, Dad's curiosity visibly growing. "So, who is this *friend* then?"

"Someone I used to know." I turned to face Dad and saw his eyes, magnified by his oval lenses, glistening with intrigue. "I met him a fair few years ago. He now knows about Mum, and because he's been through something similar, he's trying to help. Mainly by attempting to get me to talk about it."

"Oh," Dad pulled a face, mildly amused, yet softly saddened. "I'm glad you've got someone to talk to..."

I had a strong feeling that his sentence was incomplete, that maybe the words, *'Not all of us have that luxury'* were on the tip of his tongue.

"You can always talk to me, Dad," I suddenly said, the feeling urging me to comfort him. "About anything."

"I chat a lot of rubbish, Freckles. I wouldn't want to bore you with half of the nonsense I come out with, to be honest."

My phone started to ring.

"He's a persistent bugger, isn't he?" Dad joked, before tugging my duvet from around my shoulders and placing half of it across his lap. "If you don't put that poor lad out of his misery, I will."

I snatched my phone up, knowing Dad wasn't joking. "Morning, Wi—"

"Melissa! Thank goodness I caught you!" Nana Tia's shrill voice came yammering down the line, causing Dad's face and my own to fall in synchronisation. "It'll only be a quick one as I've got pilates in half an hour and I can't miss it. Your grandfather took me for afternoon tea yesterday and I've got several cucumber sandwiches to burn off," she inhaled sharply, not giving me a moment to interrupt. "Dinner tonight, I've got a lovely leg of lamb that needs eating and it's much too big for your grandfather and I. So, I had this marvellous thought. How about you and Teddy come over—"

"Tell her I'm dead," Dad grumbled, already pinching the bridge of his nose and grimacing at the thought of spending an evening with his nightmarish in-laws. Not so much Gramps, but Nana Tia was bad enough to make up for whatever sensibility Gramps brought to the table.

"Not to mention if you visit tonight, you can collect the dresses I've had set aside for you for a good long while now. What do you say?"

Piss off?

"Sounds lovely, Nana," I grumbled, unconvincingly pert. "Dad's not free tonight though, so it will just be me."

Dad's unruly eyebrows raised and he turned to me in slow motion, with nowhere near enough gratitude.

"Oh, I see. Well, we'll be eating at five."

"See you then." I hung up before Nana took the opportunity to rope me into anything else — most likely a space beside her in her upcoming pilates class. I couldn't think of anything worse than being in a freezing town hall with twenty old ladies around me puffing, panting, and stretching in lycra.

I ran my fingers through my hair, groaning at all of the possible torturous outcomes my night was likely going to have now that I'd sealed my fate.

"I was only joking, Freckles," Dad said, his brow furrowing. "I would have come. You didn't have to do that for me."

"Course I did," I sighed, pulling the duvet up to my chin and nestling comfortably into his side as if I was five again, and my Dad's arms the safest place in the world. "Your wife's dying. You've suffered enough..."

I walked into Nana's at three minutes to five, and she still accused me of being late.

"When one says, 'We'll be eating at five', that usually means food will be served at five. Not arrive at five. Or else how will you leave any time to settle yourself in? Wash your hands? Help with laying the table?"

My only response was a shrug, and a poke of my head around the living room doorway to see if Gramps was lurking nearby. The sooner he could start drowning out Nana, the better.

"Hands first," Nana pointed upstairs. "And then I'll get you a drink."

God, I hope she has tequila.

I gave her a salute, slipped off my trainers and scurried up the pale pink carpeted stairs. When I pushed open the bathroom door I almost keeled over laughing. Gramps was stood precariously on the edges of the tub, a lit cigarette lolling out of the side of his mouth, his head hanging out of the frosted window.

He jumped, nearly falling. "Bleedin' hell do you think you're playing at?! You ever heard of knocking?" he barked disapprovingly. "I could've been having a shite!"

"Then lock the door next time."

"Can't. Your Nana gets suspicious if I lock the door."

"Suspicious of what?"

Gramps inhaled the last of his cigarette. "Me, smoking in the house." He exhaled, smoke drifting and escaping out of the open window. "Paranoid nut case and a half she is."

"Why aren't you smoking in the back garden?" I washed my hands. "That's your usual hiding place."

Gramps rolled his eyes. "Oh it's a right state at the moment. Your Nana's been watching some gardening programme. Might as well be called Twits With Wheelbarras', I tell you." He coughed violently. "And it's given her *ideas*. She's been fannying about with all these bushes and paid some Manc lad to build a bloody gazebo. He ain't half made a mess."

"*Melissa!*" Nana called up the stairs, "Have you gotten lost, or merely admiring my selection of hand soaps?"

My jaw instinctively clenched and I had to take a deep breath to stop myself from swearing. "She's on one tonight, isn't she?"

Gramps cleared the black of his throat of phlegm before spitting into the open toilet. "She's *always* on one, love," he grumbled, before crushing his cigarette end between his sausage like finger-tips. "Be grateful you don't live with the wench."

"How do you do it?" I asked, genuinely baffled.

"You know, I've asked myself that question every God-damn day for the last thirty years."

We descended the stairs together, smiles on our faces, causing Nana to pout disapprovingly — fun without her say was clearly not aloud.

She shook her head, "I don't want to even know what mischief you two have been up to up there, but I'm telling you now, if you're both going to play silly buggers this evening, I'm not past putting either of you in the naughty corner."

I looked into the living room, the nostalgia of a million naughty corner memories sweeping over me. Childhood visits to Nana's, or the Fallon Christmas Clan gathering, usually consisted of at least one person being sent to the corner. Those being punished were usually sent for the most ridiculous of reasons; not eating their peas, drinking milk straight out of the carton, or in my most memorable case, giving Cousin Willow one of Nana's sealed tampons to use as a fake cigar during a game of gangsters when we were ten.

— Thirty One —

27th May

It took less than three minutes to realise where Will had got all of his flirty tips and tricks from. Jordan had me a giggly, blushing mess in no time at all. He was attentive, kind, and just the right amount of cocky. Will was nothing but the apprentice if his big brother was the master at 'women'.

"Let's go see the aspiring thespian together," Jordan whispered to me, as the round of applause for the showcase started to dwindle. "Pretend we're together to really give him a fright."

"Why would that—"

Jordan pulled me up and towards the dispersing cast, all of them clearly ready to mingle and shmooze.

"You alright, lil' brother?" Jordan swanned into them all, still holding my hand tightly.

"Jordan, I didn't know you were coming today." Will's eyes flickered my way and, laughably, he did a double-take. "What—"

"You know my date, don't you?" Jordan grinned from ear to ear. "I still don't know her name, but God, she's a lot of fun."

I felt my cheeks go red, from being flattered or mortified, I genuinely couldn't tell.

"What're you doing here?" Will asked me flatly, ignoring his brother completely.

"I got invited."

"By who?"

"A friend."

"Which friend?"

"You don't know them."

"Try me."

Jordan's eyes flicked between Will and me, his sly smile starting to drop. "Can you stop interrogating my date, Will?" he finally cut in, physically stepping between us. "You're going to make her want to leave. Which I don't mind actually..." Jordan turned to me and squeezed the hand I completely forgot he was still holding, "as long as she takes me with her."

I gulped. Even after months of dating, hooking up, and fooling around, I still felt completely out of my depth with these two — especially Jordan. Not that I would ever actually go there. That would be very, *very* weird.

Will shrugged. "Do whatever you want. I don't care. See you back at home, Jordan." He turned and walked away and I felt like I was going to vomit. Embarrassment, shame, and pain churned around my stomach.

"I better go," I sniffled, forcing myself not to cry. That would have been the cherry on the trauma-cake, for sure. "Good seeing you again, Jordan."

"Woah, woah, woah, don't let that little dick make you want to leave. We were just getting to know each other!"

"You still don't even know my name," I managed to fake a smile and a laugh. "I don't think we were getting to know each other at all."

"Course I know your name," Jordan beamed with a wicked glint in his eye. "You're Will's infamous Mel, aren't you?"

— *Melissa Bishop, aged 19, wondering if being someone's 'infamous' is a good thing or not.*

***

"So, how have you been, Melissa?" Nana asked, filled to the brim with determined ignorance and frustrating merriment.

I wanted to reply with the obvious, *I've been in hell. How do you think I've been?* But from the expectant look on her powder-puffed face, I knew she was expecting me to lie.

I cast a look at Gramps, who was already elbow-deep in mint sauce and roast potatoes.

"I've been better," I replied, shoving some broccoli into my mouth and hoping my chewing would stop her onslaught of questions before they even started. It didn't.

"Well, what are you doing to keep yourself occupied?" Nana prodded a sliver of carrot with her delicate silver fork. "I imagine you're twiddling your thumbs at home, with no job—"

"I have a job."

"Or a hobby to keep you busy. Your great uncle Matthew was in much the same way when he had his appendix removed. Didn't know what to do with himself.

But now he's taken up bowls. Done him wonders! When he's not playing on the local green—"

"He's playing with his sales assistant," Gramps interjected, causing me to nearly choke on my veg.

Nana threw him a venomous look, before re-composing herself. "I'm not suggesting you take up bowls, but a hobby of some kind might prove useful to get you out of the house."

"I'm getting out of the house enough as it is, what with all the—"

I bit my tongue, my mind reeling one way, and my mouth another.

Hospital visits. Hospice visits. Trips to see a deadbeat boyfriend, I thought coldly. *Not forgetting the sort-of dates with a bloke who has a girlfriend.*

"—work I'm doing at *Rogan's*," I finished with a sharp inhale.

"*Rogan's?*" Nana raised her crystal glass of apple juice to her thin lips. "Is that a firm?"

"It's a bar," I corrected, knowing that would give her enough fuel to fire up whatever length of time she wanted to hear her own voice, and keep her chatting about something other than *the bleeding obvious*.

"You're back *waitressing*?" she shook her head. "Not a career, dear, is it?"

"She don't need a career right now, Tia, love," Gramps chuntered, giving me a much needed wink of support from across the table. "Poor lass is only twenty-three."

"At twenty-three I was a mother of two, and a home owner," Nana chewed, pushing her one and only roast potato to the opposite side of her plate. "New generations, they're wired completely differently."

"Maybe that's a good thing," I grumbled under my breath.

"They do everything backwards," Nana continued, not that Gramps was listening, and I was doing my best to tune her out by focusing on the old clock in the corner of the room. I watched its pendulum swing back and forth, and tried fixating on its monotonous ticking rather than Nana's incessant ranting.

"Look at Amanda's youngest. Pregnant, in her thirties, with no wedding in sight. Not that I'm one for gossiping, but we all reckon she's gone about it via a turkey baster. Amanda doesn't know what to make of it. I've tried telling her that daughters are always the ones causing us mothers trouble, always up to no good. Never had any issues like this with our Kenneth, did we, love?"

"Pass us the mint sauce," Gramps replied, mouth full of food.

"What about Mum?" I asked, my heart rate quickening as Nana's face momentarily dropped. "What trouble did Mum cause you?"

Nana blatantly ignored me, proffering me the dish of carrots and peas instead of an answer. "More vegetables, Melissa?"

Is this what it's going to be like? I wondered with a sneer. *Mum isn't even dead yet and already we're acting like she doesn't exist.*

"Shame Teddy couldn't join us tonight," Gramps chewed.

"Mmm..." I mumbled back, my eyes still fixed on Nana, waiting for her to redeem herself. "*Real* shame."

"Don't know what could be so important to miss out on a family dinner, but there we are." Nana's petite shrug caused my blood to start to boil. "Suppose we all put value on different things."

"You're telling me," I retorted, wondering how much value Nana was putting on Mum at that moment.

Wonder what would happen if...

"Dad's at the hospice tonight," I suddenly started to say, catching even myself off guard. "Visiting Mum."

If Nana had given me anything other than a pleasant smile, and a flutter of her eyelashes I might've felt inclined to leave it there. But Nana was persistent in trying to act like everything was perfectly normal and I was forced to add, "You know, your daughter? The one who's *dying*?"

Gramp's whole body went stiff, his teeth clamped down on a wedge of lamb. "Mel, love..." he shuffled in his chair, uncomfortable. "Easy now, lass."

"Are you planning on seeing her?" I asked, trying my absolute hardest to keep my tone flat and respectable — not that Nana deserved it.

Nana sucked in her lips as if she'd got a wedge of lemon under her tongue. "You grandfather has seen her—"

"I'm not talking about Gramps," I bit back, dropping my knife and fork against my plate, both of them clattering against the porcelain in protest. "I'm talking about *you*."

"I... I—" she stammered, affronted by my sudden reckless change in demeanour. I'd been sitting there so polite and so obliging, why wouldn't she be thrown that I'd snapped?

"What's holding you back, hmm?" I drolled, crossing my arms over my chest and jutting out my chin. "You seemed so invested when you first heard the news. You wanted to know every little detail, and now you're literally talking about anything and everything other than Mum. Is that because you wanted to be in the know in case anyone asked? Or so you could be the one to tell everyone else?" I snapped. "You sit there and ask me how I've been, when you know *full well* how I've been—"

"Enough, Mel," Gramps ground out, causing me to bite my own tongue with a wince. "I know you're going through a hard time at the minute, But there's no reason to take it out on your Nana, who's gone to all this effort to make you a lovely tea, alright?"

I looked at the array of food in front of me; there was enough to feed a village.

I swallowed whatever I had left to say and stabbed a potato, resigning.

We ate the rest of our dinner in silence — Gramps's chewing and awkward coughing not included.

After Gramps had popped upstairs, presumably for another ciggy break, I went to clear the table. As I was reaching for her plate, Nana took my hand and held it tightly, her eyes completely dry.

"I like my memories of your mother the way they are, Melissa," she muttered, her thin lips pursed. "When our Kenneth, and then your grandfather, explained to me what this dreadful illness had done to your mother's face... I couldn't — I have no intention of seeing her like that. I don't want to taint what image I have of her. It'll be all I'll be able to think about when she..." Nana pulled out a crumpled tissue from the inside of her sleeve. "Please don't think ill of me, dear. I can't see her, not in the state she's in. No mother should have to see their child in pain... It's too much for me to take."

I wanted to shake some sense into her, but knew sense and Nana never did go together. So instead I sighed, squeezed her hand, and looked her square in the face.

"I know this may be hard for you to get your head around, Nana, but this isn't about you. It's about Mum." I inhaled sharply, desperate not to cry. "Do you think I want to see her ill? Do you think my dad wants to see her suffering, or Gramps? No. But if I didn't see her, and Dad didn't, and Gramps, where would that leave her? Still ill. Still dying. In a hospice bed, *alone*. And no one should be alone."

— Thirty Two —

27th May

I don't know how but Will caught up to me just as I was about to board the Northern Line back home. Literally, I had one foot on the Tube, the other on the platform, and he hit me like a wrecking ball from behind. I went tumbling forward, Will's hand on my elbow, the only thing breaking my fall.

"Think you could slip away unnoticed?" he asked as I stood up and spun around to face him.

"Thought you didn't care what I did."

"Have you slept with him?"

The bluntness and out-of-blueness of the question hit me round the face like a rotten, wet fish.

"Who? *Jordan?* He's your brother."

"And he's known for getting a kick out of sleeping with girls I know, Mel. My mates, sisters of my mates, he's even shagged one of my ex-girlfriends." Will rolled his eyes. "Think he enjoys making life awkward for me."

I hadn't even realised my jaw had dropped. "That's really... sick."

Will nodded slowly, his eyes staring at my face. "So have you?"

My top lip curled. "No, I haven't."

Will literally let out a breath of relief. "Right... So, your body count is still at a magical two then?"

My face burned and my lips went thin. This wasn't exactly a conversation I wanted to have with him, especially on a busy Tube with, like, fifty people around us.

"No..." I trailed off, embarrassed to admit my 'body count', as he put it, was now considerably more than two. It was the only thing that, more often than not, got Will out of my head.

Will's eyebrows raised. "Did you just say no?"

I could do nothing but nod.

"How many are we talking?" he whispered.

My hands clenched into tight fists — I was seriously considering punching him. He had absolutely no right to stand so close to me, put his lips to my ear and ask me how many people I'd slept with. Especially after he'd done nothing but ignore me for nearly three months!

"None of your damn business," I growled.

"It could be my business," Will reached out his hand, his fingertips skating across my left wrist. "I want to see what a difference it's made."

My eyes widened, my heart rate quickened, and I felt a delicious hum between my thighs. *Was he seriously suggesting we...?*

'The next stop is Kentish Town' the conductor announced, causing Will to raise one of his eyebrows.

"What'd you say, Mel? Want to take me home?"

Yes. 100% Yes.

— *Melissa Bishop, aged 19, with no backbone or standards whatsoever when her infamous Will is involved.*

***

"I have lain here and listened to these women witter on about being too tired, or too hungry, or too bored," Mum started ranting as soon as I entered her hospice room the following morning.

"Hello to you too, Mum," I sarcastically replied, putting my bag down beside her bed and kissing her concertinaed forehead.

"And it's just like, for fuck's sake—"

I froze.

"Everybody is in the same boat." Mum continued, clearly unphased by the fact she'd properly sworn for the first time in probably her whole life. "I want to tell them all to get a grip — pull up their big girl pants, stop whinging, and get on with their jobs. Because they're just sitting there chelping about their problems." Mum huffed, and weakly scrunched up the quilt draped over her lap. "And all they're doing is feeding the problem and making it bigger than it is — giving it power that it shouldn't have."

"Made even weirder when they've got someone in the next room who's dying," I added, before sitting in the chair closest to her bed. "Talk about a narrow-minded perspective."

"Exactly," Mum nodded at me militantly before beginning another spiel. "Oh, and the amount of inductions they do." She put on a silly voice and pulled a sour-puss face, "*Right have you gone through this, have you gone through that?*

And I'm thinking, have you not got a bloody book? Because I could write it now, I've heard it that many times. Give me a pen. I know where all the fire exits are. I know where the damn photocopier is."

She sounds like me, I realised, as Mum fully submerged herself into her quirky storytelling act. The voices she was putting on, the impressions, she sounded like she was reading straight out of one of my diaries. *Maybe that's where I get it from?* I wondered, Mum starting a new rant about something else. *I get my storytelling from my mum...*

"I know about the room that doesn't exist. It's just a code for 'call the police'. *Room 13*. Ugh, it's ridiculous. If anyone says they're going to Room 13, you're in trouble, Mel. Her majesty's thin blue line is on the way."

"Why would they need to call the police to a place like this?" I asked, encouraging Mum to continue her performance. It made her look healthier than if she was simply lying in her bed, staring at the ceiling.

"I don't know. Again, it's just imagined drama, drama, drama. *What if?* Yeah, what if? *Oooh, have we checked the front door, Channel?* Really? You have a policy for that. I know you have a policy for that. Seriously, Mel, get me a pen."

I laughed into the cuff of my sleeve, relishing in her enthusiasm and exuberance. If it weren't for the fact she'd clearly lost more weight, I could have even been so confident as to say she didn't look sick at all.

"Where's your father?" she asked, finally noticing his absence.

"Out parking the car, I think." I threw a look out of her large window, spotting a birdfeeder directly in her line of sight from the bed. There were birds pecking away at some seed. *I think they're blue tits.* Mum would've known, but I assumed with her right eye completely out of use and her left aching so much from having to compensate, that she couldn't see the birds well enough to tell me their breed. "Dad'll be with us in a sec."

"Hmm..." Mum grumbled, clearly not entirely thrilled by the prospect of Dad joining us. "How's he been?"

In hell, like the rest of us, I thought, before clearing my throat and replying. "He's coping, if that's what you mean."

"He looks thin—"

"He's not the only one," I cut in without fully meaning to.

Mum's eyes lit up, then her hands jazzed across her collarbone. "Best diet I've ever been on," she joked, her good eye crinkling shut with delight and matching her swollen one. "Only one that's ever worked..." she trailed off.

"How are you feeling?" I asked hesitantly, my eyes returning to focus on the birdfeeder, hoping that by not making eye contact, maybe she wouldn't feel as pressured to pretend she was fine.

"Oh, I'm alright."

Maybe not.

"I've got my books—" she pointed to the small stack of books on her bedside table. "What more could I want?"

I read up and down the pile; *Bilbo's Last Song*, *Night Watch*, *The First Fifteen Lives of Harry August*... "What's this one?" I asked, pointing to the third book in the pile. It had a dark burgundy cover and *Theresa's Written Thoughts* written in gold marker pen on the spine.

"Oh that's—"

"Have you started writing a diary?" I half-laughed, half-retorted. "That's *my* thing! You can't steal my thing!"

"It's *not* a diary," Mum tutted back at me, reaching over as quickly as she could and smuggling the book under her pillow. "It's merely some thoughts I've had in recent weeks that I thought might be worth writing down."

"So a diary?" I repeated, glaring at her with keen interest.

"*Not* a diary!" she huffed, exasperated. "A diary is a book one writes in every day. I can't, even if I wanted to, write every day. Not only will my pen not form the words as fast as I think them, but my eye," she pointed at her closed right eye accusingly, "makes it awfully difficult to focus on the words I *do* manage to get down."

"At least you're managing to get something down," I smiled supportively. "I think it's great your keeping a d—"

"*Not* a diary, Melissa," she hissed back at me. At the exact same moment, Dad came bustling through the door.

"Morning, love, how are you getting on?" he asked, taking a seat at the end of the bed.

"Don't make me repeat myself, Teddy," Mum huffed, laying back into her bleached pillows. "I don't think Melissa wants to hear me complain about the nattering nurses all over again."

I shook my head, "I'd love to, actually. Tell him about Room 13."

Dad waited expectantly but Mum didn't oblige. She simply turned her face to the window and pretended to watch the birds I knew she couldn't see.

"Freckles went to see your folks last night, Terra," Dad eventually said, desperately trying to rekindle whatever energy had been lost by his entrance.

"At least somebody's visiting somebody," Mum chirped, her lips thinning. "Dare I ask, how are they?"

"Themselves," I answered lowly, feeling Mum's good eye fix on me. "Gramps was a good laugh but didn't say much. Nana was…"

Nana's voice echoed in my head. Her tearless cries and meaningless words rattling round between my ears. *I can't see her, not in the state she's in. It's too much for me to take.*

"She gave you some dresses, didn't she, Freckles?" Dad encouraged, causing Mum's head to whip round to look at him.

"Is she sick?" Mum joked flatly. "Not like her to be charitable."

"If you saw the dresses, Mum," I hummed, puffing out my chest, "you'd know she wasn't being charitable. It feels more like pity. I'm never going to wear them."

"I thought the lime green one was quite nice," Dad cut in, nodding towards my mass of hair. "Compliments the ginger gene."

"It would make me look like an abused lime, Dad," I bounced back, watching Mum out of the corner of my eye as she turned her head rapidly from side to side, trying to keep up.

"It was better than the yellow one, Freckles. That reminded me of your Mum's custard at Christmas—"

"Crème Anglaise," Mum corrected without flinching, before holding her head in her hands and groaning. "Look, either you two need to sit together or one of you needs to go because I feel like I'm watching the final of Wimbledon."

Dad and I shot each other a mutual worried look, simultaneously wondering if she was serious. It didn't feel right having to decide which one of us should leave.

I rose to my feet and announced, "I'm going to get some air."

Then left, knowing I was leaving nothing but awkward silence behind me.

— **Thirty Three** —

27th May

I'd clearly outdone myself, since Will fell asleep shortly after I showed him everything I'd learnt the last couple of months. I was still nervous as hell, but somehow, knowing that it wouldn't hurt, and having more of an idea of what he might like, meant it didn't show. I was actually quite proud of myself.

I've got the guy, I've wrecked him, and thoroughly enjoyed myself in the process, too.

Now I just have to keep him.

He finally awoke while I was making something to eat. Clearly, the smell of melted cheese and Worcester sauce was enough to bring him back from the dead.

"Do you want one?" I asked him while he sat up, still stark naked, in my bed.

"Nah, I'm alright."

"Are you sure? I don't mind." I looked across at him and saw he was starting to pull on his boxers.

"We need to establish some ground rules, if this is going to work, Mel," he stated bluntly, catching me off guard.

I bit into my cheese melt, trying to play it cool. "If *what's* going to work?"

"This. Us."

Us? I almost choked. *We're an 'us' now? God, how good was I?!*

"I think we're good for each other—"

Agreed.

"But neither of us are exactly looking for a relationship right now."

Don't quite agree.

Will stalked towards me, his eyes hungry and voice low. "So, would being friends with benefits work for you? Or would you rather just not?"

"I dunno..." I shrugged, trying not to let on that I had no idea what friends with benefits even meant.

"We hook up whenever we want, but that's it," Will explained, evidently reading my mind, one of his hands slithering around my waist. "No cuddling, no deep conversations, no dates, no feeding each other..." Will raised a mischievous eyebrow, "Unless it's part of the fun."

"So, no cheese melts, then?" I joked.

Will then planted a kiss on my neck that almost made me buckle. "Are you interested?" he murmured against my skin. "Or do I need to convince you some more?"

— *Melissa Bishop, aged 19, trying to comprehend how she, of all people, is Will Green's go-to girl.*

***

The garden walk of the hospice was exactly how I expected it to be. Flower-clad, a vision of colour, with more than enough life in it to get its visitors to nearly forget about those dancing with death in the building it surrounded.

Birds chirped, the dusty white clouds drifted overhead, and if it weren't for the faint hum of traffic from the nearby main road, I would have thought myself to be in some sort of paradise. I supposed that was the point.

There was a cast iron, white painted bench within a small grove that stood out amongst the plethora of green. I sat and took in the scenery around me, before becoming quickly bored with it and scrolling on my phone.

I didn't go on my socials, but brought up Will's supportive messages from the past forty-eight hours. They were regular, but not pushy, consistent but not worrying in the slightest because, if I was honest with myself, I needed them.

No one else was reaching out to me. Not one family member, or friend… or Freddie. Not that the latter was in the smallest bit surprising.

What if Freddie never reaches out? I thought, unsure whether my body was tingling with hope or anxiety. *What if you never speak to him again? What if you never go back to the flat? What if it never officially ends, but 'ends' like this?*

My phone went off in my hands. Another message,

Thinking of you. Hope you're doing okay today. Xx

Define 'okay', I thought with a sigh. My thumb hit the dial button before I'd even had a chance to second guess my decision.

"Hello, beautiful," Will answered, understandably thrown by my sudden outreach. "This is a nice surprise."

"Thought I'd end your suffering," I tried to muse, a lump growing in my throat. "And let you know I'm not dead."

"I *was* starting to worry, not going to lie," he chuckled, his voice soft and soothing. "How... is your Mum?"

"Also not dead," I replied flatly. "But she's working on it."

Will, thankfully, laughed at my poor attempt at a joke. It was nice to know my sense of humour was still active, despite how very unfunny and cold I felt on the inside.

"She's no longer at the hospital. They've moved her to a hospice..." I leaned back into the ice-cold bench and clamped my back teeth together. "Currently visiting her now."

"Is she okay with you chatting to me? We can talk later—"

"She's with Dad. I'm outside, so I'm free to talk now, if you are."

"Course," Will reassured, no doubt trailing off so that I would feel free to start talking about whatever I wanted to talk about, rather than him taking the lead and unwittingly bringing up a topic I wasn't ready to discuss.

"How are you?"

"I'm fine. Busy with work, but nothing so important that I need to hang up on you."

"Not going to get you into trouble then?"

"Even if it did, I'm still not hanging up," he replied before taking a slow and considered breath. "I've missed you."

My whole body started to tingle as an echo of Freddie's voice rattled through my head. He'd said he missed me too... *Maybe I should have rung Freddie?*

I swiftly shut my internal ranting out by imagining shoving my voice of doubt into a chest, and a mini me locking it away. The lid slammed shut while the annoying voice still fretted and ferreted on. Then... silence.

"I've missed you too, Will," I said, my voice barely a whisper, in case I changed my mind on speaking my truth as the sentence was coming out of my mouth.

I swore I heard him breath an exasperated sigh of relief, and then, "Can I come and see you?"

"At the hospice?" I snorted, "Think that *would* kill my mum off."

"Tonight?"

"I'm back at work."

"What about after work?"

I couldn't put my finger on why, but hearing Will sound on the verge of desperate filled me with more joy, and more enthralling excitement, than two whole years of my relationship with Freddie. It was as though having a man indicating that he needed me - and not just to pay his bloody rent - was feeding me everything I'd been craving for years. Not even taking into consideration it was my *infamous* Will.

"I lock up, so we'd be meeting after midnight."

"So?" he cooed, his deep voice soft like velvet. "Do you want me to come and pick you up? Where do you work?"

"No, I'll—" I bit my tongue, the rest of my sentence caught in my throat. *No, I'll drive to yours.* He hadn't mentioned going to his, or anything like that, but I knew, because I knew Will, that's what he'd meant.

"You can drive here if you want," Will said, hearing the words I knew I hadn't uttered. "That'll give me longer to make the place respectable for you."

"Going to whip your Hoover out again?"

"If you're lucky," Will joked, causing me to laugh despite myself. "It's nice to hear you laughing..." He trailed off, then said, "It's good to hear your voice."

"It's been two days—"

"Still good," Will joked, but was soon serious again, "It's always good hearing your voice, Mel."

There was a heated pause, my mouth drying, and my mind reeling with all the possible memories I had of him. The good, the bad...

"Even better when I get to see you half-naked in a bit of sexy red lingerie," Will suddenly said, ripping me back into the here and now, my voice lost somewhere in my chest. "But there's no chance of that happening again, is there?"

I didn't reply. I couldn't. I tried to speak but there were no words forming, no coherent thought in my head. And a fat lot of good my internal voice was, I'd locked it away!

"Does you not agreeing with me mean that there *is* a chance?" Will practically purred. "If you have the list of things I'd need to do, I'd love to hear it."

1. *Break up with your girlfriend.*
2. *Get rid of Freddie.*
3. *Cure my mum of terminal cancer.*

"I don't—"

"I'm messing, Mel," Will mused calmly, meanwhile I was a panicking, quivering wreck. "Unless you're into it, and then I'm very much *not* messing."

I laughed, as it was the only thing I seemed able to do. "You're such a headache, did you know that?"

"Just trying to help you take your mind off stuff, that's all," Will stated. "So, I'll see you tonight then, yeah? You can chill, have a couple of drinks and relax. No sexy red lingerie. Unless you happen to bring it with you, then that's just fate, and out of my hands."

"Can't wear it even if I wanted to, it's still in London," I joked with a suppressed grin.

"Damn."

A devious thought popped in my head.

"You'll have to make do with me wearing nothing instead."

Will swallowed loudly, and I felt a smugness fill my chest and pull at the corners of my lips. It was nice to know I could get him just as good as he got me.

"I mean... that works too."

"Good to know."

I could feel Will's smile down the phone and I miraculously, for about ten seconds, felt the best I'd felt in months, if not years.

Then those ten seconds ended.

What are you doing?

"So... I'll see you tonight, then?" Will whispered, sultrily.

"Can't wait."

– Thirty Four –

2nd July

Whoever first came up with the idea of 'Friends With Benefits' deserves a knighthood or something. It's bliss — absolute bliss! I get Will whenever I want, wherever I want... *However I want.*

My sixteen-year-old self would die if she could see me now!

I feel like this is what I've been missing; Will at my beck and call. He's so responsive to my texts it's almost flattering. I wish he'd text me more, but I'm guessing that his... *appetite?*... isn't as strong as mine.

Or— *Oh God, why does my brain do this to me?* It just threw up the thought that he could be satisfying his hunger in more than one place. What if I'm not the only girl he's seeing? I know that's part of the agreement, you're allowed to see other people at the same time, but isn't it the polite thing to do to just have one?

Actually, thinking about it further, when has Will ever been a one-person-at-a-time kind of guy? *Bollocks.*

— *Melissa Bishop, aged 19, worn out both physically and mentally.*

***

Mum had been happy to see us go when Dad and I eventually left the hospice. As suspected, she'd barely uttered more than five words to Dad after I'd exited the room.

"I must not be as fun to talk to," Dad tried to joke on the drive home, though I could hear the underlying hurt in his voice. "I'll have to be more spontaneous with my subject matter when we see her again tomorrow."

"I think she struggles with us both being there," I cut in, remembering Mum's sharpness of tone when she'd accused us of essentially giving her whiplash. "How about we take turns? You do a day, I do a day. Might stop her from getting overwhelmed, or—"

"Repeating herself?" Dad interjected, glumly.

"That too..."

I pondered on how much Dad must be struggling for most of my shift at *Rogan's*. The rest of the time, my mind wandered across to greyer pastures — mainly the image of Will, half-naked doing... unspeakable things.

Katie eradicated my final inappropriate trail of thought of the day by trampling loudly on a cardboard box in the back room. When I poked my head around the doorway to see what she was doing, I realised she was actually beating the living daylights out of it.

"Are you pretending that's someone's head?" I asked, watching her stamp on it again and again, "Or are you just very against salt and vinegar crisps?"

Katie threw her head back, her blonde hair falling all over her face, manically. "Can I be frank?"

"You can be whoever you want to be, Katie. Frank, Dean, Sammy Davis Jr. for all I care—"

Katie's eyebrows furrowed as she parted her hair like a pair of sandy yellow curtains. "Are you high?"

"No," I stated bluntly, before adding. "Been a long day, I'm trying to be funny."

"I don't need you to be funny, Mel," Katie huffed, digging her heel into the cardboard box and mushing it into the floor I'd mopped not ten minutes prior. "I need you to be honest with me."

"Okay…"

"Promise?"

"Err, yes… I promise."

Kate sighed, suddenly exhausted. "Do you think I'm crazy?"

Should have crossed my fingers.

"No?" I said with little conviction. Katie then gave me a look that could have broken the heart of even the coldest of people. "I mean, not in a bad way," I quickly added, trying not to dig myself too big a hole while I backtracked. "Crazy in a unique, playful, fun sort of way."

That seemed to work-*ish*.

Katie huffed again, before leaning onto the counter with her head in her hands.

"Why do you ask?" I took a hesitant step towards her before placing a supportive hand on her shoulder. "Has a customer said something?"

"Not a customer," Katie sighed, heavily. "My boyfriend. He thinks I'm crazy... And *not* in a unique, playful, fun sort of way," Katie groaned. "And the worst thing is, I don't even know *why* he said it. Like, I was rambling on about my brother, who has got a monk on, about us, again. But I wasn't doing anything, or saying anything that could have made my fella think that I *was* crazy. He just said it, out of the blue in his stupid voice, *Katie... I think you're crazy*."

"He might not have meant it negatively either, Katie," I tried to reassure her, my hand patting her shoulder as my eyes couldn't help but drift to the clock. *Ten past eleven...* "You might be blowing this completely out of proportion and letting something that wasn't meant as an insult get to you."

"You think?"

"You told me to be honest," I said, placing my hand on my chest. "You are lovely, Katie, but you are, in the best possible way—"

"As crazy as a box of frogs."

I couldn't help but smile. "Exactly."

Katie stood up straighter and sighed heavily. "Having a boyfriend is hard."

"Tell me about it," I rolled my eyes instinctively.

Katie started to chew her bottom lip. "You think you've got a good one and then they go and call you 'crazy' and then you end up questioning everything."

"If the worst thing your fella has ever called you is 'crazy', I think you might still have a good one. No need to throw a whole relationship away over it," I quipped, thinking about all the things Freddie had called me (usually when stoned) that were much *much* worse than 'crazy' — and I was still dating him.

Freddie. A wedge of bile started to form in my throat.

I hurriedly went back to work. Mop. Wipe. Cash-up. Anything to get Freddie out of my head and Will back into it.

Katie didn't move while I manoeuvred around her. She was clearly somewhere else, thinking about her fella and looking exactly the same way I do when I think about Fre— *No!*

I poured my bucket of grubby water out of the back door and grabbed my coat. "Katie?" I nudged, pulling it on and jingling my keys at her. "As much as I would love for you to stand there and deliberate the meaning of monogamy, I need to lock up now."

She blinked at me. "I'll do it," she sighed before walking towards me and giving me a big hug. We'd never hugged before. It didn't half take me by surprise. *Who hugs their co-workers?*

"Are you going to be okay?" I asked, patting the top of her silly blonde head that smelled a lot like a jar of coconut oil.

"Yeah..." she mumbled into my shoulder. "I'll be fine." She pulled away and slapped her cheeks three times over as if trying to wake herself up. "You get home and I'll finish up here."

"Okay, if you're sure."

"Yeah, night, Mel and... thanks."

I practically ran home. The plan was to get in, 'de-work', shower, and set straight off for Will's so he wasn't waiting for me any longer than he needed to. But then, as I burst through the front door and charged up the stairs, I caught a glimpse of Dad on his bedroom floor, surrounded by piles of clothes and black bin bags.

"Dad?" I breathed, his body slumped over, facing away from me. "What are you doing?"

"Oh, hiya, Freckles," Dad croaked, turning slightly, but not enough for me to see his face. "Your mum wanted some more of her clothes at the hospice."

I looked at the array of t-shirts, jeans, jumpers and pyjamas. "I don't think she meant *all* of her clothes, Dad. You've cleared out the whole wardrobe."

"I was only going to get out a couple of things for her. But then I realised," he held up a large pale blue shirt, "none of these will fit her anymore. She's lost so much weight."

He was right. The shirt he was holding up might have hugged her rotund figure only a few months ago, but with the skeleton she had become, it would drown her.

"So what are you going to do with it all?" I asked quietly, as though fearful the clothes might have their feelings hurt if Dad were to suddenly announce he was going to chuck them.

"I don't know," he replied softly, lowering the shirt and folding it neatly.

Glancing back up at the built-in wardrobe, I noticed that every shelf was bare. "Where's all your stuff, Dad?"

Dad let out a soft mutation of a chuckle and a snort, before raising his right hand and pointing to the highest top right-hand corner where one low shelf was full of his earthy jumpers, cardigans, and jeans.

"Is that it?"

Dad sighed, finally turning fully to face me and revealing his puffy red eyes, magnified by his oval lenses.

"Your mum's always loved her space, Freckles. There never really was much room left for me."

— Thirty Five —

17th July

Will has ticked me right off! He literally came tumbling through my flat when I texted him, stripped down in the blink of an eye and got to it.

We had sex, he got dressed. As usual, I tried to slow him down, telling him I had something I wanted to ask him. His eyes widened.

"What?"

"My birthday is tomorrow. I was wondering if you wanted to join me and my acting class mates for a couple of drinks."

"Right..." he smiled. "I think I'll pass."

"You won't even think—" he kissed me silent, scrambling whatever thoughts I might have about him joining us.

"You'll be having too much fun to notice I'm not even there," he kissed me again and I hated that I just melted into him.

"Till next time," he said, just before the door shut behind him. *Ugh.*

— *Melissa Bishop, aged 19, feeling like a dirty rag... Only used when there's no better alternative.*

***

The drive to Will's house seemed never-ending. The road stretched out in front of me, the cat eyes repeating their formation over and over and over again.

Finally, I reached his driveway, and all of the contradicting, complicated and confusing feelings that had been raging inside of my already crammed head momentarily disappeared. A soft voice in the back of my mind muttered.

What are you doing?

I reversed and pulled back onto the main road. Thankfully, with it being so late, I didn't accidentally wreck Dad's car in the process by idiotically hitting someone leisurely driving past.

You shouldn't be here, the voice told me sharply.

I groaned and pulled up onto the pavement, hiding the car and myself from the view of the house. I needed a minute, a second, *an hour* to think.

I knew why I was there. And it wasn't for the chips and dip, or the chance to sup wine and reminisce about the good old days. It was purely about Will.

My Will.

Who was back in my life after two long, miserable years. It couldn't have been a coincidence that he'd come back at the exact moment when I needed someone the most. Someone to distract me. Someone to support me. Someone to listen when I spoke, and hold me when I cried.

Resting my head back into my driver's seat I looked up at the beige roof of the Mini and swore, before grumbling, "Give me a sign. What do I do?"

Nothing happened. Nothing at all.

What were you expecting?

"I don't know..." I sighed, before tightly shutting my eyes, slamming my hands onto the steering wheel, and letting out a manic, frustration-filled scream. My feet stomped in the footwell, my hair whipped my face, and after ten seconds of incessant screaming I thought my voice might break.

I rested my forehead onto the steering wheel with a final, pathetic grunt of misery.

All went very still, and very silent.

Knock. Knock. Knock.

Divine intervention had decided to take the piss.

I turned slowly and saw Will through the window, standing beside the car — a thoroughly amused yet baffled smirk pulling at the corners of his mouth.

"Having fun?" he asked with a knowing smile after opening the door for me.

Feeling miniscule under his penetrative gaze, I shrunk back into my seat rather than getting out. With as steady a tone as I could manage, I asked him sternly, "How much of that did you see?"

He suppressed a laugh. "I was walking up to your car just as you started screaming," he answered, his voice not steady at all but filled with great joy and merriment. "I saw you pull onto the drive and then disappear. Wanted to check you were okay."

"Oh... I'm—" I couldn't bring myself to lie to him.

"Do you want me to go so you can continue or...?" He proffered his hand for me to take, "Would you like to come in? I've got something for you."

Sod it.

The fire was roaring, the sofa cushions plumped, and the entire room shimmered as if it had been cleaned within an inch of its life.

Will passed me a glass of much needed wine. Not wanting to cave to my inner urges and chug the whole lot, I placed the glass on the coffee table and sat timidly on the armrest of the sofa closest to me.

"So, is this the thing?" I asked, pointing at the glass of wine between us. "Or is this ominous thing you have for me hiding somewhere?"

Will licked his lips, his eyes glistening with bubbling excitement. "I mentioned to you the other day that I'd had an idea, yeah?"

"Did you?"

"When we were at yours," Will took a few steps back and walked over to a side cabinet where his laptop was stored. "Not surprised if you don't remember as it was the day everything kicked off. But anyway, rather than wait to hear your thoughts on it, I just went ahead and did it."

I blinked at him, my heart rate quickening as he turned his laptop screen towards me. Looking back at me was my own face — more specifically, my headshot from acting class, and my showreel. A silly culmination of all of the independent projects I'd done with my fellow aspiring students.

"Why are you showing me this?"

"I sent it to my brother—"

My heart pole vaulted up and into my mouth and I clasped my eyes shut. I didn't want to look at myself any longer, knowing that Jordan had stared at the exact same photo. He, too, would have probably noticed all of the imperfections and cringed at them. No doubt he would have immediately picked up on the fact that the left-hand side of my face was slightly lower than my right, and that my freckles were uneven and far too concentrated over the bridge of my nose — God help me if he'd noticed the dark brown hair I'd forgotten to pluck, sprouting out of my chin.

"Why would you *do* that?" I hissed, hearing him place down his laptop with a clunk.

Suddenly, Will's arm slinked around my waist, causing my eyes to burst wide open. His face was inches away from mine and with every millisecond that passed he was moving ever closer.

"Jordan gave me a tip-off that his agent, Bethany, was opening her books. She's looking for new, up-and-coming actors to sign," Will whispered, affectionately tucking some loose strands of my hair behind my ear. "I asked Jordan to put in a good word for you."

The heat coming off of Will's body was not helping the already swelteringly high temperature of the room. I was unsure what would have cooled me down more, pouring an ice bucket over the fireplace or myself.

"Jordan messaged me this afternoon." Will bit his bottom lip, letting the anticipation-filled seconds stretch out.

I wriggled against him, still held tightly by his arm, desperate for him to spit out whatever news was dancing on the tip of his tongue.

"*And*?"

"She loved your showreel, and she wants to set up a meeting with you."

Will squeezed me even tighter, pressing his entire muscular body against me.

"That's..." I blinked, not knowing what to say.

Taking charge, Will lifted me up off of the ground. "It's bloody brilliant is what it is!" he cheered, before lowering me back down. Suddenly, his face fell. "What's wrong?"

"Nothing. I—"

"You're annoyed," Will summarised before I'd been able to even work out how I was feeling myself.

Stepping back from him and breaking his hold on me, I began to shake my head. "I'm not annoyed, Will," I said, my tone very much that of someone who had a bee in their bonnet. "I'm overwhelmed more than anything. And confused as hell, to be honest."

"What are you confused about?"

I found myself glaring at him, "You're being *so* different."

"Different from what?" Will asked, earnestly.

"From who you were..." I replied softly, my mind casting back over the memories I'd long tried to forget. The nights I'd spent crying over him, the mornings when I'd woken up and he'd vanished. The truths he'd kept from me.

"People can change, Mel," Will sighed deeply. "We're talking about the span of two years here. Remember how much you changed after, what, *four* months?"

"And whose fault was that?"

Will didn't know whether to laugh or get mad. His face became a strange mix of both reaches of emotion. "Are you saying you regret our first time together?"

A ghost of one of Will's many kisses brushed against my lips and I found myself muttering out a sorry, "No."

I swallowed. "Do you?"

His entire body relaxed as he let out a little laugh, then he took a step towards me and it felt as though all the air in the room had suddenly been sucked up the chimney.

"No," he reached out for me, his fingertips grazing the curve of my hip, "I don't regret any of the times we were together... Except maybe the last."

His fingers tugged on my jumper, reeling me into him. My body pressed up against his, what little space had remained between us was completely eradicated.

"W-Why do you regret the last time?" I asked, my voice betraying me, revealing my nerves by making me speak with stutters and stammers.

"*Because* it was the last time," Will groaned, leaning forward and nuzzling his face into the sensitive curve of my neck. "If I had known it was going to be the last time, Mel," he whispered, his breath hot and soothing against my skin. "I would have tried to make it last forever."

He planted a delicate, soft kiss at the crux of my jaw, just below my right earlobe, and it caused a tsunami of shivers to skate across my skin.

Will had got me. Hook, line, and sinker — and he knew it.

A warm humm started to grow between my thighs, my heartbeat pulsating in the very pits of my stomach. As he worked his lips down the line of my jaw and towards my parted lips, my mind spat out a million wild and wicked thoughts.

It was wrong for so many reasons, but I couldn't deny it felt so deliciously right at the same time.

I moaned softly as he shifted his weight towards me so I could feel the hardness of him through his jeans.

Will focused his attention on running his fingers through my hair, whispering, "The more time I spend with you, Mel, the more I find myself thinking about you. You've always come into my life and taken my breath away. I never appreciated it until now, how funny, and exciting, and *sexy* you are."

"Will," I groaned, my cheeks burning as I rested my forehead against his chest. "Don't talk shi—"

He took my chin between his thumb and index finger, tilting my face up to look up at him. I found myself taking in the sight of him all over again. He was Will, *my Will*, with his kind, laughline-decorated eyes, and annoyingly perfect face.

"I mean it," Will said sternly, holding me so I couldn't look away. I had to take in his honesty, and his need. "You're brilliant. And all I want to do, all I've wanted to do since I saw you on that train last month, is kiss you."

"Won't that complicate things?" I asked, breathless, realising our lips were already within millimetres of touching.

"Only if we let it," he murmured, before placing a fierce and passionate kiss upon me and finally crossing the line we'd been poorly upholding for so long.

— Thirty Six —

23rd November

I couldn't take it any longer! All I'd asked him was if he wanted to stay for some tea. I wasn't going to cook for him, maybe order us a takeaway or something.

"Don't do that," Will reprimanded me, pulling on his boxers.

"Don't do what?" I bit back at him. "I'm asking if you want some food."

"You're asking me to stay," Will softly laughed, though I don't think he or I was finding the conversation in the least bit funny.

"So?" I bit the inside of my cheek, desperately feeling like I should just tell him that's what I wanted, purely for my own sanity.

"We already agreed that wasn't part of the deal." He pulled on his jeans, finally turning to face me. "We use each other for sex, that's it. That's the benefit, nothing more, nothing less."

"Don't you want to stay, though?" I tried to keep my voice as steady as possible, hearing it shake was mortifying. "I'm not asking for much. I just think this all feels a little too..." I couldn't find the word. Then, "Animalistic?"

Will's eyebrows raised, a smirk pulling at the corners of his mouth. "And you're complaining about that because...?"

"It's not like we've never talked to each other before, Will. Or hung out. Jesus, when we first met we were close because that's *all* we did."

"Only because we couldn't do *this*," he retorted, causing me to physically recoil.

"So, what you're saying is the only reason you were my friend back when we were sixteen was because we couldn't shag? That's nice," I drolled, sarcastically. "*Real* nice."

"God, this is why we're not supposed to talk, Mel," Will huffed, trying desperately to find his socks. I pointed to the one hanging off top of the curtain pole. "I came here to chill, not be nagged — that's what girlfriends are for."

"Do you have a girlfriend?"

I don't know why I asked. I was preemptively mortified to hear the answer, because in my gut I wasn't one hundred percent certain that the answer would be no.

"Do you think I'd be here if I did?" he replied with a sharp coldness to his tone.

"That didn't answer my question," I bit back.

Will left without another word and one of his shoes not yet on.

— *Melissa Bishop, aged 20, feeling like she can't handle the heat, so it might be time to get out of the kitchen.*

***

Will's kiss stirred my soul and rekindled the dwindling light of lust that I'd suppressed inside of me for the longest time. It felt so good to be kissed so fervently, held so tightly, and wanted so desperately.

Will groaned irresistibly against my mouth, his hands roaming all over my body. We sunk into one naturally, as if our muscles were working via memory. We'd perfected how to dance with one another in a past life — it was so easy.

I pulled on Will's shirt, causing us both to stumble forward and bump against the sofa's armrest with a thud and a burst of laughter.

"Come here," he whispered, after our laughter had eventually subsided. He pulled me to the sofa and onto his lap. He pushed my frizzy hair out of my face, then planted kisses across my collar bone. His fingertips played with the hem of my shirt, teasing at the idea of removing it.

"You're amazing, Mel," Will sighed, looking up into my eyes with the same hunger as before, only this time with a flicker of sadness. "Never let *anyone* make you feel anything less." He planted one soft kiss on my lips, then, "I'm sorry if I made you feel less..."

My heart felt as though it was going to seize from the speed it was beating at. I took his face in both of my hands and watched as he melted into my touch with delight.

"The last time we met, you said—"

Will cut me off with a kiss, holding me to him as though he never planned on letting go. Then, as he went to remove my shirt, I found myself thinking the most ridiculous thought. It rendered me into an unfit state of uncontrollable giggles.

It had come about because, as before, when being kissed by Will, my sixteen-year-old self seemed to be hooping and hollering in the back of my head, her jaw practically on the floor of my brain, unable to believe, but thrilled all the same that we were going to be having sex with Will.

Although, this time, she wasn't cheering and squawking with adolescent joy as per, she was daring me to do something ridiculous and absurd.

Will pecked a flurry of kisses over the bridge of my nose, worsening my giddy, tickled state. "Are you going to laugh the whole time?" he whispered, wrapping both his arms around my waist. "I'm all for it, but you may need to let me in on the joke."

"Can you do something for me?" I asked, catching my breath and starting to unbutton his shirt with my trembling hands.

"If you're going to ask me to *be gentle* again..."

My laughter cut out, and my cheeks burned red with embarrassment. "No..." I trailed off, cringing at the memory and pulling Will's shirt off of his shoulders, to reveal his smooth, olive skin. "Can you play for me?"

"Play?" Will repeated, his dark eyebrows furrowing. "What do you mean, play? Play with *you*? I thought I already was."

I rolled my head to the side, and glanced across at Will's shiny, perfect, black piano in the centre of the room. "I've never heard you play it."

"I haven't played in years," Will said, leaning against the plush cushions with a huff.

"I don't believe you," I teased, discarding his shirt over the back of the sofa. "No one who doesn't play has a piano in their living room."

Will smirked and I knew I'd won him over. He lifted me off his lap with breathtaking ease and plonked me back down again.

"I assume," Will began unbuckling his belt, "you want me to play naked. To get the full effect?"

"You read my mind," I giggled, grabbing a sofa cushion and covering the bottom half of my bright red face as Will stripped for me.

He stood there, in all of his magnificence, wearing nothing but a merry grin. "Any requests?" he asked, before moving over to the piano and stretching his fingers.

"Whatever is your fav—"

Before I'd even been able to finish my sentence, Will was playing a series of notes, recognisable almost instantly as *Claire de Lune* — I'd heard it enough times through the door of Mum's study.

Suddenly, I wasn't laughing anymore but holding my breath. Our joke had turned serious in the space of four notes.

As the melody quickened in pace, so did my heart rate.

I was transported to watching a sad movie with Mum on a grey day, the noise of the popcorn machine whirling in the kitchen, butter sizzlingly in the microwave, rain cascading down the window.

While Will played, I slowly rose to my feet and undressed. There was comfort in knowing he wasn't watching me, and an excitement in anticipating the moment he'd turn to realise I'd joined him in his nakedness.

I crossed the room to his side, then traced my finger across his bare back, causing him to shiver, but not miss one note.

"I think you proved me right," I whispered into his ear, watching his fingers dance across the keys.

"Oh yeah?"

"Yeah." I revealed myself beside him, and was unsurprised but thrilled all the same that Will's playing ceased. His eyes widened as I placed myself between him and the keys. "Playing the piano while naked is *very* sexy," I lowered myself onto him, both of us letting out a satisfied moan of release as I guided Will into me.

"Now all we need is for you to get your accordion," Will joked, gingerly brushing my lips with his thumb.

"Shall I go and get it?" I giggled, causing him to scrunch up his face in pleasure and let out another satisfied groan.

"Don't you dare leave now," he growled playfully, moving me to his liking with emphatic skill.

Both of us moved as one, building our pleasure together with dizzying enthusiasm. When Will and I were like this, I didn't blame my younger self in the slightest for believing with all her heart that we belonged together. Or that deep down she knew one day we would be together — as though all of our ecstasy went rippling back through time, washing over us with a sense that something great would one day pass between us.

This was that greatness. That pinnacle of joy that we would share as a pair — never to be matched, never to be repeated.

The front door bell rang and we both froze, our breaths caught in our throats, our heights of pleasure plummeting swiftly to the ground.

"Is that going to be *her*?" I breathed, my stomach starting to churn.

Will shook his head slowly before looking up at me with deep sorrow in his eyes. After half a second, the sorrow turned to heart-wrenching panic.

"Do you want me to hide in the bathroom?" I said flatly, lifting myself off of him and hurriedly grabbing my clothes off the floor. "Or shall I save us the hassle and climb out of the window?"

"Mel—"

I pulled my pants on, and my shirt over my head. "Point me to the exit, Will. Don't make this harder than it needs to be."

The doorbell rang again which seemed to be the wake-up call Will needed to realise the crap-storm currently tornadoing around him. He grabbed his jeans and pointed at a set of double doors doors with a pitiful bow of his head. "They lead into the garden..." Will groaned. "If you wait, though, I can get rid of her. I'll end it with her—"

I cut him off, already heading for the double doors, one shoe on, one shoe off. "We both know that's not true."

"Mel—"

"At least this time I knew you had a girlfriend though, ey?" I said sarcastically, before stepping out into the garden. "Goodbye, Will," I snapped before slamming the door behind me.

As I hobbled around the house, I tried to not let any tears form in my eyes. I heard the doorbell ring again, followed by a soft shout from Will.

"I'm coming! Two secs!"

Pressing my back against the wall, I clasped my eyes tightly shut. She would be on the front door step, which I would need to pass to get down the drive and towards my car on the road.

The door opened with a thunk. "Babe, what are you doing here? It's nearly two in the morning."

"I know, I know, but you know what they say, couples shouldn't go to sleep aggravated with each other."

My blood ran cold. *I know that voice.*

"Can I come in?"

I heard Will sigh, then, "Sure, Katie."

I have to quit my job.

— Thirty Seven —

30th November

He has a girlfriend. He hadn't – he didn't – have one while we were messing around. At least that's what I have to keep telling myself. Either way, I *know* he has one now. It's only been a week since we had our fight.

Feels like some cruel trick of fate that I decided to check my socials before texting him this evening; firstly to apologise, and then to see if he wanted to come over.

When I opened up the app the first thing that popped up on my feed was a photo of Will with his arm around a pretty brunette.

I just can't believe it. He has a bloody girlfriend.

— *Melissa Bishop, aged 20. Heartbroken.*

***

The following day, Dad and I had decided to take shifts visiting Mum, hoping that, by going separately, she might not feel as strongly as she had about repeating herself. It also meant that Dad could try and discuss whatever he needed to with Mum, which evidently was next to nothing, as when I asked Mum what she and Dad had talked about in my absence that morning, she replied with, "The usual."

Mum and I had spent that particular afternoon discussing books (no surprise there), the possible existence of angels (some surprise there), and the possibility that if Jesus hadn't specified *'Lazarus*, come out' in John 11:43, then all of the dead folk might have come out and thus started a zombie apocalypse (lots of surprise there).

Kara popped her head into the room as Mum was reciting a random poem off by heart.

"Sorry to interrupt you, Theresa, but visiting hours will be ending soon." Kara gave me an awkward, apologetic smile. "Hope that's okay?"

"Going to have to be," I joked, getting my things together and checking the exact time on my phone. Kara had disappeared when I'd raised my head again. I turned to Mum, "Right, you have exactly eleven minutes to share your wisdom with me."

"Oh, very good," Mum paused, the lines between her nose reflecting how deep in thought she needed to be to form her life-altering wisdom upon the world. She exhaled, "I had a nice quiche for lunch."

I threw my head back involuntarily and laughed heartily. "Excellent wisdom, Mum," I lovingly teased, tears of deep joy actually forming in the corners of my eyes.

"I love you," Mum suddenly said, one eye staring at me from across the room, the other tightly swollen shut.

"I love you, too," I replied, my bottom lip and heart trembling. "A lot," I added, though it hardly seemed necessary. The love I had for Mum flowed in abundance, and it had only grown the more time I spent in her bizarre company.

"I think you're mad though," I concluded, right at the point where I couldn't take the seriousness of the conversation any longer.

"Good," Mum sighed deeply. "I'm quite happy with my madness." She threw a limp thumb towards the door where Kara had popped her head through. "They come in and ask me, what are my aspirations, what am I wanting out of this, blah blah blah. Pain relief?" She gestured to her body. "No, no pain. No regrets. The fact that I managed to raise a daughter who has a level of awareness way beyond what I had at her age is a result." Her good eye crinkled, and her smile was bright. "I am happy with this. And I don't feel like I owe anybody anything else. I've done what I was put here to do. And if you are what I was put here to do, then I am content. That's my level of wisdom at the moment. You know?"

Is she saying...?

"Are you saying that you're *dying*, Mum?" I finally asked hesitantly, fearful that I might scare off her new, and long overdue, acceptance.

She gave a miniscule shrug. "Not as such. More that, if I were to die anytime soon, I'd be content with how I've conducted myself throughout my life."

That's as good as you're going to get, I thought to myself, with a knowing smile gracing my face. "Do you want to decide on any arrangements?" I quickly added, "In case you *do* go anytime soon?"

"No harm in it, is there? Do you have a pen?"

"I can use my phone—" I said, already holding it in my hands. "Where would you like to start?"

"Preferably with my service," Mum cleared her throat.

"Would you like a burial or a cremation?"

Mum hummed, deep in thought. Then, "I do believe there's a tribe somewhere that leaves the deceased body out in the mountains for nature to pick away at it. You know, till there's nothing left but bone. Then, the leftover skeleton hardens in the sun and they grind down the bone into dust before putting it into a tube that's illustrated with a tapestry of the deceased person's life story. The tube is then placed into the ground with all of the other tribe members who have passed, and essentially, one becomes part of a horizon of history."

I blinked at her. "Does that tribe happen to *be* in West Yorkshire?"

"I don't think so."

"Then, do you have a plan B?"

"Cremation, probably."

I couldn't help but softly giggle as I typed out 'cremation' into my phone. "Flowers?"

"Lilies. Always been severely allergic but I don't think my allergies will be a bother on the day."

"Music?"

"Classical," Mum sighed deeply, "Anything with a good woodwind solo. Or a french horn... I love a good french horn."

"Noted. Err, guest list? Do you want to invite specific people, or have an open invite put out?"

"Don't let anybody come to my funeral that I wouldn't want there. I'd rather the crematorium be empty than filled with people I don't like, and I *know* don't like me."

"It won't be empty," I reassured. "I'm definitely going, and Dad's RSVP'd as a 'maybe'—"

Mum laughed, though it swiftly mutated into uncontrollable coughs. She held a tissue close to her mouth, letting it be speckled with blood. "Your jokes are going to kill me one day," she croaked. Her eyes crinkled at the corners as she smiled, but they all swiftly vanished when she noticed I was silently crying.

"What's wrong?"

I choked on my own breath before stammering out, "I don't — I just don't think I'm ready. The world isn't going to be a world I recognise when you..."

Mum's eyebrows furrowed. "This is one of your things, isn't it? That, because I'm in it, the world is a certain way. And it's going to go *pfft* because I'm not."

I felt myself start to sob. A timid "yeah" fluttered out of my mouth.

Mum let out a half-bemused laugh. "I'm not that special, actually, to tilt the world on its axis."

"Mum," I assured her sternly, "you really are. You are to *me*."

She laughed weakly, flattered at the sentiment but still not acknowledging that I meant every word.

"You'll be fine, Mel. I know you will."

I couldn't help but scooch to the edge of my chair and take the hand that was resting on her chest. Her skin was as soft as ever, though there was an added delicacy to her that I couldn't fathom. She felt so fragile, as though, if I squeezed her hand too tightly, I might break her.

"And what if I'm not?"

"You're a *good* person, Melissa. You have a *good* life, and a bright future ahead of you… Whether I'm in it or not, is not up to us." Mum closed her eye and rested her head deeper into her plethora of pillows.

"I'm not a good person," I confessed with a soft whisper, not sure whether I wanted Mum to hear me or not.

"I don't think anyone is. Not really," she finally replied, her face turning ever so slightly towards me. She looked so ethereal as a soft beam of sunlight came in and shone upon her pale skin.

"What makes someone a good person?" she asked me, sounding as philosophical as ever. "Is it from doing good? Or being good? Or good thoughts and good morals?"

"All of it?" I countered, my voice soft and quiet, like a sinner seeking repentance.

"If you had 'all of it' you would be perfect, not human. We are learned beings Melissa, who hopefully grow from our mistakes. If anything, our bad makes our good better because we appreciate it more knowing the alternative."

"What do you mean?"

"Well," Mum inhaled deeply, "someone who lives their whole life in a bright white room of goodness, never knowing the dark, will not appreciate light in the same way as someone who has lived in the dark for their entire existence. The person in the dark will appreciate dim light, a twinkle, or shade even, because they know what it is to be in the centre of an abyss."

"So, what you're saying is our bad choices make us better?"

Mum pulled a face; clearly, I had butchered her analogy. "No, dear, what I'm trying to say is that if we do good our whole life, we won't feel the full benefits of what it *is* to *do* good. When we've done bad, hopefully we learn from it, see the repercussions and consequences of it, and actually strive to do better because of it." Mum paused, assessing me as best she could with her good eye. "I think you're good, dear," she smiled weakly. "Because you do good everyday, consciously or not. Don't get me wrong, you make poor choices–"

I felt my eyes instinctively roll, *You have no idea.*

"—but it's the little things, the droplets, that amount to a tsunami of goodness." She hummed to herself, in pensive amusement. "One thing I've always noticed is when you make someone a cup of tea, you fill up their mug with boiling water before your own. That way, if you run out, no one is waiting for the next boil but you. It's a minor thing, but very, *very* considerate."

I found myself shaking my head, slightly baffled. "I don't think me making brews for everyone else first makes up for..."

My mind, without want or warning, spat out the tortuous memory from the previous night. I'd done well over the past couple of hours to control my thoughts of Will, but in that moment, when discussing my moral worth, the image of Will could not be suppressed any longer.

We'd crossed that line, thrown aside Freddie, not cared about Katie — not that I had even known it was her I would have been hurting. But did that matter? It was someone. Katie or not, I'd willingly put my own desires above someone else's relationship. Had sex with someone else's boyfriend. Had sex with Will.

He wasn't my Will, I'd merely justified my sordid actions in the heat of the moment by convincing myself he was.

Considering Will hadn't tried to reach out to me since, he'd proven my point. He was Katie's Will, not mine.

Never mine.

I convulsed.

Mum looked at me quizzically, her face forming a lop-sided frown. "Melissa, if you were *truly* a bad person you wouldn't even be reflecting on it. Cruel people are the last ones to know that they're cruel, malicious people don't question their own malice."

I raised her hand and kissed it lovingly. "Thanks, Mum. I'll try to remember that."

She closed her eyes, and inhaled contently, as if my thanks were the permission she'd been seeking to finally go to sleep.

"Do," she breathed. "I'd hate to leave this world with you thinking anything less than the truth about yourself."

If only you knew the truth.

Later, in Dad's car, when I'd signed out in the visitor's book and prepared myself for the drive home, I found myself crying. I didn't even know why I'd waited so long to finally let all the torturous emotions out.

I cried for my mum.

I cried for my dad.

For Katie, for Will... even Freddie.

But more than anything, I cried for myself.

— Thirty Eight —

5th December

Right! It's decided! Time to stop feeling sorry for myself and keep my pathetic excuse for a brain occupied with something other than Will crap-bag Green. I'm throwing myself into work, friendships — anything!

I need to get a grip on whatever the hell this is before I turn into one of those psycho ex-girlfriends.

But that's the thing, isn't it? I wasn't even his girlfriend!
I wasn't good enough to be his girlfriend! He said he wasn't looking for a relationship! Said he wasn't READY for a relationship! So how come he's all loved up with Miss Tits-Too-Big-To-See-Her-Toes? Posting every other five seconds all over his socials about how lucky he is?!

Make. It. Make. Sense.

— *Melissa Bishop, aged 20, thinking she may have already turned into the dreaded psycho; ex-girlfriend or not.*

***

I ignored Will's calls that evening, tempted to block his number, but I couldn't quite bring myself to go through with it.

My mind tormented me with all the possible things he could be calling to say, but I knew the truth, deep in the pits of my soul. He was ringing to say we made a mistake — which I was in full agreement with, no matter how much my stupid heart was trying to convince me otherwise.

I took distracting myself to the extreme and decided to join Dad in his mission of clearing the house.

We were determined to get rid of anything of Mum's that was going to be of no use to her for however long she had left, which turned out to be near enough everything she owned.

With every bag that was filled, box that was packed, the house gradually became bearer and bearer.

"Haven't you got work tonight?" Dad asked, tying a black bin bag with its luminous orange strings.

"I'm not going," I admitted glumly, stacking more of Mum's books that I knew she'd never read again in a pile in the corner. "I quit this morning."

"You *quit*?"

"Sort of," I replied, recalling how I'd literally rung Rogan on the way home from Will's and left him what will probably go down in history as the most horrifying voicemail ever. Rogan would have most likely thought I'd rung him out of my nut, or high as a kite, blubbering over and over again that I won't be coming in to work anymore.

How could I?

How could I walk into *Rogan's* ever again and look Katie in her sweet, innocent eyes and know I'd had sex with her boyfriend? I couldn't.

I let Rogan assume it was because whatever reason I'd actually moved home had come to fruition. He accepted my resignation with a simple text of 'kay', no questions asked.

"Did something happen?"

My lips pressed tightly shut to stop them from trembling. It was taking everything I had to keep it together, but then Dad's hand rested on my shoulder and I fell apart completely. He enveloped me into a hug that smelled of tea, and slightly musty wool.

"We're going to get through this, Freckles," he said, his voice muffled by my hair as he kissed the top of my head affectionately. "Your mum is in the best place, with the best people around her–"

"It's not Mum," I blubbed, feeling overwhelmingly guilty even admitting that. "It's..."

"Your *friend*?" Dad summarised quickly.

I pulled away and gave him a look, my eyes already sore and straining to see him through my tears.

"How'd you–"

"I saw you leave," Dad shrugged, "and heard you come back a couple of hours later."

"You were asleep."

"I *don't* sleep these days, Freckles," he admitted with a soft sigh, immediately drawing my attention to the soft lilac circles under his eyes, that most of the time were hidden by his lenses. "I assumed you would talk about it in the morning, but then you didn't, and I didn't know how to be the one to approach you about it. You always talk to your mother about this sort of thing."

I haven't even been able to tell her.

"Do you want to talk about it?" Dad asked, unsure but determined. It was admirable.

I shook my head. I *couldn't* talk about it. It would make him disappointed in me, and the thought of disappointing Dad hurt my heart more than hearing Katie's sweet voice outside of Will's house.

"I can have a good guess and you can simply nod or shake your head, if that makes it easier?" Dad tried to joke with a gentle squeeze of my arm. "Believe it or not, I wasn't always a silly old man. I was in my twenties once."

"Okay...?"

"And I know first-hand that going round to a friend's house at one in the morning makes them significantly more than *just* a friend."

Ew. Not an image I need in my head.

"Did it not go the way you expected, or...?" Dad pinched the bridge of his nose. "Did they hurt you?"

"No, Dad, no," I reassured, not even realising that was where his poor mind had been taking him all day. "No one hurt me, Dad," I breathed, deciding to put him out of his misery. "You got it right the first time. It didn't go how I thought it would. He has... a girlfriend. She showed up and I ran."

"Right." Dad nodded slowly before asking, "Did you know he had a girlfriend before you went over?"

My silence screamed 'yes', and amplified my shame. "He knew about Freddie, too."

Dad's eyes widened in slow-motion. "I thought you and Freddie weren't–"

"We're *technically* still together. Like, I'm still paying my half of the rent, and the bills–" I started to vent, a verbal diarrhoea spewing out of my mouth. "But with my job at *Rogan's* gone, I'm either going to have to find something new to keep up the payments, or take you up on that offer of helping me out. Because to be honest, Dad, I don't know what I'm going to do. I've managed to save enough to hopefully see me till the otherside of Christmas–"

"What if you're still living *here* at Christmas?" Dad cut me off, the colour of his eyes darkening. "Freckles, at what point do you stop paying for a flat you're not living in?"

"I don't know."

Dad crossed his arms over his chest and furrowed his brow, looking more like a put-out, frizzy-haired toddler than a disapproving parent. "What has Freddie said about all this?"

I didn't answer.

"Have you and him *still* not spoken?" Dad's mouth dropped open slightly before he threw both of his cardigan-clad arms into the air. "Freckles, you cannot be serious! You cannot be paying rent on a flat you're not living in, and paying for your supposed boyfriend to live there when neither of you have spoken in nearly a month. That's utterly ridiculous."

"You think I don't know that?"

"It doesn't sound like it. Freckles, what are you *doing*?"

Your guess is as good as mine, old man.

"When are you next planning to go down to see him?" Dad asked bluntly, going over to Mum's calendar on the coffee table. "Every third weekend would make your next visit... *this* Saturday."

"Saturday?" I echoed, "That can't be right. It can't have been three weeks since I saw him already."

Dad then looked at me, saddened by the sorry situation I'd gone and gotten myself into, and sighed deeply.

"I think Freddie's a prat," he said matter of factly, catching me off guard. "But if Freddie's no longer *your* prat then the lad needs to know. Not only so he can move on, but you can too. Not to mention you can stop this ridiculous rigmarole of paying for the rent. It needs to end, love, and you need to end it face to face."

"I can't leave–"

"You also can't avoid this any longer, Freckles," Dad said, picking up the tied bin bag and throwing it over his left shoulder. "You've got enough going on with your mum. Make your life a little easier for yourself and cut the rest of the crap out."

God, I think he might be right.

Dad looked around the room, as if suddenly realising how empty it had become from our decluttering.

"Your mum is going to hit the roof when she sees what we've done," Dad noted, before a dark thought crossed his face.

"She'll only see it if she actually manages to come home," I replied. "Which, if she has her way, we all know would be tomorrow."

"Your mum has said she wants to come home?" Dad's bushy eyebrows raised over the rim of his glasses, crinkling his forehead. "When did she say that?"

"This afternoon," I replied hesitantly, trying to not recall how frail and gaunt she'd looked. "She was rattling on about preferring to spend her days in her own bed rather than a hospice that constantly smells of bleach."

Dad remained pensive. "What else did she say?"

My chest tightened. *She's not told him she has accepted she's dying*. Not that she'd really told me in so many words.

"That..." I sighed heavily, flicking aimlessly through the pages of the book I was holding. "That she feels as though she's waiting for Monday."

"Why what's happening on Monday?"

"Nothing, it's a — it's an analogy she's come up with to explain what dying feels like." I dreaded looking at Dad in case I found him crying. Surprisingly, his composure had remained unchanged. He merely looked at me, intrigued. "You work Monday to Friday, right? As do most people, so most of the time you crave the weekend as it's your only real time off, and you dread Monday because it means that you're going to have to go back to work, start all over again. Mum said that waiting for death is like waiting for Monday. It's inevitable, and the weekend is going too fast for her. The seconds are speeding by and she feels as if Monday is going to be... *it*."

"She said all that?"

"Pretty much."

Dad scratched his head, messing his already wild, greying hair. "There's only one problem with that analogy," he began. "If Monday is death, then she isn't the one waiting for Monday... We are."

"*Us?*"

"Well, she won't actually be aware of it when it happens, will she?" Dad continued, "Our death isn't something we experience, Freckles. It's experienced by every one who loves us that we leave behind."

— Thirty Nine —

9th December

The epiphany finally hit me this morning while I was in the shower.

It's not that he didn't want a relationship... It's that he didn't want a relationship *with me*.

— *Melissa Bishop, aged 20, no longer heartbroken... Just broken.*

***

"I'll be back to see you on Monday," I told Mum, bending over her hospice bed that Saturday morning and planting a soft kiss on her forehead.

"Why?" she croaked, her eyes remaining closed.

She's deteriorated even more, I thought with a pang of pain going off in my chest like a gong. "I'm going to London for the weekend," I told her again, "Got some things I need to sort out with Freddie."

Despite Mum being barely able to lift her head or mutter more than three words at a time, she still managed to purse her lips. "Hmm," she burbled disapprovingly. "I'll be home... by Monday."

"I hope you mean literally and not spiritually, Mum."

Her pout became a weak, peaceful smile. "Funny girl."

I kissed her forehead again and squeezed her delicate, frail hand. *I'm not ready.*

Dad was waiting for me in the corridor, holding my rucksack out for me. "Are you sure you don't want a lift to the station?"

"No, I've already got a taxi coming, but thank you." I pulled my bag onto my shoulder. "I'll be back late tomorrow night, the cheapest train I could get was half eight, so that should give me enough time to talk to Freddie, but I'll let you know. Either way, I'll be home tomorrow. Okay?"

Dad nodded before pushing his oval glasses up his nose and walking us towards the hospice's exit. "Okay."

"Also, will you let me know how you get on with Mum's transfer talks this afternoon? If they actually decide to get her home today, I want to know."

"Will do." Dad watched me sign out of the visitor's book with a hurried scribble. "Do you know what you're going to say to Freddie?"

"No," I confessed with a half-manic laugh. "But as you said, I've got to tell him, haven't I?" A nauseous wave washed over me, "Got to end it."

Dad gave my arm a supportive squeeze. "Are you going to be alright?"

"Doubt it," I resigned, before hearing a blaring honk from outside. "That'll be my taxi." I kissed his beard-covered cheek. *He seriously needs to shave,* I thought, before starting to make my way down the front stairs. "Rest, eat something, and try to stay sane, yeah?"

"Bit late for that, Freckles."

The journey was sickening. My already toxic thoughts were worsened by the rattle of the carriage, and the stifling humidity of the Underground.

The book I had with me wasn't making any sense. Words were merging into one another and I found myself reading the same sentence over and over again, unable to remember what had happened on the previous page.

The scenery whizzed past me, the track seemingly endless.

I tried to plan what I was going to say to Freddie, how I was going to tell him and end it with him, but nothing came to mind — except for the memory of him standing on the balcony, screaming that he would jump if I took another step towards the door.

As Peterborough station disappeared out of sight, my phone started to ring. I answered without checking the ID, assuming it would be Dad ringing to check how my journey was going and no doubt fill some of the silence that was now encasing him.

"Hello, beautiful."

God's sake.

"Hiya, Will."

"You okay, stranger? Been trying to get a hold of you for a week."

"I've been a bit busy."

"With work?"

"No, with my mum."

The line went quiet.

"Oh..." Will took a hesitant breath, "How is she doing?"

I leaned against the large pane of glass beside me and scoffed. "She's dying, Will, how do you think she's doing?"

"Sorry, I didn't—"

The line went quiet again.

I don't know how long we went without speaking, but the train was pulling into Kings Cross before Will finally broke.

"I want to talk to you about what happened the other night."

"I can't right now, Will."

"Mel, *please*," Will groaned, pained and frustrated. "I can come to you, or you can come here. I just want to talk to you."

"I'm in London," I said bluntly. "So I couldn't come over even if I wanted to."

"*London*?" Will repeated, his voice ghostly. "Are you going to see Freddie?"

"Yeah." I held my breath, then, "When are you next seeing your girlfriend?"

Will paused. "Tomorrow, after she finishes work."

"*Rogan's?*"

"Err, yeah? How do you—"

"So, are you two still together then?" I cut him off sharply, people around me beginning to collect their things.

Will cleared his throat. I knew what that meant, he didn't need to expand, "We're trying to make it work."

Said the sailor, with the bucket, in the sinking ship, I thought.

Silence. Again.

I found myself clenching my back teeth together. "Look, I'm literally about to get on the Northern Line, so I best hang up now before I lose signal," I lied. The train hadn't even fully pulled into Kings Cross yet. "I'll talk to you when I'm ready."

"Okay."

I hung up and threw my phone into my bag, not needing to hear another word.

A faraway dog barked as I approached the looming block of flats. As I looked up at the grotty grey and blue building, my heart sank.

God, I hate it here.

As if the universe agreed with me, a tumbleweed of trash was sent rolling down the pavement beside me.

The lift, as usual, stank of stale piss and lingering smoke. Knowing I didn't have my keys, I instead went straight for the handle. With a kick and a frustrated grunt, the door opened.

The lights were off and all the curtains drawn.

Anyone else would've believed the flat to be empty, but I could hear the faint murmur of a phone playing music, and smell the tang of cheap weed lingering in the air.

Well, he's definitely home.

"Mel?"

Freddie reared his head over the top of the sofa. A lit spliff lolling out of the side of his mouth.

"Jesus, I didn't know you were coming home this weekend."

"Clearly," I bit, flicking on the big light and revealing the bombsite of a living room in all its grim glory. "We decided every third weekend, didn't we?"

Freddie propped his spliff on the side of his makeshift ashtray and got to his feet. He looked around at the abandoned pasta bowls, the cigarette ash, and the array of grubby clothes discarded over every possible surface. "I haven't even cleaned. Give me like five minutes." He started scrambling for the trash, as if that would somehow stop me from seeing it all.

"Don't bother. I'm just going to make myself some tea and head to bed, if that's okay."

"Yeah, sure. Though, like, we've got no food in, so..." Freddie looked sheepish, his eyes bloodshot, as he pointed to the ashtray in his hands. "I was just about to take this outside."

Course you were.

Freddie was right, there was absolutely no food in. Not even a forgotten tin of Minestrone soup at the back of the cupboard.

I was resolved to go to bed without eating, and ended up staring at the ceiling, unable to sleep, forced to listen to the hum of the never-ending London traffic and my stomach grumbles harmonising. From the open window, I heard the wails of a cat fight, and someone yelling drunkenly into the night, like a wolf howling at the moon.

Rolling over onto my side, I glanced at my phone.

1am. Usually the point at which Freddie comes to bed, strips down to his boxers, crawls under the covers, rolls onto his side and goes swiftly to sleep. *If he even manages to make it off the sofa.*

As if it were rehearsed, he did exactly that.

I looked across at the shadowed outline of his body once he'd clambered under the quilt beside me.

How are you going to tell him? I asked myself, staring into the back of his head.

The voice wouldn't shut up, it nagged and screamed, tittered and tormented me. The next day was going to be hell, but I had to tell him, I had no choice.

How are you going to tell him without killing him in the process? I screamed at myself internally, resulting in me scrubbing my face harshly with the palms of my hands trying to rid the image of Freddie running out onto the balcony.

"What are you doing?" Freddie grumbled into the dark, disturbed by my vigorous movement as it shook the headboard.

"I can't do this."

"Do what?" he sounded distant, as if he wasn't really paying attention, just asking out of habit rather than genuine concern.

I sat up and turned on the bedside light, blinding us both.

Freddie recoiled, covering his eyes with the back of his arm. "Jesus, Mel, I was sleeping."

"You've only just come to bed."

"Yeah," he groaned, rolling on to his side, away from me and the light. "To *sleep*."

I'd decided that staying in bed wasn't going to be safe for either of us. He stank, and snored, and I would throttle him if he uttered another word, so, I grabbed Mum's jumper off of the floor and pulled it over my head. I was momentarily relieved to smell something other than weed. The soft fabric smelled of home, *real home*, not this pathetic excuse for a home that I hated from the mould in the bathroom, to the grease in the kitchen; from the furniture that reeked of smoke, to the pathetic inhabitant who was the cause of it all.

At least he hasn't slept with someone else.

"What?"

Looking up, I only then realised I'd spoken aloud. Freddie was sitting bolt upright behind me in the bed, looking like he'd momentarily seen a ghost.

"I slept with someone else..." I repeated, this time a little louder, so that I could be confident that I had actually spoken and not merely thought it.

"Are you fucking serious?"

Air escaped my lungs as a fire began to swell in the pit of my stomach. "Yes, I slept with someone else."

"God, you don't have to keep saying it!" Freddie panicked, holding his hands over his ears as if that would somehow keep my words out.

"But I did."

"Yeah, I gathered that," he spat, before rubbing his bloodshot eyes with the backs of his hands. "Look, I'm a bit too stoned to do this right now. How about we talk in the morning?"

I shook my head, fueled by the fact he was talking to me as if I was a nagging child, and more than anything, that he was quite happy to let what I'd said slide.

"Why don't you want to talk about it now?"

Freddie groaned, "Because I care more about getting some sleep than I do about you shagging around."

"I *haven't* shagged around, Fred!" All the saliva glued to my teeth as I sneered at him. "I slept with one person, one time, and—"

"I don't need to know the details. *Jesus*, Mel. I don't care," Freddie bit back, pulling on his hair fiercely. "You can do what you like."

What?

"You don't... *care*?"

Freddie threw his hands in the air manically. "Honestly, Mel? No. We already established that I'm not going to sleep with you any time soon. So, if you want to go find someone else to meet that need then that's *fine* by me!"

"Are you being sarcastic?"

Freddie rolled his eyes. "What answer will make you shut up?"

He's serious. I realised. *He genuinely doesn't care.*

"We can talk about it in the morning," Freddie concluded, collapsing back into bed with a final grunt.

"I won't be here in the morning," I stated softly before the room around me started to blur.

My body was moving faster than I could comprehend. Cramming my phone and charger into the rucksack with one hand, I swiped up my diary off the nightstand with the other. Freddie started to growl under his breath.

"Are you taking the piss?" he asked sternly, still lying in bed.

I grabbed my suitcase from on top of the wardrobe and started to throw all of my things in it manically; my books, my laptop, my favourite coat, my most expensive pair of heels. I knew I'd never be able to pack everything I owned so I cast aside anything that I would be happy to never see again — Freddie included.

"This is insane," Freddie said, his voice and temper starting to rise. "You literally just got home!"

I ignored him and started to fully get dressed.

Is this really happening? I thought with a hopeful, terrified yelp, as I pulled a pair of grey sweatpants over the top of my pyjama bottoms. *Am I really doing this?*

As I zipped up my suitcase, I felt Freddie's hands wrap themselves tightly around my wrists. "You've had your fun, now stop it, Mel. You don't get to drop a bomb on me like this, tell me you've shagged someone else and then just leav—"

"Why not? You said it yourself that you don't care."

"I don't!" he shouted. "You've not spoken to me all month, why *should* I care what you do?"

"A phone rings both ways, Fred. You haven't spoken to me either," I bit back, trying to free my arms from his grasp.

"I've been busy. God, you don't know the hell I've been living this past month. I had to fork out thirty quid last week to get my glasses fixed because some git on the bus decided to knock them off my head with his bag. Not to mention the warehouse sacked me for not putting up with their stupid rota."

"You lost your job?"

Freddie looked as though he was on the cusp of swallowing his own tongue. "Well, yeah."

"When were you going to tell me?"

Freddie's eyes steeled. "About the same time you were going to tell me you'd had sex with someone else."

"Don't you dare throw that in my fa—"

Freddie started to smirk, which set my blood boiling. "You haven't got a leg to stand on, Mel. You're the one who cheated, not me. I haven't done anything wrong."

"Exactly," I hissed at him, "So, I should do us both the favour and be the one to leave." I ripped myself away from him and could see that my wrists had already started to redden.

"For God's sake, you're not leaving, Mel!" Freddie roared, done with it all. "We're not doing this now. We're not doing this *ever*. Without you I have nothing, okay? So, get back in bed, go the fuck to sleep, and we'll talk in the morning."

I froze, Freddie's words ringing in my ears. "What did you just say?"

Freddie rolled his bloodshot eyes. "I said, get back in bed—"

"No, before that," I breathed, my heart rate quicking. "You said, you *have* nothing without me... But that's not the saying, is it? It's 'I *am* nothing'. Not *have*."

"Jesus, Mel, does it matter?" he snapped. "Have, am, it's the same thing!"

"But it's not, is it?" I gasped, my brain slowly starting to put every toxic jigsaw piece of our decaying relationship together. "You're right, without me... You *have* nothing. You don't care about me cheating or leaving because you don't care about *me*. You care about this lifestyle. If we break up, you lose it."

Freddie looked at me with a condescending sneer. "What *lifestyle*? Have you seen this flat?"

"I don't mean the flat, Freddie. I mean the freeloading, weed-smoking, don't-have-to-keep-a-job crap you've been pulling for two years." I pulled my suitcase off the bed. "You've had it *so* easy and it's only now that I realise... You've *known* it the whole fucking time."

Before he could stop me, I was bolting out of the door with my rucksack on my shoulder and my suitcase trailing behind me.

"Mel!" Freddie called after me, the desperation in his voice deceptively real. "You can't do this to me *again*!" he screamed, but it was too late.

If he gets on the balcony, I'll tell him to jump, I thought with deep contempt.

"What am I supposed to do?" he yelled as I got to the front door. "What about the flat? I haven't got the money for any of this month's rent."

"You'll work it out," I spat back, wrestling with my keys in the lock.

"I'll have to move back in with my parents, do you know that?" He swore, pulling on a pair of trousers that had been thrown over the back of the sofa.

"That's good," I cheered back at him unironically. "That's a start. They'll help you find your feet. Get a job. Get off the weed."

"This isn't a joke, Mel!" he screamed at the top of his voice, the veins in his neck puckering as they strained.

I blinked at him, realising I hated him.

I never thought I'd be able to hold hatred in my heart for anyone, but Freddie had, without me even realising, become the exception to the rule.

He'd made a home for himself in the centre of my being, and picked away at it, like a child with a scab. I felt as though I was now bleeding freely, hating the life I'd made with him, and hating myself for putting up with it for so long. *Not anymore.*

"Who said I was joking?"

Freddie breathed deeply, his voice low and threatening. "Mel, this isn't fair."

"Nothing in life is fair, Fred," I replied, thinking of my mum's frail body in her pristine white hospice bed.

I threw my front door keys at his chest, and he caught them with a seething grunt. "You can't do—"

I didn't let him finish; merely stepped out into the hallway and slammed the door behind myself. As I walked towards the piss-stained lift, I checked my bank account. I had money saved to pay for rent for the next couple of months, but knowing that I wouldn't have to worry about that anymore, I decided to blow a month's worth on a 2am taxi home.

— **Forty** —

8th May

The club Tilly from acting class had dragged me to was heaving. The whole bar packed, everyone sardine-tinned up to one another — not that anybody seemed to care. They were all too drunk, too out of it, or too busy having fun to notice that the person next to them was close enough to have their sweat mix with their own. *Gross*.

Tilly had forced me to join her as some band was supposed to be playing and she fancied the pants off the drummer. I was sure we were in the wrong place as there was no stage, and after an hour of being pushed about, still no band.

I tried to convince Tilly to leave but she wasn't having any of it. Blokes were buying her drinks and she was enjoying herself. So, I decided a French exit was the best thing for it. I headed for the back door, only to be blindsided by a ring of drunk-in-the-face frat bros, all clearly on a stag do.

"We're waiting for a round of tequila shots, love," one of them shouted into my ear that was already ringing.

"I don't work here!" I shouted back, determined to get to the fire exit before any of them asked to see my non-existent manager.

"Oi-oi!" a loud, bellowing voice called from behind me, causing me to spin around and look at the shirt he was wearing. An embarrassing photo of the groom-to-be, poorly printed in black and white, the words underneath reading 'R.I.P Greeny'. I felt myself falter, looking at the photo again.

It was Will.

He's getting married...? I internally screamed.

"Here he is!" They all cheered as the lonely straggler came wobbling back into the group from the direction of the bar, precariously holding a round of tequila shots.

"Will...?"

He couldn't have heard me — there was no possible way he could have heard me, not with all the cheers, heavy music, and carnage surrounding us. But he looked up at me all the same.

"Mel."

I bolted out of the fire exit and out into the back alleyway. There was no way this was happening. Not to me. Not after I'd spent months refusing to think about him. I wasn't about to witness his stag do. Not a chance.

— *Melissa Bishop, aged 20, wishing she'd never met Will pissing Green.*

***

I'd never been more grateful to see Mum and Dad's house than when the taxi finally chugged up the hill at half six in the morning. Due to it being early November, the sun was still tucked tightly away behind the horizon, and the sky a deep, dark shade of blue. Moths hovered around the lone streetlamp and I could have sworn I could see Christine peeping out from behind her first-floor bedroom curtain — the taxi's headlight had probably alerted her to fresh movement, and therefore, fresh gossip.

"It's the one on the right," I said to the taxi driver, who looked almost as relieved as I felt as he parked up outside.

"Got to go all the way back now," he joked, hopping out to assist me with my bags. He'd been gentle company for the four-and-a-half-hour drive, never really saying much but always happy to converse for a few minutes if I felt like saying something other than, "Sorry about this". I never got his name.

"Have a safe drive back," I said as he passed me my suitcase from out of the boot.

"And you have a lovely rest of your day," he replied, before giving me a lop-sided, sweet smile and getting back into his car.

I looked up at the house as he drove away and smiled to myself. Not caring that Christine was watching me with great interest.

It's good to be home.

"Morning, Dad!" I cheered, coming into the kitchen a few hours later with a spring in my step.

Dad was settling down at the kitchen table with his cereal, my entrance causing him to jump and nearly drop the entire contents of his bowl over the floor. "Son of a—"

"Miss me?"

"You wazzock!" he hissed, but I could see his smile hiding behind his bushy beard. "What do you think you're doing other than trying to kill me?"

I kissed his cheek and pulled up a chair beside him. "Couldn't resist."

"Thought you weren't coming back till late tonight. What the hell are you doing home?"

"Got everything sorted a *lot* quicker than I thought," I replied with a tired huff, folding my arms across my chest. "There was no point in me sticking around."

Dad raised a suspicious eyebrow. "Did you tell your glorified house-sitter the truth?"

I nodded with a puff of my chest. "And that it was over, and that I wouldn't be living in or paying for the flat anymore."

Dad looked borderline impressed. "How did Freddie take it?"

I didn't answer, merely reached across to the fruit bowl on top of the microwave to swipe a banana.

"What time are you going to see Mum today?" I asked, peeling it and avoiding making eye contact.

"I'm not," Dad replied bluntly with a shrug. "She's coming home."

I nearly choked on my banana. "What?"

Dad nodded slowly. "She got her wish. The hospice and I organised a care plan yesterday after you left. We've sorted district nurses, Mum's meds, a bed. It's all been scheduled and sorted."

"I *told* you to tell me—"

"You had enough on your plate," Dad snorted, before taking up his spoon and finally going about eating his breakfast. "Plus it's still not definite. They may change their minds and keep her at the last minute."

"Like Mum will let them."

Dad and I shared a knowing look. Despite Mum's frailty, loss of eyesight and inability to talk in full sentences, she was still as stubborn as ever.

"It'll be good to have her home," I sighed, missing her deeply.

Dad reached across the table and squeezed my hand. "It's good to have *you* home."

Mum was home by two that afternoon. She arrived on a plush stretcher, brought into the house by two very attractive paramedics; so handsome even Dad commented on it. "It should be illegal to look that good."

Once settled and the house quiet again, I decided to head up to Mum's bedroom with a steaming hot chocolate in my hands.

She appeared to be in her usual state when I entered; eyes closed, head relaxed back into a mountain of soft pillows, her quilt up to her protruding collar bone.

She's lost even more weight, I thought, looking across her once round and full face and seeing the outline of her skull. She winced as I placed the hot chocolate on the nightstand, as though the small tap had gone off like a foghorn.

"What's wrong?" I asked, kneeling beside the bed and taking her left hand.

"Nothing," she groaned back, the word sounding too big for her mouth, almost as if her tongue had swollen again.

"Your body just being silly?" I joked, trying to sound sweet and calm, even though I felt nothing of the sort.

"Yeah."

I needed her to say more than one word, needed reassurance that she hadn't lost the ability to say three words in a row in the space of twenty-four hours. "Hearing's alright though, still?"

"Yeah."

"It's just your body?"

"Yeah."

"Has it got worse? Or is it just today?" I pushed, thinking that maybe something other than a 'yes or no' question would make her expand a little further.

"Just today."

Two words? We're getting somewhere.

Mum's face scrunched with pain, her throat clearly sore. Every word she uttered no doubt took a lot of effort, but I needed to check she was still with me.

"Would you like some water?" I asked, already picking up the glass on her nightstand and jingling the metal straw.

"No..." she croaked.

"What about something else? I have a hot chocolate here, but we might need to let it cool down a bit." I placed the glass back down. "Do you want me to read you something? Or tuck you in?"

Mum shushed me before rolling onto her other side and revealing a flurry of bed sores across her face. I tried my hardest to keep my stomach firmly in place. "Mum?"

There was no response, but I could see the gentle rise and fall of her chest so decided it best to leave it there. As I left the room, three words fluttered around my head.

I'm not ready.

— Forty One —

8th May

He showed up at the flat. I genuinely believed that he would do us both a favour and leave me alone. And then that would be the end of it — *all of it*. I would be able to finally get over Will because I could move on with my life knowing he was getting married and there would be no chance of him ever, *ever* wanting me again.

But there he was, his tiny little image in the keyhole of my front door when I heard a fist beating against the wood in the wee small hours of the morning. He was wearing the exact same clothes he'd been wearing at the club, including the eye sore of a stag do shirt.

"What are you doing here?" I asked him, slowly prizing my flat door open to the width of a penny. "It's like, four in the morning."

"You never came back," he stated, his body swaying slightly from side to side.

You still haven't texted me back, I thought viciously, wanting nothing more than to slam the door in his face.

"I waited for you," he scrunched up his face, drunkenly. "I stayed at the bar and waited for you, but you never came back," he laughed nervously, "I've missed you, Mel. I've not seen you for months."

"And whose fault is that?" I opened the door a little wider and found myself snorting derivatively. "You're a joke, you know that, Will?" I snapped, "*You* ghosted me and now you're standing there in a stag shirt, saying that you *miss* me?!"

Will looked down at his own black-and-white face, stumbling backwards, drunkenly confused. "What's wrong with my shirt?"

"You're sick in the head, Will. I actually think there may be something wrong with you. Anybody who thinks it's okay to be engaged to someone and then stand at somebody else's door and tell them that you miss them is sick. It's *so* sick—"

I looked at Will and began to boil as soon as I noticed he was laughing at me. The corners of his eyes were crinkled in merry delight. I could have slapped him.

He pointed at the black-and-white fuzzy face on his shirt and grinned widely. "That's my brother."

"What?" I blinked, my mind and heart rate starting to race. "You're *not* getting married?" My bottom lip was trembling so much I was struggling to form my words.

"*Me?*" Will laughed again, "Jesus, Mel, I thought you of all people would know me well enough to know I'm not the marrying type."

"I don't know you," I replied, my grip on the door tightening. "I thought I did, but then you... You disappeared." Both of my hands flew to my face and I stumbled back into the flat. *I'm not going to let him see me cry*, I scolded myself, turning away from him. *I'm not going to let him know how much I like him or how much he hurt me.*

"I didn't disappear—"

"*Twice!*" I hissed, my hands falling to my sides. "You've ghosted me twice, Will!"

"I have not!" Will shouted back, stepping into the flat and shutting the door behind him with a thud. "I may have forgotten to text back now and then, but I've never purposefully ignored you."

"Bullshit!" I swore, the blood in my veins starting to boil. "You don't just wake up one day and *forget* to text someone who you've been shagging for six months." I snivelled into the cuff of my sleeve before shooting daggers at him and sneering, "More like you were too busy with your girlfriend, to have any time left over for your bit on the side."

"You have never been my *bit on the side*, Mel," Will took a step towards me, his looming physique enough to make my brain glitch and all of the air in my lungs evaporate.

"I've also never been your girlfriend," I stated bluntly, before building up enough foolish courage in my stomach to ask him the question that had been burning away in the back of my mind since I saw the picture of him and his pretty brunette on his socials. "Why didn't you want me as your girlfriend?"

"Because I like you too much," Will said softly, before frowning dopily and leaning against the wall.

"What kind of an answer is that?" I retorted, turning my back on him and pulling at my hair, frustrated. "What kind of wanky, crap answer is—"

I then felt Will's arms slink around me, whip me around, and all of a sudden, his hot mouth was on mine.

I could taste the tequila, smell his sweat, and feel the heat rising off him as if he were a newly-lit fire. He kissed me in a way he'd never kissed me before; passionately, lovingly, and with more than just want, but need, too.

I pulled myself away. Will whimpered in distress.

"Mel... You don't want to be my girlfriend. *Trust me*," he groaned, allowing me to push him off and away from me. "I lie to the women I date. I pretend that I'm something that they want me to be, or think that I am... I've never felt that pressure with you. I can be *me* when I'm with you," Will confessed solemnly. "If you were my girlfriend, I'd hurt you. And you mean too much to me for me to ever want to hurt you."

I looked at him and for the first time really saw the broken, damaged and pathetic excuse of a boy that he was. "You've hurt me, Will. Girlfriend or not," I pointed over his shoulder and at the door. "I think you should leave."

He left, and I can't believe I'm writing this but... I was happy to see him go.

— *Melissa Bishop, aged 20, praying she never lays eyes on Will Green ever again.*

***

The following week passed in a haze. Days filled with sitting by Mum's bedside and watching her. By Wednesday, she had stopped talking altogether; by Friday, she was refusing to do anything other than sleep.

Dad spent most of his time sitting in her room reading quietly in the corner, the rest by the kettle making him, or me, or Gramps, who visited every other day, a cup of tea.

The house was becoming emptier as I spent my time continuing where Dad had left off. Going through Mum's endless hoard of stuff. Art supplies, baking utensils, jam making equipment and enough books to make the local librarian actually utter the words, "I'm afraid we can't take any more donations from you. You've almost doubled our stock this week. We simply haven't got enough shelf room."

"Would you not be able to send them to another library?" I asked, the vegetable box in my arms weighing me down into the worn orange carpet.

"We have," she admitted sheepishly, before giving me a small smile and returning to typing away on her computer.

"What would you suggest I do with the rest?"

She tapped a few more keys. "How many more have you got?"

"Six more boxes, and there's about fifty books in each," I said, knowing full well that summary didn't include the two bookcases in Mum and Dad's garage that I hadn't even gone through yet.

"As a librarian, it pains me to say this," she sighed, looking up at me over the top of her computer screen. "But if you've tried selling them, donating them, *and* giving them away... Paper recycling is the next option on your list."

"Right. Thank you," I'd replied before turning on my heel and heading out of the library as fast as I could — which is turtle speed when carrying about fifty paperbacks.

The stand-out event of the week was on the Sunday afternoon when, having a cup of tea with Gramps in the kitchen, I got an unsuspecting email.

Afternoon, Melissa Bishop,

Hope you're well. Would love to have a chat with you if you're free. Face to face or over the phone, whatever is easiest. I understand you're a very busy bee and apparently very hard to get hold of. Nevertheless, I'd love to speak with you. Sometime early next week, maybe?

Let me know when would be good for you!

All the best,

Bethany Rollins & Co

"You don't half look like you've seen a ghost, sprog," Gramps said, holding his brew to his lips. "Summat happened?"

"I've had an email..." my voice trailed off, the name 'Bethany' taking me back to the night at Will's. "From an agent."

"FBI?"

"Actor," I replied, showing him my phone screen and a load of words that meant absolutely nothing to him. "She wants to speak to me... Maybe even sign me."

"And what does that mean?" Gramps grunted, his eyes crossing slightly as he tried to focus on the shaking phone in my trembling hands.

"I would have an agent. Someone to send me to auditions, help me get work." The excitement in my chest started to build, "Most people go to drama school to *get* an agent. But this, *this* would mean—"

"You'd be leap-frogging over the lot of them." Gramps summarised, giving me a curt nod. "Good on ya, lass."

Dad then entered the kitchen, his empty mug of tea in one hand, his glasses in the other. His shoulders were slumped forward, and he yawned loudly as he dragged his brown tartan slippers across the kitchen tiles.

"Christ, you don't half look like shite, Ted," Gramps noted, not even attempting to sugar-coat it. "When did you last get some sleep?"

Dad yawned again as he rinsed out his mug. "Well, what day is it?"

"Sunday," Gramps and I both said in unison.

Dad grunted then flipped the kettle on and scratched his caveman-like beard. "October?"

"November," I corrected him, passing him the half-eaten packet of custard creams from the table. "How's Mum doing?"

"She's the same," Dad sighed, pulling up a chair and sitting between Gramps and I. "Though the strange rattling noise has stopped, thank God."

"Yer what?" Gramps asked, his forehead crumpling into a frown. "What noise?"

"Yesterday, Mum was making this weird croaky noise every time she breathed. Like snoring, but worse," I shivered, remembering how unnerving it was to hear it through the walls throughout the night. "Didn't seem to bother her but it wasn't... pleasant."

"Yer mum was probably putting it on," Gramps tried to joke, "give you all a bit of a fright, and have a good giggle to herself."

I looked across at my dad and saw him nodding along, though not really paying much attention to either of us, his mind somewhere far, *far* away.

"I'll go up and sit with her, Dad" I said, patting him on the back. "You make a brew and have a rest."

Up in Mum's bedroom, the curtains were partially drawn, causing a soft evening glow to cast itself only half-way up the bed. Dust particles floated and danced gracefully between the rays of light. The whole room felt peaceful and still — as it should have been.

Mum lay on her back in the centre of her bed, her cracked and dry lips parted slightly, her eyes closed, her chest gently rising and falling. If it weren't for the unnaturally long gaps between her inhales and exhales, I would have thought nothing wrong with the scene before me.

I sat in the chair beside her bed, the seat still warm from Dad's presence for the majority of the day. Leaning forward, I took Mum's hand, and kissed it gingerly.

"How're you doing, Mum?"

No answer.

"Dad's gone to make himself a cuppa, so you've got me for a little while. I hope that's okay…" my voice trailed off as I waited for her next breath. "Mum?"

Nothing specific differed from second to second, but I *knew*. My world was about to end.

"Why wait for Monday when you can go on a sunny Sunday afternoon, ey?" I mused aloud, squeezing her hand, before closing my eyes and thinking, with a tight chest and a broken heart, *I'm ready*.

— Forty Two —

16th November

— Melisssa Bishop aged 23, living the first day, in her entire life without her mum in the world. No words. Just love.

***

I held Mum's hand for what felt like an eternity. I'd never seen anything as still as her body in my whole life. There was no rise and fall to her chest, no twitch beneath her eyelids that made me wonder what she was dreaming about. There was nothing.

Somehow, in a completely unexplainable way, I found myself believing that she was still in there somewhere. Almost as if her body was the car she'd driven her entire life in and now the engine was cut, yet there was still the gentle hum of the heater cooling down. The driver still sat in the driver's seat, waiting to get out. What she was waiting for, I'll never know.

Dad appeared at the doorway, his phone in his hand, limp by his side. "Your gramps has finally gotten off the phone with your nana. She's going to let the rest of Mum's family know..." he trailed off, his feet teetering on the metal strip of the threshold.

"What did the coroner say?" I cleared my throat, not able to look over my shoulder at him, my eyes fixed on Mum's ever paler and stiffening face.

"They said they could either collect her now, or in the morning. I hope you don't mind, but I asked for them to come now."

"I don't mind."

I loved her dearly, but the idea of Mum's corpse being in the next room while I lay in bed did freak me out a little. Knowing Mum's sense of humour, she'd revive herself, come into my room and scare me awake, purely for the hell of it.

"How are you holding up?" Dad asked me, his voice distant. "I mean, obviously..." he was trying to fill the silence.

I turned to him and suddenly came face to face with a stranger. I'd never noticed until that moment how all the lines on his face deepened when he smiled and practically vanished when he frowned. Every wrinkle, every pucker of skin was a nod to his humour. His face was etched with all the jokes he'd ever told, all the laughter he'd ever had. And in that moment, all of them were lost as he looked at me with an unspeakable amount of sorrow and heartbreak.

The coroners came, Dad and I stepping out to let them do their thing.

When I came back into Mum's room, my eyes filled with what felt like an unlimited supply of tears.

It looked *so* empty.

Gramps's large hand landed on my shoulder and I heard a gruff sort of snivel. "Your mum's at peace now, ey?" he murmured, before wrapping his beefy arm around my neck. "You did good, lass. Proud of you."

I heard another snivel and within the next few seconds Gramps had scarpered down the stairs and out the front door.

I remained frozen in the doorway looking at Mum's empty bed, and still seeing the faint outline of her body in the sheets.

Then, my eyes flicked over to the burgundy book on the nightstand with gold writing on the spine. *Theresa's Written Thoughts*.

With great trepidation, and a deep suspicion that I would be in big trouble with Mum if I were caught, I reached out for it. Curiosity got the better of me and I flicked open to the first page.

With my heart in my mouth, I saw Mum's poor handwriting scribbled across the paper;

'Theresa's Written Thoughts' — diary sounds too tawdry!

— Forty Three —

I believe in miracles because I am one. Let me tell you a story, and call me Theresa.

Theresa, meaning 'summer', and 'God danced with me'. He danced with my daughter and my whole soul family.

Where does the story start? Well, it's a long story, so let's get comfortable.

As a child, it was why I didn't make sense. My mother used to say, "If there was an awkward way of doing something, Theresa would find it".

I didn't fit in, was picked on and bullied at school. No real friends, except for Great Uncle Matthew.

It got better when I moved to secondary school. There I could do art, but even my art teachers struggled to understand me, unless I did clay or lino. I was excellent at it – my work was even submitted, accepted, and printed in a local magazine.

I wanted to flee into the art world but it was never an option. My mother demanded that I get a 'proper job' – cowardice and scared rubbish!

I chose podiatry. Grew and grew and grew.

Cancer diagnosis. Terminal diagnosis.

Today's date? 25th September – and now I live the rest. Signed,

Theresa Bishop (formerly Fallon)

– Theresa's Written Thoughts, Entry 1

***

The three days that followed Mum's death consisted mainly of sympathy cards coming through the letterbox. The first one came from Christine next door, who managed to post hers directly, *one hour* after Mum had been taken away by the coroners. Balls have left cannons slower.

On the Wednesday morning, I decided it was finally time to get out of the house. Food supplies were running low, not that Dad and I were eating much, but I felt as though if I stared at the interior walls of Mum and Dad's house any longer, I would officially go mad. *Just your Dad's house now*, I thought with a grimace as I pulled up into the big shop's car park.

I'd left Dad sitting on the garage floor going through Mum's remaining books, so when my phone rang, I assumed it was him.

"I know you said you would ring me when you were ready, Mel, but I really need to talk to you. It's been weeks, and I'm worried about you."

Surprisingly, Will's voice didn't make my blood run hot like the last time he rang me, or my heart rate quicken as it so often had. It didn't affect me at all. I continued to feel nothing.

My response of silence caused Will's voice to trail off. Then, "Welcome to the half-orphan club," he stated suddenly, causing the first smile in three days to actually appear on my face.

"Thanks," I blubbed, a fraction of myself actually feeling a little more human than I had four seconds prior.

"How long have you been a member?" he asked, a sorry softness to his tone.

"About three days," I croaked, my throat dry and voice hoarse. "She died on Sunday."

"Oh God, Mel... I'm so sorry."

"Why?" I quipped, recalling his joke from before. "You didn't kill her."

Will chuckled slightly, calmed by my poor attempt at normality and humour. "How are you?"

"Shit," I exhaled, my cheeks stinging as fresh salty tears ran down red raw skin. "Dad's worse. Other than talking about Mum's funeral plans, he isn't saying much. Neither of us are eating or sleeping... Surprised I managed to even get it together long enough to have a shower, to be honest."

"A shower after only three days?" Will whistled through his teeth, "That's impressive... When's the funeral?"

"Next Thursday at half eleven in the crematorium your way." I placed my phone on the dashboard and ran my fingers through my wild hair. "Thank God, Mum had made plans... Don't know how anyone makes these decisions blind. Like music and flowers. Even though she told me what she wanted, I still second guess every choice we make, wondering if she'd agree... And knowing my mum, she probably wouldn't."

"You're doing your best, Mel," Will reassured me, his voice soft and soothing. "That's all anyone can ask of you."

I didn't reply, merely rested my head against the steering wheel and took deep and steadying breaths.

"Jordan has said that you haven't got back to his agent—"

"Well, ya know," I groaned sarcastically, "had a lot on."

"Would you be okay with me updating them both, save you losing out on the opportunity?"

"Do whatever you want, Will," I cut off, sitting up straight and letting out a petty laugh. "I'm honestly not arsed at the minute what you do."

"Okay..."

I found myself shaking my head, not knowing why I was even wasting my breath on the conversation. "Anything else?"

"Nothing urgent," Will replied faintly. "Try and get some sleep, and I know I'm probably the last person you want to talk to right now, but please remember I'm here if you need me."

"Noted."

"Are you going to be okay?"

"No," I answered honestly, surprising even myself. "But I've got to be, haven't I? If not for me, then for my dad."

— Forty Four —

There's something missing in the cafe scene in London and I'm not entirely sure what it is. A cultural divide or something lost in translation; but the last time I visited my daughter, we had breakfast in a rather quaint, and supposedly competent, cafe.

I ordered extra hot water with my pot of tea and it came in a latte glass. I was utterly lost for words, to such an extent that I just looked at it thinking, *how?*

How did we ever progress from a pot of tea, which always came with a pot of water without asking, to the hot water arriving in a latte glass. How did fusion cuisine mess up a pot of English tea in the capital city of England?

Lost for words, as you can see, I rapidly leap-frogged over the 'WTF?' response of my teenage daughter, and into a full-blown rant on the loss of basic tea science.

In a London cafe. Coffee, yes, *coffee* you can have pretty much any way you like, as long as you're happy with skimmed milk, but tea?

REALLY?

Asking for a real decent cup of tea exactly the way you would like it is extraordinarily difficult.

One feels like Sally on the inaugural road trip of meeting Harry just asking for hot water, never mind a saucer for the tea bag or heaven forbid, '*Lady Grey*' tea.

The English have an obsession with tea. We are known the world over for being obsessed with the stuff and have even fought hard and fast to maintain the Nation's supply.

The world changing industrial revolution only succeeded because of tea. Not coal, not canals, and not Victoria herself either. Tea made with boiling water pretty much enabled people to live together in large communities without killing each other with waterborne diseases, simply because they boiled the water before drinking it. With a few dried leaves sleeping in the bottom of the pot —

Oh, and beer. Alcohol also helps prevent waterborne diseases (but large groups of people and large quantities of alcohol have their own disastrous consequences).

I can feel the rage stirring in me now. Offer me a cup of tea, promise me tea, and agree to deliver it to me at my table for the price advertised, and then serve up something less, and it's going to rile me beyond being slightly miffed. Or even, rather, put out.

I am disgruntled.

It should be obvious to any spectator to not disagree with me on the matter; then again, it should be obvious that additional hot water for tea belongs in a pot, not a latte glass.

As Teddy would say, "Common sense isn't very common". Rare as hen's teeth if you ask me.

— *Theresa's Written Thoughts, Entry 4*

***

I don't know whether it's a blessing or a curse that I don't remember the details of Mum's funeral. Sometimes I try to make the hazy memories more clear, but I quickly give up when I either find myself crying or nursing a blistering migraine.

What I can remember about the day either comes from what other people have told me, what I can see in the pages of her order of service, or what comes back to me momentarily when I play the music we chose to have accompany her into the next world.

'Nimrod' from the Enigma Variations serenaded her as she was carried into the crematorium.

When I relisten to that piece of music, it makes me remember Mum's pale green, bamboo lattice coffin. When I first saw it, making its way towards us in the back of the hearse, I thought, *It looks like something she would make herself.*

Would have been morbid as hell, but no doubt, if Mum had been presented with the idea of having a go at weaving a bamboo coffin, she would have jumped at the chance.

La Mer makes me recall the fact I wore pink, and Dad didn't cry. He didn't do much, to be honest. Stared blankly ahead, aware a lot of intrusive eyes were on him for what should have been a very private moment.

Gramps sat behind us, with Nana Tia in full mourner's garb beside him. She had the black net fascinator and the coal coloured pashmina and everything — if I hadn't been so bloody miserable, I would have laughed.

As I was called up to say a few prepared words, Gramps placed a heavy, large hand on my shoulder, giving it a supportive squeeze.

"You can do it, kidda'," he whispered when I appeared to be frozen to my seat. "You can do it."

I rose to my feet, unfolding the crumpled-up and sweat-stained ball of paper I'd had clenched between my hands. The ink I'd written in had smeared, making some words intelligible, but it didn't matter, I knew the damn thing off by heart. Mum's eulogy had become merely lines to learn — it had occurred to me when I stepped up in front of the tiny black microphone that the reading had to be a performance. The sea of eyes staring at me didn't need to see a genuine display of affection. I didn't owe them that, especially when it meant probably crumpling up beside Mum's coffin and never getting back up. It had to be an act. It was the only way they, and I, were going to get through it.

I steadied myself and read,

"Mum was one of the most creative people I've ever met. Be that creating art, or a delicious meal... Or an argument out of nowhere."

There was a titter of laughter.

"Mum created every day. If you wanted to try something, without a doubt Mum had already done it. And excelled in it. Except for maybe... I genuinely can't think of anything Mum was bad at. She created so much. Me for a start, with the help of Dad, but I won't go into the details of that."

There was another echo of laughter that caused me to raise my eyes from the page and look across at Gramps and Dad. Gramps was staring back at me with heartbroken pride. Dad, on the other hand, was... somewhere else entirely. I pushed on.

"She raised me to be like her, strong, independent, and as stubborn as she was. Mum co-created a twenty-six-year-long marriage, which in this day and age, deserves a medal.

"Mum created a safe hearth, a home you always knew you were welcome in no matter how much she protested your presence when you were actually there in front of her. Getting in her way, eating the food in the fridge, or putting the TV remote somewhere she couldn't find — which usually meant it was right in the middle of the coffee table, in plain sight.

"She created art right until the end, and I know she will continue to create even though she is gone in body.

"Her art will create more art.

"Her recipes will create more delicious meals.

"Her home is still forever a home.

"Mum was... Mum was my mum. The person I rang when I was sick. The person who read my work first, critiqued it, and watered every idea I've ever had to help it grow. Mum wasn't perfect, no... But she was really intelligent, and loved those closest to her inexplicably deeply.

"She read a million books, and so lived a million lives from the comfort of her study.

"Mum was mad, but as she told me herself, she was quite happy with her madness, and content with how she spent her time on this earth. I think that's something we could all maybe take away from this... Let us all live as my mum lived; mad, happy and content."

Gabriel's Oboe was the song that took her home. It makes me think of... *Her*.

Just her.

And, ultimately, what a pleasure it was to have her as my mum.

— Forty Five —

How to be Happy.

First, unleash the shit that makes you sad. This is difficult and sometimes needs repeating several times to thoroughly get rid of the years of crap.

Being happy is as much a simple process as that of learning how to climb a mountain. If you are unhappy, you first have to learn to swim to get out from under the water of sadness and despair.

Then wade through the tough mud – through the undergrowth of guilt, shame and fear. So many obstacles, so many chances to turn around and sink back into the water, but you must be steadfast and strong.

Each step up the mountain will be more gruelling as you become fatigued and dragged down by others who do not want to see you succeed, who do not want to see you happy.

Onwards and upwards. Identify the crap. Isolate it. Minimise it, or better yet, ignore the why. Reject and evict it, and once you become skilled enough, you may even be able to place it underfoot and use it to raise you higher up your mountain.

Strive for happiness; for being happy is that which makes life worth living.

— *Theresa's Written Thoughts, Entry 17*

***

Mum's wake felt like too many rats crammed into a cardboard box of a country pub. My relatives scurried around the place, not knowing whether to give Dad and I their condolences first or head straight to get a round in at the bar.

"It's what she would have wanted," Uncle Kenneth hiccuped, nursing a gin and tonic the size of his head.

Yeah, a woman who was teetotal would have absolutely wanted you all to get trollied at her funeral, I thought coldly, standing beside Dad at the door as more delusional relatives arrived.

"Beautiful service," Nana Tia noted as she kissed me on the cheek and nearly stabbed me in the eye with her black tulle-covered hat. "Shame about the lilies though, orchids would have complimented her casket so much more."

I bit my bottom lip to stop myself from swearing. "Maybe we'll do orchids for your funeral then, Nana," I swiftly replied, causing Gramps to throw his head back and let out a roar of laughter. The whole room seemed to be caught off guard — rule number one of funerals and wakes, no one is supposed to enjoy themselves.

"That's made my day, has that," Gramps said, wiping one of his large sausage fingers under his eye. "Not that the bar was set very high to begin with, but that's properly tickled me walnuts."

My mood remained flat. "Glad I could help, Gramps," I replied stiffly, motioning for them to head towards the bar.

Nana Tia patted me on the shoulder, "Try not to look *so* glum dear," she whispered, ever the matriarchal nightmare. "Your mother's passing was a blessing. We wouldn't have wanted her suffering, now, would we?"

If Dad hadn't grabbed hold of my tightened fist, or Gramps physically got Nana by the shoulders and swept her away, I would have hit her.

"I don't think I can do much more of this," I hissed to Dad, my blood sizzling in my veins. "If one more person tells me, 'Mum's in a better place now', I'll scream."

"Try and hold it in till everyone's here, Freckles. Then I give you full permission to bolt," Dad managed a weak smile. "I might even flee with you."

A woman swept Dad into a hug before I could respond, tittering in his ear, "I'm so sorry for your loss."

"Thank you, Christine," Dad said, patting her back in a way that screamed, '*You can let me go now*'.

"I saw you both dressed up this morning, leaving the house, and it broke my heart, it really did." Christine finally withdrew, "If there's anything I can do for either of you, please let me know."

Dad forced a smile. "I'm sure you'll know before we do if something comes up, Christine," he replied as she finally carried on into the room, not forgetting to throw me a sympathetic frown as she passed.

"Mr Bishop—"

I froze, my head whipping round to see Will shaking my Dad's hand.

"Sorry, you'll have to forgive me, I don't—"

"It's Will. I'm a friend of Mel's, sir. Purely here for moral support," Will glanced at me and all I could do was blink at him.

"*The* friend?" Dad asked, shaking Will's hand and throwing me an amused side-eye. "Nice to finally put a face, *and a name,* to you."

There was a small cough and a woman stepped out from behind Will.

Holy shi—

"Oh, and this is my mum, Harriet," Will said, stepping to the side to reveal her in all of her pale blue glory. "She's here for—"

"For the free buffet, to be honest," Harriet cut in, her eyes crinkling as she laughed. "Of course, I'm joking. The son needed a—"

"Taxi service?" Dad interjected, a faint smile hiding beneath his beard.

"Exactly," she nodded back before rolling her eyes. "Some things never change, no matter how old they get."

There was a smash of glass and all eyes turned to see Uncle Kenneth looking sheepish by the bar, the remains of his G&T pooling around his loafers.

"Ooopsies," he chimed, the bartender already at hand with a dustpan and brush.

"Can't take him anywhere," Auntie Angela chuntered, swooping in beside me and shaking her head so much that I thought her black fascinator might wriggle itself from her back-combed bird's nest. "Lovely do," she said, turning to me and clocking Will immediately. "Is this your boyfriend, Mel?" She pressed her manicured finger to her lips. "Freddie, am I right?"

Will's jaw clenched.

"No, Auntie Angela," I quickly interjected, feeling the mortification rising in me like an overflowing well. "Freddie and I broke up."

Will nearly gave himself whiplash.

"This is my friend, Will," I stated curtly, hoping my tone was blunt enough to stop Angela from poking her angular nose in any further. It wasn't.

"Are *you* seeing anybody, Will?"

"Drink?" I snapped, already taking his hand and pulling him towards the bar.

"Love one," Will chuntered, energetically following my lead. "Nice to meet you, Mr Bishop," he tried to say, but his voice was lost in his throat as I tugged him harshly in the opposite direction.

We got to the bar and passed it, heading straight for the back door and out into the beer garden.

The freezing air hit me like a punch to the lungs. In a strange way, the pain of the chill was refreshing, almost as if it was forcing me to think of something other than the fact I was at Mum's wake surrounded by unfeeling morons — Dad and Gramps not included.

"What the hell are you doing here?" I snapped as soon as we were out of ear shot. "*How* are you here, actually?"

"You told me the time and date of your Mum's funeral. The wake details were announced at the end of the service, so I—"

"You were at the crematorium?"

"At the back. I tried to hide."

"*Why?*" I hissed, continuing to pull Will further and further away from the raucous building. "You didn't know my mum. You never even met her. Why on earth would you go to her funeral and then to her wake?"

"I did say I was here for moral support, to be fair," Will shrugged, not letting go of my hand even though I'd finally stopped dragging him.

"And your mum is here to what?" I snorted, "Keep you in check?"

Will scratched the back of his head with his free hand, "Genuinely, my car broke down this morning, she offered to give me a lift."

"Was Katie not available?" I couldn't help but ask, despite knowing it would open a can of worms neither of us needed to discuss.

Will pursed his lips, then sighed. "We broke up."

"Right..." My voice escaped me, and I looked at him with a rainbow of emotions coursing up and down my body.

I didn't know whether to laugh, cry, hug him or hit him, so I just continued to glare.

"You're really brave, you know?" Will exhaled, his hand still grasping tightly onto mine. "For breaking up with Freddie. How did it go? In the end?"

"He didn't kill himself, so it could have gone worse," I shrugged, before adding, "It was long overdue but still hell." I bit my tongue, then thought with a pithy sneer, *sod this for a game of soldiers.* "How come you finally ended things with Katie?"

"We simply couldn't make it work," Will confessed, placing his free hand in his front pocket and rocking back and forth slightly on his heels. "Certain people just aren't meant to be together."

Including us, I thought, my hand slipping out of his and falling to my side. It took nearly every ounce of self respect I had in me to take a step back away from him.

I knew Will was important to me, he was a pivotal moment in the makings of my history. He was a homing beacon from the moment I met him in that damn dance studio... Every time we reunited after those fateful two weeks, our chemistry felt effortless, instantaneous, and in that moment I knew why. My sixteen-year-old self had allowed him to burrow so far deep into the pits of her making that I had a special place for him in my soul, in case he ever wanted to stay forever.

It seemed that moment had come, but that space was filled with grief, and pain, and the loss of my Mum. There was no room left for even hope, let alone Will and all the baggage he carried.

"Does it ever go away?" I asked him suddenly, my heart feeling as though it were being constricted by electrified barbed-wire. "The grief... and the pain?"

"Not really," Will sighed with a heavy heart. "It never gets easier either, no matter what anyone tells you, it just becomes... *different.* You learn to live with it."

"I miss her," I confessed, my bottom lip starting to tremble and my eyes starting to fill. "I don't know what I'm going to do."

Will stepped towards me, breaking the space I'd made, and tucked a few stray bedraggled ginger hairs behind my ear. "You keep going. That's all you can do."

Will then planted a soft kiss on my forehead, before wrapping his arms around me and smothering me in the loveliest, most genuine hug I'd had in years.

"I don't think we should see each other anymore," I said, my face pressed, and voice muffled against his chest.

Will took a long moment before planting another kiss on the top of my head. "Okay. But *if,* in a few years, when you're doing the big filming jobs and only have time for a weekend boy... You know where to find me."

I actually laughed.

— **Forty Six** —

A long, long time ago, someone spoke words of prophecy over my daughter in church. Powerful, believable words about her future. Not anything trivial, you understand, like tall dark strangers, nothing entertaining about this — It was church after all and therefore *very* serious.

They got in trouble for it after, or so I heard, but I have no recollection of who told me about the reprimand. It was just a whisper that it should never have been said over the children, where other people would hear.

Afterwards, many years later, when all hell and many secrets emerged, the people who would have done the reprimanding were revealed to be less honest, less Christian, and less respectable than all the standards they preached so righteously for decades. So in hindsight, I have no issue with the people who spoke the words of prophecy.

None at all.

They believed what they were doing was stating the intentions and purposes of God as they believed Him to be.

Exactly the role of the prophet, and like prophets of The Book, sometimes that got them into trouble (it's a sign of a good prophet!). Not so bothered about the P.R just relaying the message.

Sometimes they were believed, people changed their ways and 'bad stuff' didn't happen — everyone was happy, *mostly*. Other times, prophets were not believed and then things got really interesting.

But all that is in The Book, no point me retelling it here, apart from the most interesting thing about prophets, which is The Cloak. Like a badge of office, job uniform, special hat, or whatever, The Cloak went with the job, it followed the anointing.

Interesting thing about uniforms, they are supposed to show the job, not the person. Powerful stuff uniform — could probably write a whole thesis on it but not just now — as that would get in the way of my daughter.

Like I said, people to whom words of prophecy are given have a choice — several choices actually;

Believe the words.

Believe the prophet.

Act on, or disregard, either or both.

Daily choose how far to take those beliefs and actions.

At the time, my daughter was very young, no more than three, and I don't believe she ever noticed what was going on, nor did she understand the significance of the prophetic words. However, my daughter is no fool, and could well have understood the whole thing and chosen accordingly.

I have no idea.

I never discussed it with her. I only ever discussed it with my mother, who whispered about the "inappropriateness" of it. So, like many in The Book, I just stored the memory and thought about it from time to time. Mostly because events seemed to prove the words false.

Until my daughter started to be able to speak proficiently and write in excess.

With pen or pencil in hand, and mouth running wild, she began and continues to demonstrate the words of the prophecy. As if during the last few years, choosing not to accept The Cloak, had left it unused but safe and somehow, when finally ready, took up the mantle, anointed and compelling.

"When she speaks, people will listen. Many people will listen when she stands and speaks to them."

All else is speculation, how and where and why and about what. That will all come out in time. All I can say is that it was God ordained that my daughter would be a great communicator in words both spoken and written.

The choice to act on that ordination *is* hers — *daily.*

Always was, always will be.
– *Theresa's Written Thoughts, second to last entry.*

***

For weeks after Mum's funeral, I saw her everywhere. Still don't know if that's a universal thing or simply something a griever's brain does to them to really screw them over.

I heard Mum's laugh when the cutlery draw was opened and the forks rattled together. I saw her eye colour in a strained and slightly dried out teabag. Felt the softness of her hand whenever I picked up a fresh sponge. No matter where I went or what I did, the memory of Mum was there, causing me pain and making me cry.

A piercing smash of glass had me running into the kitchen at full speed. I found Dad, standing on a chair, the remains of one of Mum's trifle dishes, like a puddle made of shards, surrounding him.

"Never liked that one anyway," he commented, slowly getting down from the chair and letting the glass crunch beneath his tartan slippers. "Can you pass me the dust—"

Before he'd even finished his request, I was already rolling up my sleeves, grabbing the dustpan and brush from under the sink and going about cleaning up the mess myself. "No, no, Dad. I'll sort all this out. You go into the other room and get some rest."

"I don't need rest, Freckles, I need the dustpan and brush. I dropped the dish, I should be the one to clean it up. Now, give it here."

His voice sounded coarse; not that I was surprised, his voice usually sounded dry in the morning. *Maybe he's dehydrated?*

"Seriously, Dad I've got this. Make yourself a cuppa."

"Freckles."

"Or some lunch," I suggested, starting to pick up the larger pieces of glass and put them straight into the bin. "Have you eaten today? Had any breakfast? You know you really should eat something, even if you don't feel like it."

"Mel—"

"I tell you what, I'll make you some scrambled eggs on toast after I've cleaned all this up. Or shall we go out for something to eat?" I swept up the last of the glass, Dad sitting down in his chair at the end of the kitchen table and putting his head into his hands. *He must be exhausted, bless him.*

"I know it's hard, getting out, but I think some air and a fresh scene will do us some good. We don't have to talk, we could just go and grab a takeaway coffee or something—"

"Melissa!" Dad snapped suddenly, hitting the kitchen table with the base of both of his fists. The unexpected thud reverberated through the entire house. "Will you just stop?"

"Stop what?" I blinked, genuinely befuddled. "I'm only suggesting things we could do to help you."

Dad sighed, looking at me through his large lenses, a smile gingerly tugging at the left corner of his mouth. "Exactly... I don't *need* any help, love."

Of course you do.

"Dad, you don't have to put on a brave face. Like, you lost your wife a month ago. Pretty understandable that you would need some help."

"But I don't," Dad shrugged, his subtle smile disappearing beneath his shaggy grey and ginger beard. "I'm fine."

"You're not fine, Dad," I tutted, feeling a little like I was being too harsh with him. "And that's okay."

"I *am*—"

"You're not. God, Dad," I gestured to the barren house around us before emptying the dustpan into the kitchen bin. "I've been doing a lot around here since Mum passed—"

"Because you won't let me do anything! I can't even wash my own pants without you coming in and swooping the fabric softener out of my hands telling me, 'Oh, I'll do it, Dad'. I can't even make myself dinner—"

"You can't cook!"

"I've never had to!" Dad cut me off sharply, "Your mum did all that — and now you are! Not that I ever asked either of you to. You just do it and I stand there like a wally looking like I can't take care of myself. Melissa, I'm not a mess. I'm fine!"

Full naming me? I must be in trouble.

"Look at me, Mel." He strode across the kitchen and took my free hand before getting down to my level and squeezing it tightly. "I mean, *really* look at me."

My eyes ran across his face, not sure what I was supposed to be looking for. Was there a lump? A bruise? Skin discoloration he was worried about that we needed to go and get seen to?

"I'm fine," he repeated, the tension dropping out of his shoulders. "I didn't think I would be... Not to this extent so soon, but I promise you, I'm *fine*."

The more he said it, the more my eyes honed into what he was talking about. He'd showered, he'd trimmed his beard, he was even wearing a new jumper... *When had he been shopping? When had he been out of the house?*

"I thought that when your mum died, it would be like losing the ability to breathe." Dad's eyes started to shimmer behind his large lenses, "But I found that, actually, I'd been holding my breath for so long... That her dying was almost like..."

He was trembling, I could feel the little vibrations in his fingertips.

"I won't say it was a relief, or that I'm glad it happened, because I'm not. I'm simply saying that I have to see the positives in all this or else I wouldn't be able to get out of bed. I love your mum very much..." he whispered under his breath, "...but by God, she was a hard person to live with.

Look at this house. Without her things in it, the bugger is empty. I have nothing here, I never did, because she took up space before I even had a chance to claim it.

"Her mood was like a yoyo, not just day to day, we're talking hour to hour. One minute she'd be singing some musical number in the bathroom, and the next spitting feathers, throwing her arms in the air, scolding the world for something or other. I was so often the only one in the house so I got the brunt of her outbursts. Being yelled at for something I hadn't even done, or lectured at about something I barely understood. Her thoughts were not coherent, more so as we neared the end of things.

"It was hard and it was exhausting. I constantly felt like I was waiting for it most of the time—"

"Waiting for what?" I pushed, wondering if this was the first time Dad had ever said any of this out loud.

"One of her turns," Dad chewed the inside of his cheek nervously, his eyes darting from me to the door, as if part of him was still worried Mum was about to miraculously come bursting through it, offended and outraged by his confession. "Retrospectively speaking, hindsight makes it seem obvious to tell you the truth... I think she was sick for a lot longer than any of us realised." Dad's eyebrows furrowed, "I think those tumours had been playing havoc in her brain for years."

I couldn't help but instinctively think of the rare times Mum had completely and utterly lost her rag for such an irrational reason. Mothering Sundays turned on their axis because I'd got her the wrong type of flowers. Christmases ending in tears because someone had bought her a present that made her feel as though no one understood her at all.

Hell, when I lost my school jumper on the walk back home and she made me search, in the dark, late at night, up and down the road until I found it because it cost twenty quid.

Dad was right, it had to be more than just her upbringing or her personality, it had to be because she was sick. That was the only way of looking at some of those memories and not viewing her as a bad person.

Dad squeezed my hand even tighter, his gold wedding band glistening under the kitchen lights. I'd never noticed how battered and scuffed it was. All those years working, pottering, and labouring away had tarnished it.

I didn't know what to say. *What can I say?* Dad had already said it all.

Losing Mum was simultaneously the hardest and easiest thing to do — hard for reasons that are bleeding obvious, and easy because there was absolutely nothing either of us could have done to change her fate.

Dad went back to the table and drank some of his abandoned tea.

"So, what are you going to do?" I asked him timidly, looking around the kitchen and seeing nothing but empty shelves, and sparsely filled cupboards. "Downsize?"

Dad's upper lip twitched, a flash of his old self breaking through the cracks of his grief. "I've always liked the idea of living in France..."

"Oh, yeah?" I laughed softly, rolling my eyes and blinking back a few unshed tears. "Because *that's* going to happen."

"What about you?" Dad snivelled, amusement lacing his tone. "What are you going to do? You still have to set up that meeting with that agent, or are you thinking you want to go back and try drama school?"

"I don't know, Dad," I sighed. "I haven't a clue *what* I'm going to do."

Dad sipped his brew, "Maybe that's a good thing, Freckles," he replied with a smile. "Means you could end up... anywhere."

— *Epilogue* —

Today! 18th October. I do not believe I will be dead in twelve months' time!

I get to write my own story!

— *Theresa's Written Thoughts, Final Entry... 4 weeks before her death.*

***

"This Piccadilly Line train will be terminating at Cockfosters. The next station is *Arnos Grove*," the half-arsed conductor announced on the tannoy.

Cockfosters and Shepherd's Bush could make even the most grief-stricken mourner smirk – if they were immature enough. And I happened to be very immature, and not so grief stricken or mournful as I had been in recent months.

Christmas had been hell. New Year was even worse, but then the sun had started to come out earlier, the nights became shorter and by the time daffodils had started to bloom I finally felt a little more with it. Enough so that I'd decided I was going to move back to London. I wasn't going back for another attempt at drama school — Bethany had been more than patient with me, understood my situation due to a mysterious tip off, and after our meeting was kind enough to sign me to her books. With an agent, and the first flutters of hope in my heart in months, I was eager to start my own path into the industry.

Only problem being, I had nowhere to live.

Until now.

"The next stop is *Arnos Grove.* Arnos Grove will be our next stop."

I stood and hauled my rucksack onto my right shoulder. My left hand swooped up my black bin bag full of bedding, and my right hand grabbed the dark blue overhead handle so that I didn't fall flat on my face when the Tube jerked to a halt.

I found out about the house share opportunity through Tilly, of all people. She said that an old friend from secondary school was looking for a house mate, since the last one had suspiciously left with no notice. I checked out the details and fell near enough in love with the quaint house on the roundabout.

The advertisement said that the house was a fifteen-minute walk away from the station, but with all my belongings weighing me down, it took me closer to an hour.

When I finally arrived, I looked up the pothole-ridden driveway and felt a fizzle in my stomach; anticipation? Excitement? Or perhaps just a desperation to pee — it was a very similar sensation.

I placed down my bags, rolled my shoulders back and knocked gingerly on the dark blue front door.

"*Two seconds!*" screamed a voice from inside. "I'm just – *For God's sake!* Get in the cupboard you jammy bast—"

There was a clatter and a thud before the door swung open and a tall, thin, quirky looking young man was beaming at me. "Sorry, I was just trying to put the damn Hoover away. It's just decided that it can't fit in the cupboard under the stairs even though that's where it's been for the last four months! Bloody thing. Come on in! Come on in!"

He stood to the side and waved his right arm manically like a windmill, causing a literal draft to waft over me.

I juggled with my things, practically falling over the threshold and into a warm and bright hallway.

"Living room is through there, kitchen down there. Your room is the door at the top of the stairs, mine's on the right. Bathroom is on the left," the man babbled on, waving his hands about in all the appropriate directions. "Rent is due first of the month. We split the bills fifty-fifty, unless you're the type who showers for forty minutes three times a day, then the water bill is all yours, babe."

He turned on his fluffy red-slippered heel and led me into the kitchen, where he wafted his hands some more. "Your cupboards are all on the right, mine are all on the left. Tried doing the up and down way with the last one but it just ruins your back if you've got the lower cupboards. All that bending down just for a tin of tomatoes, do you know what I mean?"

I was unsure why I nodded in reply as he wasn't actually looking at me, but I couldn't speak; there hadn't been a chance to, and I was too busy trying to take in all of this magnificent person. "Kettle has just boiled, so I'll make us a brew." He finally stopped and looked at me, his smile wide and friendly. "I think that's everything, unless you have any questions?"

"Yeah," I half-laughed. "Who are you?"

"Oh!" He threw his head back and let out a piercing, infectious, bird-like squawk. "I'm Ian! Sorry, I should have started with that." He laughed some more before asking, "It's Melissa, isn't it?"

"Mel, yeah."

I shook his hand, admiring the array of colours painted across his nails.

"How do you have your tea?"

"Milk, two sugars."

Ian pouted as he waltzed over to the kettle. "Funny, you don't look like you take sugar."

I wasn't even sure what that meant.

"What do I look like?"

The question seemed to surprise both of us. Ian's eyes twinkled with delight as he looked me up and down with a merry smile.

"You look like the kind of person who thinks Wednesdays are purple," he laughed, "when everyone else thinks they're blue."

He reminds me of…

"You're mad," I concluded, unapologetically out loud, unable to suppress the biggest smile I'd had on my face in six months.

"Absolutely," he nodded enthusiastically before turning to make the tea. "And I hope you are too, or else what's the point?"

Oh, I'm mad too, I thought with a soft smile, *and happy with my madness.*

Ian passed me my tea.

"Welcome home, Mel."

THE END

Special Acknowledgments
My Cheerleaders

Of course, Dad is first. The man, the myth, the legend that he is. It took me roughly around ten thousand words to realise *Waiting for Monday* wasn't about Theresa, it was about Mel and her Dad, and the love and laughter the two of them share while they go through hell. I feel like I've only been able to capture a fraction of the strength, humour, and faith my dad has. He truly is my hero.

I'd like to thank Jamie, and our beautiful cracker-jack of a daughter, Boo.

Thank you to my sisters, Esther & Zoë. The besties, Emmy, Grace, Rose, Paige, Annie and Rhys.

My bonus family: Nana Rachel, Big Al, Martin & Gill, Auntie Mandy & Auntie Mary, Fancytart & Alys. Bumble & Rubble. Plus my agents, Oliver, Natalie, Humphrey and Ruby.

The incredibly talented Kayla Coombs for the cover, and for bringing Mel and Teddy to life.

And I'd like to thank my brilliant mum.

Not forgetting to mention all of the incredible NHS staff at Airedale Hospital, the district nurses, and every single person at the *Sue Ryder* Manorlands Hospice in Oxenhope, who cared for my mum.

Thank you all so much for your unwavering love and support. Wouldn't be here without you.

A Note from the Author

Apologies in advance for the tsunami of mush that's about to come oozing off this page. But there's something I would like to tell you. My mum *was* mad. Gloriously, weirdly, and lovingly mad, but mad all the same.

Her end-of-life diary did consist of the entries you see at the start of chapters forty four through to the epilogue (with obvious name changes). The words of *Theresa's Written Thoughts* are Mum's words, not mine — I simply cannot take the credit.

Mum really did believe she would live on *way* past her terminal prognosis... And in a weird way, I believe she has. Here in this book, and in *Melodramatic*, her story, her essence and her bloody stubbornness and lunacy will live on.

She spent her whole life between the pages of a book; why would she spend her death anywhere else?

I love my mum dearly, and writing *Melodramatic* and *Waiting for Monday* has been such a blessing. In fact, it's been like therapy. I've forced myself to look at what we went through, and reflect on it, see it for what it was, and in some places, rewrite history.

Mum wasn't my north, my south, my east, or west... She was my mum, and a part of me will miss her for the rest of my life.

I still write with the expectation that my mum will be the first one to read it. She edited everything I ever wrote (including her own eulogy), and watered every idea I ever had.

I'll never be able to fully understand her, but I think, since her death and becoming a mum myself, I've been able to get my head around why she was the way she was. Why she encouraged my weirdness, fed my creativity, and set me on a hard but magical path of sharing my voice with the world.

She truly believed I could make a difference.

I just hope I'll have done enough to make her proud, when that blissful moment comes, when I see her again...

I hope you're in the garden, Mum.
Surrounded by the children, Eve, Louis and Peanut.
I hope you're teaching them to bake, to paint, and to sing.
I hope you're with Dorothy, pip-spitting sunflower seeds
while sitting on stone steps.
I hope you found your God, your Grace, and your Light.
I hope you found your peace,
And a place to read forever.

Thank you for believing in me,
And for everything else too,
I love you, Mum.
Always x

Other Works by Megan Parkinson

Melodramatic
Book 2 in the *Melissa Bishop* Series

Told in a series of diary entries in which Mel muses on everything from booty calls and all-butter croissants to grief and family bonds, Melodramatic is a candid look at the mess of wires behind those big flashing lights of fame — wonderfully witty, refreshingly honest, and ultimately hilarious.

The glitz and glam of showbiz isn't all it's cracked up to be. As a 26-year-old actor living in London, Mel would know. Three years after the events of *Waiting for Monday*, Mel is now wasting her time at fruitless auditions, dealing with constant rejection and batting off back-handed compliments. It's no wonder she's starting to reach the end of her tether with it all. That's until she lands a semi-substantial role in a hit movie alongside superstar heartthrob, Jack Hart.

Jack is super confident, super handsome, and, at face value, super arrogant — everything Mel can't stand. But when Mel gets the opportunity to break industry protocol and get to know the person behind the pretty face, she soon realises that even the most famous and successful actors have their problems.

Megan Parkinson & Mollie Winnard's
Playlist to The Apocalypse

'Parkinson and Winnard's *Playlist to the Apocalypse*' is a stage-play that follows two sisters, Anna and Stacey, who, with the threat of a nuclear bomb, find themselves at the end of the world. They spend their final hours on the phone with one another deciding if it's best to finally voice their secrets, or take them to their premature graves.

It is a dark comedy that explores the complexity of sibling relationships, parental pressures, and the humour we find when faced with dire situations.

Taking from the shared experience we gained during the pandemic, *Playlist to the Apocalypse* is an insight into that bizarre and terrifying moment when we don't know what tomorrow will bring... *So what is there to lose?*

Megan Parkinson's

SKYWARD

Coming Soon...

— Prologue —

The rumours were true, the war was over. *'The Smoke had won, and London was to move Skyward.'*

New London had been completed just three years into the new millennia. An immaculate feat of engineering, the first of its kind.

It had come at great expense to the Loftier class. Though some may argue that was only in the realm of pounds and pence. The Gutter class had paid for New London with their lives.

They'd welded the new city above their heads, the death toll rising with every new man who, devoid of strength, from pure exhaustion, fell daily to their premature demise.

A grievous amount of Gutters were crushed when the New Blackfriars quarter collapsed under the sheer weight of itself. And more devastating than that — a paint, layered plentifully onto New London's steel foundations to prevent rust, had revealed itself to be toxic to the touch.

Those same workers who'd spent all their working hours with the paint had returned to their homes, held their children, embraced their wives, and before the fortnight was out, carriages full of corpses were being pulled down the cobbled streets of Old London in inconceivable succession.

Despite all this, New London's completion was met with astounding celebration. Without remorse, or guilt, the Loftiers ascended to their new home, saved, and free from *The Smoke*. While what little remained of the Gutters were forced to stay below, their torturous fate just as sealed as they were.

New London was to be a fresh, clean-aired start for those who could afford it, and a shackle to the poisonous past for those who could not.

— 1 —

Daniel found himself outside of a pleasure house. He grimaced. What was pleasurable about it? They were always filled with feral men, poking at model one or two automatons, whose programmings were barely functional and appearances anything but appealing.

His first experience of a 'Pleasure House' was on his sixteenth birthday. His father of all people! And his elder brother, Simon — who Daniel was now on the hunt for — had dragged him through the doors and demanded Daniel be given his birthday reward.

He assumed his father had paid for an automaton to take his boyhood, but no, into his blackout-curtained room walked a woman. A *real* woman. Thrice his age, and clearly not pleased to see someone as young as he was at the time, standing before her.

She was smiling, but behind her eyes, she looked disgusted... Not at him but at herself, for what she had been paid to do.

She reached out to remove his coat, but before her fingers had even touched the top, solid gold button, he'd stopped her.

"I'd like to talk," Daniel had said, surprised by how unstable he'd sounded.

"What is it, my love?"

Daniel winced. He'd never been called 'love' by anyone, not even his mother, and he would've liked to have kept it that way.

She mistook his hesitation for shyness and smiled at him encouragingly, while making her way to the worn four-poster bed.

"Is there something specific you wanted to try? Don't be shy, my love — I've heard it all before."

Daniel placed a frustrated hand to his brow. He felt sixty, not sixteen, tired of the ways of the world already. His mother had once remarked that he'd been that way since age two. An impossibly bright mind, with a soul that had clearly walked the earth, perhaps too many times, before.

"You misunderstand me, miss. What I want, and the *only* thing I want, is to talk."

The woman on the bed stared blankly at him. Her bottom lip wobbled for a fleeting second as she sat in the suspicion that this was some new, fashionable, school boy trick. "I've been payed to please you, my l—"

"Talking to me would please me. You can keep the payment as long as you talk to me, and nothing... more." Daniel swallowed some bile that had crept up his throat.

His elder brother, Simon, on the journey to the God-forsaken place, had given Daniel not-so delicate descriptions about what his birthday reward would entail. He'd had to endure vulgar details, describing how degrading a woman, or an automaton for that matter, would suddenly make Daniel a 'man'.

The woman on the bed nodded, agreeing but still wary of the surprising turn of events. "What would you like to talk about?"

"Anything," Daniel breathed, seeing a chair in the corner of the room and sitting in it. "But it seems practical to start with your name."

She flashed him a flirtatious look, a reflex no doubt, as she said. "My name is whatever you wish it to be."

Daniel shook his head at her, leaning back into his seat. "We're not doing that. We're *talking*, remember?"

Her eyebrows furrowed, before she answered softly, "Alma... And your name, sir?"

Daniel smiled, satisfied that however long he was destined to spend with this woman may no longer be a thing of nightmares.

"Daniel Moore."

Her eyes widened as he assumed they would.

Her lips parted, a breath escaping her as she suddenly took in the sight of him all over again. "You're a *Moore*?" She no longer focused on the innocence of his face, or the shortness in his height. She instead noted the famous Moore family features, spread across his appearance. His mother's legendary, flawless, mahogany skin, his father's cold, steel-grey eyes, and the tight curled, charcoal hair both he and his brother shared. If all that were not enough to confirm his identity, there was the broach, engraved with the *MM* crest, pinned to his lapel.

He was a Moore. Second son of Malcolm Moore, the most well known man in New London, and therefore the whole of Britain. Original creator, engineer, and manufacturer of all automatons — better known as *Moore Models*.

Daniel heard a raucous of laughter as he stepped through the wooden carved doors, his mind and body back in the present, and focused on the hunt for his brother.

He sauntered up to the automaton model one stood to attention behind the front desk. His right hand instinctively reached into his coat pocket for his hacker.

"I'm looking for Simon Moore," Daniel stated, thinking it worth a try before he broke the damn thing.

Its glass eyes focused on him, the lenses whizzing and whirling, no doubt recording his face onto its system.

"I'm afraid," it chimed, "I cannot assist. Any information we receive about our patrons is completely confidential and—"

Daniel rolled his eyes, his hacker, already on the machine's steel neck, flashing red. "Shut up, you overgrown rivet."

It started to fritz, spasming under the hacker's touch, its eyes turning from clear to red. Daniel started again.

"Location needed for Simon Moore, likely using an alias. Dark skin, black hair—"

And when I get my hands on him, an eight ball shiner around his right eye socket, Daniel thought, watching the model skim through their visual records.

"Simon Moore, identified. Frequent patron, currently using the alias Master Tobias Cullingworth. Current location, second floor, room six. He is currently with model—"

"That'll be all," Daniel flipped his hacker from its neck and back into his pocket before, patronisingly, patting the automaton on its shiny, metal, bald head. "Thank you."

It collapsed to the floor with a clang, and Daniel made his way to the stairs.

As he passed each room he heard grunts and curses, yells to God, and amusingly, artificially engineered recordings of praise and encouragement.

"Sad gits…" Daniel grumbled under his breath before finally spotting something he recognised at the end of the hall.

Tinking. His brother's personal automaton model two, standing guard by the door engraved with a large 6.

"Master Daniel," it began, bowing its head slightly, as was customary practice. "Master Simon is currently occupied at this time, may you wait for him to be finished before you—"

Daniel had already reached the door and was knocking harshly against the wood.

"Occupied!" he heard his brother bark from the other side.

Tinking looked from the door to Daniel and back again. "I must repeat, Master Simon has asked that—"

Daniel ignored it, chuckling as he knocked a few more times. He found disrupting his brother's current 'enjoyment' pleasantly satisfying, to a point where he felt he might not even need to blacken any eyes.

"I said, *Occupied!*" Simon's voice could've rattled the whole floor, so Daniel thought it best to wait — a good three seconds before knocking again.

There was a thunderous crash, no doubt the automaton Simon was with having been thrown against the wall. After a series of stomps, the door finally swung open.

"I'm going to *kill*—"

"I'd like to see you try," Daniel grinned, mischievously.

Simon's face fell, before he tried desperately to cover himself with the door.

"It's nothing that I haven't seen before, brother," Daniel chuntered, letting himself into the room. Despite being three years his junior, in recent years Daniel had surpassed his elder brother in both height and size. There was little Simon could do to stop him, and by the dishevelled look spreading across his brother's face, he knew it, too.

"What is the point of having you Tinking, if you can't even hold a door?" Simon hissed at his unfortunate companion.

Tinking responded by placing one of its hands firmly on the door handle. "Correction, Master. I *can,* in fact, hold a door."

Daniel couldn't help but laugh — God, sometimes these things could almost come across as though they were intentionally being funny.

His brother's curses became distant as Daniel's eyes scanned the room. The automaton, as Daniel had expected, was indeed on the floor, unresponsive after being abruptly shut down. It was a pretty thing, dressed up to fit its seductive purposes. Amusingly to Daniel, it was even sporting a blonde wig.

Daniel crouched down to remove the wig from its head when suddenly he noted, with widened eyes, the hair was fused to its scalp. Which only meant one disastrous thing. This was, in fact, a new, yet to be released, model *three.*

"Simon, what the hell do you think you're playing at?!" Daniel became enraged. "If you've stolen this, I swear to God—"

"Keep your britches on," his brother scoffed. "It's a prototype, and a recalled one at that. Father sells them off on the cheap once they've been discarded from the warehouse. They're all over the place."

"All over *certain* places," Daniel grumbled, proceeding to give it the once-over. Upon closer inspection, yes, he could see the errors. It looked so drastically more realistic than the relic downstairs, and Tinking, but there was, most definitely, poor craftsmanship here. Its cream-coloured synthetic skin was hanging loose across its collarbone, its nose slightly off centre, and its left ear, amusingly, had been fused upside down.

Daniel pressed the reset button located on the back of its neck.

A vein appeared along Simon's right temple as the model began to stand. "What are you turning it back on for?"

"I need to wipe its memory," Daniel raised an eyebrow, "Or are you happy with the idea of being blackmailed with a scandal again?"

"That happened one time!" Simon barked.

"Pleasure to meet you, sir. How may I be of assistance?"

Daniel's attention snapped towards the automaton, now batting its eyelashes flirtatiously in his direction. Its voice was crystal clear, melodic in fact. If it weren't for its overly formal language setting, with his eyes closed, it would have taken even Daniel a good minute to work out if it was a model or not. That's how good the model threes are — Daniel internally praised himself.

Simon clearly read his little brother's mind and sneered. "If you're here to brush your own ego then please find a room, pay for your own model and leave me alone with mine!"

The automaton smiled. "I am fully equipped to satisfy both of you at the same time, if that is what you require."

Daniel felt his stomach turn, the image playing in his mind — locking eyes with Simon was very much the wrong action to take, as it caused both men to retch and gag into their hands.

"Jesus, no!" Simon shook his head, and recoiled. "That's officially killed my mood!"

Daniel grabbed his brother's trousers from the floor and threw them at him forcefully. "Good, that means you can get dressed. Mother needs you."

"*Me?*" Simon asked, trying to keep his balance, while he dressed himself. "What the hell does she want with me?"

Daniel shrugged, focusing on swallowing the acidic saliva that was still lingering in his mouth. "Beats me. I was just ordered to retrieve you."

Simon started to chunter under his breath. "I'm not a bloody child, I don't need retrieving. I'm a grown man — twenty-eight next month, for God's sake!" Simon pulled on his shirt, almost ripping the sleeve, "And you don't help, enabling her coddling!"

Daniel passed the automaton its dressing gown from the nightstand. "Put this on," he commanded, before turning his attention back to his now respectably dressed brother. "I'm merely doing as I'm told."

"You *always* do as you're told," Simon grumbled, pulling on his black boots. "I'll need to get my money back from downstairs before you drag me home. I'm not paying full price for an unfinished lay."

Daniel took offence at the vulgarity, but decided it best to ignore Simon and, instead, pull his hacker out from his pocket. "Shouldn't be too difficult, the model one has already been dealt with."

Simon scowled, looking disdainfully at the hacker. "You didn't?"

With a satisfied smirk, and a flip of the handy device, he then popped it back into his pocket. "Oh, but I did."

Simon turned to Tinking. "Right, well, you can actually make yourself useful then and retrieve my cash from downstairs."

Tinking nodded, taking on the command. "Understood, sir. I shall meet you by the entrance." It turned and left, Simon visibly ticked off with it, more than usual.

"God, I can't wait for an upgrade," he remarked under his breath. "Fat lot of good that one is anymore."

"You've had Tinking for five years, Si," Daniel stated, "I would've thought you'd be transferring them into a model three?"

"God, no," Simon sucked his teeth. "I want a restart. Tinking has a habit of reminding me of my past failings."

"Of which it has many to chose from, I'm sure."

"In addition, I can't transfer Tinking when I want a female three, their personality is too masculine," Simon rubbed his hands together, apprehensively giddy. "Do you know how much money I'll save by having my own personal chit, clucking at my heels every second of the day, rather than Tinking?"

Daniel glared at his brother, a curse on the tip of his tongue. "That's *not* what your assistant is for Simon, and you know it."

Simon clearly ignored him and instead shrugged on his coat. "Shall we?"

Daniel motioned towards the model three still functioning beside him. "Aren't you forgetting something?"

Simon cursed before strutting up to the thing and relaying, "Memory reset, preceded by full system shut down, override code SM446 732." The thing whirled at him, before bowing its head, as if dislocated at the neck, its hair falling forward over its face.

"Not bad," Daniel noted, impressed, before following Simon out of the door.

"More efficient than your methods," Simon jeered, casting an eye to his brother's coat pocket. "If father ever catches you using that thing, or better yet, finds out you have it—"

"You really think I'm that careless?" Daniel mused, refraining from using the bannister, thinking of how unsanitary the surface was.

"No, I think you're that smug, Danny."

Daniel considered. "Well, you've got me there."

Printed in Great Britain
by Amazon